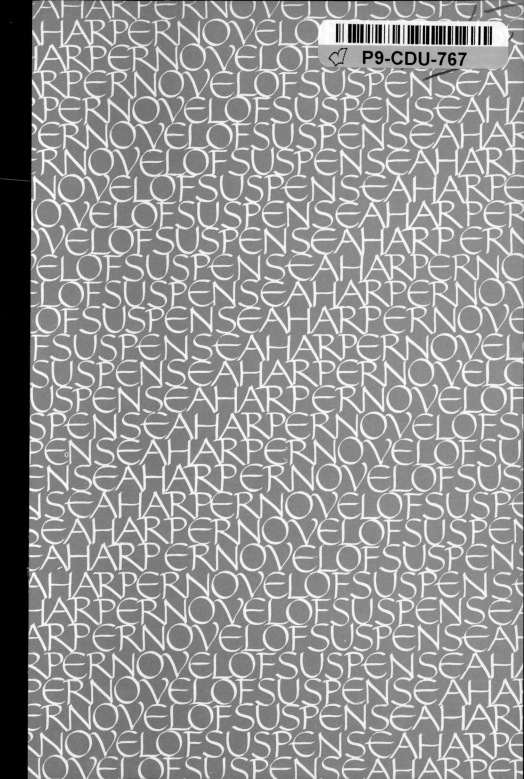

The Bitter Tea

Books by Gavin Black

Gavin Black

The Bitter Tea 🙚

HARPER & ROW, PUBLISHERS
New York, Evanston
San Francisco, London

For my niece, Diana Jesperson

A JOAN KAHN-HARPER NOVEL OF SUSPENSE

FIRST EDITION

STANDARD BOOK NUMBER: 06-010371-X

LIBRARY OF CONGRESS CATALOG CARD NUMBER: 72-80373

Poisoned leaf
Of betrayal
Makes bitter tea.

—Japanese hakai
attributed to Bashō,
seventeenth century

I

The casino made me angry, an irrational anger, the kind that comes to a businessman looking at something he dislikes which is nonetheless going to make money. There was also a moral irritant of sorts. I couldn't be dead certain that if I had been offered a twenty-percent cut in this development when it was starting up I'd have said no.

It's not that I object to classy gambling. Casinos are all right in their places, provided these are silly enough places, like Monte Carlo, which no one in his senses could take seriously. I take Malaysia seriously, and what I was now standing looking at represented a new bid to get with it in the international scramble to grab a share of tourist fool's gold. In my view, the country could do without this kind of gold and be the better for it. Also, if they had to have a damn casino, why plank it down right on top of my favorite mountain?

It was that which hurt, really. The mountain has long been a unique hill resort, within an hour's drive of the capital city, half of this up a road carved through climbing jungle and the final stretch offering killer bends every hundred yards on which a fractional oversteer means a drop of anything up to a thousand feet. I had always reached the top feeling glad to be alive, suddenly cool, looking forward to a log fire in the evening.

1

There had been an inn offering those fires. Now there was a hundred-bedroom hotel with a casino in its vital parts, the whole thing looking as though it could have been a prefabricated export from Las Vegas.

The view was still there, one of the world's most stunning when the mist cleared, down to Kuala Lumpur's lights and then beyond flat lands to a sea on which moonlight shone nearer gold than silver. Some nights a horizon about fifty miles away seemed to promise a sudden appearance of Sumatra's mountains. But no one was looking at a panorama; air-conditioned behind plate glass, everyone was watching croupiers imported from Macao.

The clientele was as yet mostly our South Asia jet set. A lot of them had come by plane, but on the shorter flights: Hong Kong rich with their girls of the moment taking in a long Malaysian weekend, Thai rich ditto, and some ladies from the Philippines wearing butterfly-wing sleeves. The Americans weren't in evidence; it was a bit too soon for charter-plane loads from San Francisco, though advertising would soon bring them—there aren't many five-thousand-foot mountains with casinos on top.

Emotional jaundice was compounded by the fact that I was just back from a trip to Britain and tired, having found my little specialist shipyard on the Clyde deeply involved in the crisis of Scots shipbuilding and continuing to lose money. It was going to go on doing this, too, as long as I kept it open, which put me in a position of forced philanthropy upsetting to my commercial instincts. There were just two more ships to be built there for my Singapore company, and after that an empty order book, which was worrying. Also, I'd felt a bit alienated from the new social mores in Britain. If it's reactionary to feel that permissiveness is being carried a shade too far these days, then I'm a reactionary, and I got on my plane at Heath Row feeling like one, wanting to be back in the relatively healthy Orient. And almost the first thing I'd hit when I arrived was a casino up on my retreat mountain.

I could have postponed seeing this place, but had suddenly wanted out of a Kuala Lumpur blossoming with flags to mark the splendid new understanding we've just reached with Peking. As part of his current tread-softly-and-keep-smiling policy, Chou En Lai had sent a top member of the Politburo on a goodwill mission, one Li Feng Tsu, who had stepped out of his plane wearing a Mao tunic, but of the finest Shantung silk and beautifully tailored. He was also wearing the smile his boss had ordered. For many of the waiting dignitaries at the airport this state visit must have been something that three months earlier they wouldn't have expected to live to see, and there was still quite a degree of reserve among Malay officials. It was the local Chinese who were really playing host and throwing the big banquets. I was pretty certain that the taipans drinking their shark's-fin soup nearest to Li Feng Tsu at the parties were all heads of those companies which had never fallen behind with the premiums on their Great Motherland life-insurance policies. These are fat premiums, too, accounting for a good deal of Red China's foreign exchange, arriving in Peking from all over the Far East, and, being strictly unofficial, are sadly not tax-deductible. A friend once admitted to me that his safety payments are fifty thousand Singapore dollars a year; when sober next day, he denied this, but I believe wine tells the truth.

I stood back from one of the tables where the play was for stakes that hadn't yet warmed up into anything very exciting. Very few of the men in the big room were young, but there didn't seem to be a matron in the place, which suggested that most of the males had left wives at home, relaxing in other company. Evening dress wasn't insisted on, but it was popular and I looked about at a great glitter of Bangkok silks, sarongs worked in gold, and embroidered suits. I noticed a girl who seemed to have noticed me.

3

She was standing by herself, looking as though the night hadn't in any way begun for her, almost certainly a Thai, probably from the Chiang Mai area, which produces a high percentage of the country's beauty queens. She wore a green silk jacket and trousers, perfectly plain, but from one shoulder was draped a tartan silk length which came down over one breast and then went around to her back. Her earrings were pagodas in red gold with four verandas from which hung pendant diamonds. Holding the sash just below the collarbone was a brooch also liberally splashed with the glitter jewel. Her face was a Javanese carving, a shade broad-jawed, and with lips that might be too full for some tastes. She had a long neck, her head held just slightly forward on it.

There was no invitation in her look, just appraisal. She seemed totally unembarrassed at being on her own. She might, of course, have a man gambling somewhere, but I didn't think so. I went over.

"May I buy you a drink?"

"Yes," she said, but didn't smile.

The bar was behind a concrete lattice, attended by a near-elderly Chinese cynic. Muted piped Hong Kong jazz contended with the gambling noise. The lady drank malt with water. Whisky is one Scotch business I wish I had a stake in and don't.

Her name was Ranya Nivalahannanda. She had learned English under strong American influences and hadn't been lazy like so many Oriental girls, doing a partial job and leaving it at that. Ranya's use of the language was crisp and efficient, only the tones of her voice giving away Thai origins; these were rather like the sound of small bells, pretty to listen to, though you might get tired in time of all those notes in the same octave.

"You don't gamble, Mr. Harris?"

"Not at the tables. I just came up for a look. What about you?"

"For me it's business."

"Professional interest?"

"I run the Ponchana restaurant in Bangkok. You know it?"

4

"I'm not often in your city."

"It has been very successful."

"So now you're thinking of a casino?"

She shook her head. "Not in Bangkok. We have a recession."

No one ever uses the word *depression* anymore, as though it has overtones that are too spine-chilling. I gave Ranya another malt and we talked about the economic dumps that have hit her city, as a direct result of partial U.S. withdrawal from Asia. American taxpayers' money created a real boom in the entertainment and good-eating industries of Bangkok, a highly popular rest and recreation center, but the great days for this are over. Already, even on peak nights, a third of the Ponchana's deeply padded seats stayed empty and no one bothered anymore to make reservations. She was considering closing the place before keeping it functioning started to make heavy inroads on her capital holdings. She told me that in this connection she had just made quite a killing on one of Hong Kong's thirteen stock exchanges and had invested her take in Swiss francs. A shrewd girl, with a marked reverence for money.

But she had her problems, quite aside from the restaurant business, the biggest being Mr. Nivalahannanda. She had divorced him two years earlier, but in her country that didn't mean a clean break at all; he still had her on a leash, and a pretty heavily restraining one. In Thailand a woman cannot own and run a business in her own right if she is married. Everything has to be done through her husband, who remains in titular control of joint property even if the enterprise is all the wife's. In her nominally free state she still had to take every document and contract to him for his signature and approval if there were any legal strings back from it to the time when he had been lord and master. There were these strings to everything she tried to do, and to keep Mr. Nivalahannanda quiet she had to pay him fat alimony, most of which he spent on call girls. I gathered that he had never worked, considering anything like that far beneath the dignity of a cousin of a prince of the blood.

5

Her candor after only twenty minutes on a bar stool seemed a bit surprising until I realized that she had probably never talked to a man about her situation before, male ears in her country being unsympathetic. The men up there had things exactly the way they wanted them, totally unmenaced by Women's Lib. It was no wonder that the poor girl rationed her smiles. After years of hard slogging, all she had in the world to call her own was a nest egg deposited under a number in Zurich. The apartment house bought with restaurant profits was in Mr. Nivalahannanda's name, as was also a bus concession up north, not to mention a fleet of twelve Bangkok taxicabs running over the filled-in canals.

She used her hands to express frustration. These were perfectly beautiful, fingers with oval nails like outsize pearls. The pagodas from her ears set up small light-and-music performances every time she turned her head. Fresh from Europe, I was sharply conscious once again of how wonderfully most Eastern women move, even when sitting on a stool. They can get fat and still use their bodies as though the excess pounds were a gift from the gods. In about twenty years Ranya might get fat and it wouldn't matter too much, but right now she was a piece of Sung porcelain with that extra-special glaze on it, her skin the color of clover honey. It was the kind of skin which could stand up to an enlarged candid-camera photo and never show an outsize pore. She made me feel too big and slightly greasy, which is probably how I looked to her. When Oriental women are attracted to us, it is almost always because of our minds, not our bodies.

It was certainly my mind that interested her now. Ranya was down in Malaysia doing an in-depth study of the country as a possible new field for her activities. The American withdrawal doesn't really affect us at all and there still seemed to be plenty of money about. She had spent three days considering Kuala Lumpur, where the only good cooking is Chinese and that not of the best, for in spite of being a capital and having an international airport, it's not really a cosmopolitan town at all. The Malays and Chinese hate each other and both stare at foreigners. Indians squeezed into odd corners do quite good business, but Thais are suspect, mainly because before the British Raj the Malay sultans had to pay tribute to what was then Siam and no one has ever forgotten this. I couldn't see a Thai girl, even one who looked like Ranya, building up the sort of prestige eating house where all races would mix harmoniously over eight-dollar entrees. I told her this. She had already come to that conclusion herself. What did I think about Singapore for her?

I thought a lot of it for her, especially as I was now living down there most of the time. I felt that the city-state had a deep need for its hundred-and-eightieth expensive restaurant. From the way she looked at me then, I could see that business instincts made her suspicious of my enthusiasm, and suddenly, as though to define our contact, she announced that the next round was hers.

I watched those beautiful hands open her bag and saw a comfortably filled billfold, but she didn't tell the bartender to keep the change from a note—she counted this when it arrived, then pushed over one coin I'd have been ashamed to leave on a tray in a snack joint. The old man looked sour.

At first I thought the noise was a sudden attack by a mountain electric storm, but the roaring had a curious beat through it, a pulsing. It got loud enough to disturb the play at tables. Ranya and I got down off our stools. Everyone was staring out through plate glass, but not at the view: a great white ray was beaming down from the heavens onto hotel lawns. It could have been a UFO landing and about half the guests looked as though this idea had struck them, too, a sudden judgment from outer space on earthling vice. Then a man in a white dinner jacket appeared at the top of the three steps which led up into the foyer. He raised both arms and shouted:

"Please pay attention. A very important person is arriving by

7

helicopter. But continue with normal play and take no special notice. He wishes this to be completely informal."

I could think of better ways than dropping in by whirlybird to keep things informal.

"The King?" Ranya asked.

I shrugged. Croupiers attempted to whip up interest in their tables again, but though a few of the rock-faced professional gamblers settled back in their chairs, most of the rest of us stayed expectant. The white-jacketed man came down the steps looking worried.

"Please go on with the play!" he shouted. "I am instructed to ask you to do this. Please!"

He repeated the plea in Malay, then Chinese. No one seemed to hear. The helicopter had come into view, blasting itself down onto grass, rotors continuing to scream for a moment or two, then letting sound escape on a long, diminishing whine. The ray from under the craft's belly went out, but was partially replaced by terrace floodlighting. To the disappointment of us all, they opened a door on the side away from plate glass and whoever was getting out over there was at once surrounded by what looked like a concentration of all the motorized police in the district. A clump of bodies moved across lawn toward the main entrance beyond the carpark and then disappeared.

The major-domo went from table to table exhorting patrons to get on with losing their money, and some stakes were placed, but most eyes were now focused up toward the foyer. Waiters came around with trays of poured champagne that had lost its fizz and looked tepid. Ranya and I passed up our chance of a free drink. I gave her full marks for not insulting a good malt even under conditions of stress excitement.

"What's your King like?"

"We've never met. I believe he doesn't gamble."

"You don't think it's him?"

"Probably just a prince."

"You have many?"

"Dozens."

"So do we."

She didn't think much of princes, having been related to one by marriage. On a good night at Ponchana's, princes who hadn't made a reservation got turned away at the door.

The Muzak suddenly flared up with a new tape of what sounded like a Sousa march. A number of guests looked ready to thrust their arms down to their sides and stand to attention. These days you find true patriotism only among the very rich. The gorgeous birds fluttered and swayed. Ranya's pagodas glittered. We all saw a party advancing across the foyer.

The very important person was a top member of the Peking Politburo, this a considerable surprise to everyone. The Chinese used to come close second to the British as the world's most hectic gamblers, but Chairman Mao, about the time he ordered the swatting of all flies in his country, also ordered the termination of a bourgeois vice. There are now no flies in China to speak of, and also none of those games of chance that used to keep the workers from their work.

I would have thought that a new casino somewhat difficult of access was about the last place where one would see Li Feng Tsu during his goodwill mission, but perhaps he was reacting to one banquet too many. Also, up where he lives there is no night life anymore; everyone goes to bed at nine after a hard fifteen hours following the precepts in the little red book in order to get up at six and start all over again. There was a rumor that in his early days Li hadn't been a horny-handed peasant at all, but a pretty wild student in Shanghai with a factory-owner father and a sports car. It could be that while traveling abroad he wanted to renew his youth just a little. In his report to Chou this particular side trip could be put down as inspecting the deep penetration of Western decadence into Eastern patterns. Chou would understand—in his time he's done a lot of traveling, too.

The great man came toward us with his bodyguard packed in pretty close behind him. It surprised me that none of these

9

tight-faced characters were wearing Mao tunics. Then I realized that an unbuttoned jacket facilitates the quick reach in to
a shoulder holster. Those suits, too, were a kind of uniform,
standardized Peking turnouts in some sort of blue serge, obviously designed with the idea of making the guards inconspicu-
ous among foreign crowds. This they completely failed to do,
identifying the wearers as positively as if they had been garbed
in bright red. The party also included five or six local Chinese,
all of them aggressively cheerful, but I couldn't see any Malays
among the entourage. Li himself was small, compact, relaxed,
but with the bounce in his step which indicated muscles kept
in trim. His hair was clipped to his skull, leaving sprouting
eyebrows as the only growth on his head.

I had seen plenty of photographs, these unavoidable since my
return, but none did the Minister justice; he was much more
impressive in full color than in newspaper black and white, with
surprisingly bright pink cheeks for an Oriental. Everything
about the man seemed to suggest that nearly a quarter of a
century of Communist regulations is the only real way to
spiritual happiness, which is more than rival economic philoso-
phies do for our politicians. He also looked much younger than
what must have been his years and the girls were quickly aware
that he was noticing what they had to offer. Disappointment
that he wasn't royalty was replaced by expectant interest.
Ranya, a staunch enough supporter of private enterprise, was
showing this too, suddenly a long way from me.

If you've achieved greatness in this life, either by inheritance
or working up from the ranks via one of the other formulas, the
gift of presence seems to be added automatically to your pretty
full cup. Royalty always have it; so do even bad generals, most
presidents, and all Greek shipowners. People want to touch you
for luck. I'm pretty certain that having everything stop when
you walk into a room is adequate compensation for a loss of
privacy. It is only the unsuccessful who make a fetish of privacy;

the characters who have really arrived shun it as a symbol of failure.

Everywhere Li Feng Tsu went everything stopped, and his reaction to this was standard: a regal gesture with one hand, just a small wave which said, graciously, that there had been quite enough pomp and the world could now carry on. That wave of the hand was a personal triumph over ideological barriers; it at once identified a member of the Chinese Politburo as an in man, a maker of lesser destinies, and a little thrill of acceptance ran around the gambling hall.

The wheels of chance were still. Girls stood about like debs at a 1920s ball wondering who was going to have the first waltz with the Prince of Wales. Li took his time over the selection, then chose Ranya. She stood perfectly still, as though she hadn't really noticed this, but the pagodas were shivering.

Li spoke in Mandarin first. All this did was produce a tiny, frozen smile of incomprehension. He then tried French, odd in a former British colony, and the reaction was a breathless "Oui."

The Minister smiled. He asked her if she was a Malay and diamonds glittered as she said no, a Thai. He told her he would be in her country in a couple of days and that he understood it was very beautiful. She was afraid he would find it very hot. I didn't think they were establishing much of a relationship until I saw the way he was looking at her, an unblinking hot stare from a woman-eater which gave particular significance to his suggestion that he hoped she would one day soon visit Peking.

There was no doubt at all that I was redundant. Li's guards thought so, too. They were checking to see if there were any suspicious bulges in the inner or outer pockets of my dinner jacket. I remembered a half of a glass of malt sitting waiting for me on a bar counter, but there didn't seem any graceful way of getting to it.

"Venez avec moi," Li said.

That didn't sound to me much like an invitation, just an order. Ranya might have put one glance over in my direction before she obeyed it, but she didn't, just went, moving toward the tables in the company of a Gauleiter for eight hundred million people.

I walked on grass. It was a beautiful night—no mist, three quarters of a moon. Forty miles away the capital city shone brighter than Ranya's diamonds, a great brooch pinned on the downslopes of Malaya's bosom. From up here you got the feeling you could see the country right to its edges, a vast area incorporating man but putting him in perspective, with at least two thirds of it black jungle. I needed the perspective.

None of the other guests were using the gardens. My feet sank into lawn with a still rough, spongy texture from its newness. An enormous sweep of it led to the edge of a ravine where the view had been much increased by slicing out a section of encircling forest. Behind me the hotel glowed like an acute inflammation on what had been until recently a perfectly healthy mountain. The copter, all its lights out, looked like an obscene insect from a species out to defeat man via a runaway breakthrough in genetic size-control. I kept well clear of the thing.

The drop beyond grass wasn't quite a cliff, just a very steep slope on which giant hardwoods had all been butchered; new growth coming up was not yet high enough to cover stumps. To my left, and almost due south beyond the parked aircraft, forest had been left intact on flat ground, the grass running right up to a hundred-foot wall of huge trees and dense scrub under them. Between this reprieved jungle and a continuation of the peeled, sharp-angled hillside a strip of what looked like an adventure trail had been laid down, a nicely asphalted path twisting away into mystery. I went down this and after ten yards was completely screened from the hotel. There was no breeze and almost total stillness, not even insect noise. Then monkeys in more jungle across the valley heard me and protested.

As a species they must be sharply conscious that their world is under increasing threat. All they ask of us is to be left alone, but we keep cutting down their trees and air-freighting the survivors from the destruction of their environment to zoos where they are offered substitute trees made of cement. These monkeys, close to a new development, sounded especially bitter.

A couple of big birds weren't too happy about man, either. I looked up at a fluttering of heavy wings to see two vultures circling out from their roosts on treetops to my left. That helicopter's arrival had upset them. Usually they spent reasonably quiet nights staring hopefully toward the hotel which seemed to contain such a high carrion potential.

A recess carved out of forest offered me a teak seat on a platform of stones. At night in black-panther country it was a damn silly place in which to sit down, but I risked it, lighting a cheroot to fend off mosquitoes. After five minutes the vultures perched again and monkeys stopped yattering, but a deep peace and that view didn't do much for me. I tried to tell myself that I was suffering from too much air travel recently, plus worry about the imminent bankruptcy of my small Scottish shipyard on the river Clyde.

Thoughts about that shipyard do quite often bring me from deep sleep to a sudden, chilly wakening. It's a small concern, and rationalization would close it down tomorrow, but if I did what made economic sense a hundred and eighty men weren't going to get other jobs. I'm probably handicapped in business by the fact that I just can't train myself to see this world as a free-for-all in which a man's duty is to make himself and his immediate family safe and to hell with the other animals roundabout. Human factors keep intruding, and when they do I lose money. I've never yet had management consultants inside one of my enterprises, which labels me a hangover from paternalism.

I had started a second cheroot when the copter engines came on. It felt as though the whole top of the mountain was being pressured to an eruption, but the din was only a warm-up; the roar cut out again, leaving two birds circling the ravine and monkeys screaming. The vultures came low enough to let me see drooping heads and moonlight glittering on weapon beaks.

A pilot checking his engines suggested that he'd had word Li Feng Tsu was going back to bed in Kuala Lumpur, having had enough of gambling even with Ranya as his partner. The great bore easily. Or maybe she was going with him. I decided to sit out the departure where I was, not much liking the idea of those gun-toting guards watching for shadows moving at the edge of the hotel lawn.

The two rifle shots had the space of about one second between them. There were another two seconds of dead silence, then a howling, this time from men, not monkeys. A barrage of rifle fire drowned out human noise. The jungle behind me was a baffle and the racket didn't really sound lethal, more as though a platoon were shaking big cans filled with pebbles. But it was intense, killing fire that I was suddenly certain was being poured into the forest wall beyond the parked copter. Also, I was roughly in the line of those bullets even if a ricochet was unlikely to home on me through a few hundred yards of fat tree trunks. I established personal neutrality by moving fast down the path away from the action.

I didn't get very far. The asphalt ended in an octagonal summerhouse embraced by jungle except on the cliff side, and with no hint of a path beyond it. Anyone wanting to go further would have to take either to the forest or a five-hundred-foot slide down into the valley. I wasn't dressed to do either, but in the white shirt and black bow tie of a bourgeois evening out offered an almost irresistible target to the first man with a gun rounding a corner of the path, especially if he was a Marxist.

14

The summerhouse held shadow, but would not be bullet resistant. I needed cover in some depth and went back into the jungle for about four feet. I had a leaf-patched view out into moonlight and was provided with a stout tree trunk which, if this became necessary, could take the lead instead of me. The thought came that I was sharing a piece of jungle with an escaping assassin, but I didn't nurse it.

Firing stopped. Monkeys seemed frozen in terror and didn't even croon to their babies. There was no shouting. It became very still. I told myself that the pursuit wasn't coming this way, a nice idea. I had another thought which wasn't so nice: what I had heard was almost certainly an assassination attempt, and the only man really worth a professional's killing time up on this mountain tonight was Li Feng Tsu. There was a very good chance that a member of the Peking Politburo was now dead.

It was hot and I began to sweat. This mountaintop was an almost perfect set-up for a political murder. The helicopter was parked on grass within easy range of one man hiding back in the jungle. The killer wouldn't even need a telescopic sight and there had been plenty of time for him to assess range, even rig up some kind of sling mounting for his weapon. Bodyguards can offer no cover to a man climbing steps to a cabin, and for at least half a minute Li must have been totally exposed. Also, the murderer's getaway was assured. He was already back in cover that would shelter him right down to the highway leading to Kuala Lumpur. Pursuit of a man through tropic forest is practically impossible. Police can't use dogs in it—even the best-trained animals, offered such a delectable assortment of alternate spoors, just go amok.

There was shouting at some distance, then another sound that jabbed my nerves: a padding on asphalt—not leather, soft soles. I took a careful step or two toward the edge of my cover and risked parting branches. A man was running toward me, slim, not very tall, wearing camouflaged military-looking fatigues and a soft, floppy-brimmed hat. He carried the rifle as though ready to use it again, balanced from his left hand and arm. He had come out from jungle to make speed on the path and meant to go into it again just beyond the summerhouse, carrying out a plotted retreat maneuver. The runner couldn't be much more than a youth, but I had the feeling at once of a dedicated professionalism. He knew what he was doing. He was trained.

Then he looked back. When his head jerked forward again, I saw his face, lifted to moonlight, sweat streaming down from under the hat, mouth wide to suck in air. My neutrality was shattered. I had taught the killer to swim.

2

I couldn't have stopped the assassin. I didn't try to. I just stood there listening to the sound of a body crashing into jungle growth, no attempt made to keep silence, none needed with the pursuit din swelling. Li's bodyguards must be responsible for the noise. They were strangers to this forest, and if they went into it after their quarry, five minutes would see them thrashing about, hopelessly lost.

I had myself to think of. Frustrated men could so easily start pumping bullets into trees and undergrowth. It would be madness for me to emerge. If these were Li's personal support troops from north China they wouldn't understand Cantonese, and even if that thundering herd had Malay police among them I still stood a good chance of stopping a bullet before I could identify myself.

It couldn't be more than four hundred yards to groomed gardens about the hotel. I started off in what I thought was the right direction, any noise I made fully covered first by shouting out on the footpath and after that what I'd been expecting, the rattle of automatic fire. This was now loud and unpleasantly close. I went faster. Filtered moonlight ended and it was pitch black. I had to contend with huge ferns, roots, vines, thorns, and heat. Malay police might also be moving into this stuff up near the lawns, looking for the killer's hide, but I was pretty sure I'd hear them before they heard me.

One voice became louder than the others, fighting for control. I thought the man was using Cantonese, but I couldn't make out words. It was some time before he got what he wanted, a silence for listening. That was when I had to go quiet, very quiet.

I've never really been trained in jungle work, hating every minute of the few times I've had to contend with the rain forest and on these occasions traveling with guides who told me what to do. But I've picked up a few of the tricks needed for getting through the horrible stuff without announcing too loudly that you're doing it. The basic one is a matter of balance, not allowing body weight forward on a testing foot until the very last moment just in case there is something down there waiting to snap. You don't walk, you probe with your toes. It's essential to protect your face the whole time, particularly eyes; the really rich flourish of thorns is nearly always at head level. The smell doesn't help much, either, this from deep layers of the leaf-mold compost on which the jungle feeds itself, as pungent and as suggestive of inevitable death as the scent of canna lilies in a crematorium.

I began to find darkness bad for morale and decided to risk striking a match, but the box had been against sweating thighs in a trouser pocket and was sodden. I might have been swimming in my shirt and jacket. Jungle needs only five minutes to turn civilized man into the most uncomfortable and ill-adapted animal under its cover. I loosened collar and tie, enlarging a mosquito target area, the insects already homing down on the wet landing surface of my face like a squadron of fighters coming in to a carrier deck. I mopped them away with a soaking handkerchief, remembering that I don't balloon up from the bites and by morning there oughtn't to be any evidence at all that I hadn't just gone quietly to bed in the hotel either during or after a gun battle outside it.

18

This thought came to me obliquely. The next one arrived straight on. I knew that I had no intention of making a report on what I had seen and heard to the police tonight, and maybe not even tomorrow. There were pressing personal reasons why I shouldn't do this. I didn't tick these off, but could feel their cumulative strength. When sweat rash is imminent over large areas of your body, a moral argument doesn't carry anything like the weight it does after you've had a shower and used an expensive cake of French soap. I reached a decision without any hint of a struggle with my conscience. I was going to become an accessory after the fact.

Helicopter engines came on, the racket so tremendous it was impossible to place where the noise was coming from; again it just seemed to take over the mountain. I heard the altered tone of motors at the lift-off, and a moment later the forest was belabored by downthrust and I was showered with bits of dead branches. This was splendid cover for movement and I used it, blundering on much faster than made sense and getting scraped in the process, but still not slowing down until the clattering had almost faded. Then I stopped to listen. There was no shouting. No one was trigger happy. Yet the peace was uneasy and I distrusted it. Li's guards might have gone off in that machine with the Minister's body, but the Malay police would still be about in force, and probably more coming.

Another engine revved and this time the sound was useful. It was rough and could only have come from a truck or jeep, probably a police detachment off in a bid to intercept the assassin down on the main road. They hadn't a hope.

I knew now that I was pretty near to the hotel lawns. A couple of minutes later I had light again and moved around a tree trunk to a view.

The hotel guests were back at the tables, immunized from the night beyond by plate glass, the scene in that glowing salon grotesquely normal, as though all those salvos of gunfire hadn't upset the jet set too much. Shining security in there looked like

19

a kind of heaven from which I was now disbarred as the result of a decision not to play honest citizen. Society was saying to hell with me via policemen patrolling terraces, discreet policemen taking care not to be seen by anyone inside who happened to glance out, but still very much on the prowl. I counted eight men around the front of the building. It was probable they all had Lugers handy. Policy was to seal off the hotel, to make it an impenetrable box, and from the look of things inside the gaming room it was also policy to do this with such discretion that the guests wouldn't even know what was happening.

What I saw didn't tie in with Li being dead. Even the police couldn't keep a monster story like the murder of the Chinese Minister quiet for a few hours. Perhaps someone else had stopped those two bullets from a rifle, a guard who didn't matter?

I did a careful check of the deeply shadowed forest edge. There was no patrol along the outer margins of the lawns and, insofar as I could see, no stationary sentry on duty. I stepped out from cover and, moving very cautiously, made for the carpark. This looked like a kind of annex to the celestial city, illumined and glistening with highly polished Mercedes and Jaguars. The key to my rent-a-car was in one of my damp pockets, but a sudden dash down the mountain in that Ford would not be sensible. If I used a car at all, it would only be for a short distance and I'd borrow someone else's. My objective was to get back inside that hotel to reestablish myself among the righteous rich, and, from the looks of things, these special people were going to sleep tonight better protected than they ever had been in their lives. Angels mightn't be watching over them, but a good third of the motorized police in the state were.

There were no guards in the carpark, which offered reasonable areas of shadow between lamp standards. To get into it, all I had to do was step over a low hibiscus hedge, where the first row of parked vehicles provided shelter at once. A view through the smoked-glass windows of a Rolls showed me the big glow up at the hotel entrance. The police weren't actually functioning as doormen, but I saw two in attendance just outside the first arc of brightness and there were sure to be more on mobile patrol. I counted at least six jeeps tucked into various places among the play cars. It was obvious that I had no hope at all of getting into that building unless I could attract away from it at least a considerable number of the men on duty. I thought I saw how this could be done, though it was going to involve pinching a car. If I tried to use the hired Ford, big red arrows would point from it to me.

I must have been looking remarkably disreputable as I stood there—like a convention delegate on the night of the last booze-up who has, among other things, fallen into the hotel pool. Sweat was beginning to dry, but I had the feeling it was leaving me streaked, and if the police caught me I wasn't going to be able to put on a very convincing act of a guest from inside who had somehow been able to sneak past their watching eyes to be sick among the cannas.

My experience of stealing cars is limited and the new safety locks defeat me. What I had to do now was look for a job with a careless owner, and the rich so rarely are careless with property. For half an hour, using shadow cover and making dashes between the rows, I searched and drew a total blank. Then, at the far side of the park I found it, a Volvo station wagon loaded with water-skiing equipment for the next round of fun, this including a couple of scuba masks lying on the front seat. The key was in the lock. The owner must be nouveau riche. I opened and closed a door quietly, settled behind the wheel, and plotted the action. I also took time to consider my motivations. In terms of personal affairs, what I was trying to do still seemed the only possible course. It was imperative that I avoid a police interrogation, at least the kind that would be beamed toward me if I was caught out in these grounds tonight. I wasn't afraid of routine questioning as a hotel guest—I could ride that all right. Also, running away was out of the question. I'd be missed, tracked down, and pounced on, my flight clear evidence that I knew something the police also wanted to know very much indeed. What I had to do was exactly what I had decided on in the middle of a patch of jungle: get back into that shining building and my role inside it as a temporary playboy.

Most of us carry for a while a mental videotape of the roads we have been over recently, and though mine of the drive up here was already beginning to fade, I did remember that branching off from the last gradient to the hilltop there had been a side track marked in both Malay and English: SERVICE ONLY. A car turning in there couldn't be seen doing this from above, and there was just enough moonlight to let me keep driving after I had doused lights. What I wanted was to have my departure attract a great deal of attention but at the same time give me an adequate head start on police jeeps. If I tried to leave by the only designed way out from the parking area, which meant passing right by the hotel entrance, I'd get the attention but practically no start at all on pursuers. The answer to this seemed to be to put the Volvo down a bank planted with ornamental shrubs and onto the road out that way. It was going to be a bit hard on the car, but the owner was certain to be well insured and it would also teach him a lesson.

The engine grumbled into life. The car had been conveniently parked facing toward the bank. I put her in first and bumped front wheels over a three-inch curb. They whined a bit on long grass and I had to accelerate to give the tires traction. We moved. The rear end cleared the obstacle with some rattling from the load. I switched on full heads to astonish them up at the hotel. Apparently they were. Above a groaning from the transmission and a terrible rattling of water skis I heard the shrill peep of a police whistle. The descent began with brakes hard down, a terrible bouncing in and out among ornamental plant life.

The Volvo is a very well-bred car indeed, but this one had never been asked to go down a bank before and didn't like it.

There were some moments, as the gradient increased, when I didn't either. Headlights showed target asphalt ahead, but the drop to it looked disturbing. The car started to slew, and in fighting this we hit a palm tree. It was a small palm, not very well established in life and I doubt if it ever will be now, but it helped to bring us about, front wheels pointing to hit a hard surface straight on.

The bump was about what you might expect from an air hostess forced to land a jumbo jet because both pilot and co-pilot had passed out from eating poisoned sandwiches. The bang was horrible, independent springs were tested to maximum, and for seconds I thought we would either end with the Volvo capsized and skidding along on its shiny roof or else go straight across the road and down another bank. But the back wheels made a landing, too, and I got the car around in the direction I wanted, accelerating at once, aware as I did it of a decided steering wobble. But I had my head start. A rear-view mirror showed no following lights.

The service road was farther down the main gradient than I had remembered, but I reached it before any pursuit came over the top of the hill behind, managing the sharp-angled turn even with increasing wheel wobble. There wasn't really enough moonlight to drive by—much shade along this way—but I used intuition and with doused lights managed about five hundred yards before we skidded on red clay, jerked across truck ruts, and smacked into a bank with a crunching that said something about the near-side fender. I cut the engine and listened. The night was filled with a great roaring of police transport. Headlights stabbed the sky, then dropped. I was pretty certain those jeeps would go belting away down the hill, but I couldn't rule out the possibility that one of them would decide to check on the side track. It would take time and some maneuvering to get the Volvo moving toward the hotel service area, so I got out, leaving the owner with something like three quarters of a this-year's model. I ran.

Cross-country sprinting in the tropics is a lunatic's sport, leading straight toward strained heart muscle and probable emphysema. On my last medical in Kuala Lumpur, I had been pronounced sound in all parts, but the old doctor who did the checking up is really interested only in tropical viruses and had given himself a couple of quick whiskies before getting to work on me. I keep going to him because one day I might catch one of those viruses and also because his verdicts are likely to be what the patient wants to hear, but I still can't quite forget that he passed as totally fit a business contact of mine who three days later dropped dead in the men's washroom at the country club.

The thumping of my heart was much louder than it should have been, and no sauna could have produced anything like those streams of sweat. A mountaintop usually chilly from mist had escaped it tonight, and rising heat from the plains kept the air clammy. I listened for the sound of jeeps returning, and when I didn't hear this, used it as an excuse to reduce speed. I'd learned that it was high time I took up lapsed daily exercise sessions at the Singapore Swimming Club. It's just not enough to cut down on your smoking and watch carbohydrate intake.

The hotel came into view again, this time more or less from the servants' angle. The design is a sprawl, a three-story center portion with the bedroom and service wings on two floors built out from the hub like spokes on a half-wheel. My objective was a second-floor bedroom in one of those wings, the most expensive, nearest to the pool. I didn't have a private balcony, just shared a deck with all the other rooms on my level. This ran past a selection of sliding glass doors to a ramp which curved gracefully down to the swimming area. The design sacrificed privacy in that people kept walking up and down past your windows, but no one seemed to be complaining about this, probably because that deck was really handy if you had any reason for a small-hours visit to one of the other mini-suites on your floor and didn't want to be seen out in the brightly lit corridors going to it. Civilized living becomes more subtle every year.

24

I was coming up toward the staff wing, a utility block without a deck and obviously without air-conditioning, for most of the windows were open and lit, inviting in those insects that aren't supposed to bite the natives. A gun battle and police clamp-down after it didn't seem to have upset the servants too much, for transistors blared and there were shrieks of laughter from what might be a late party thrown by chambermaids. I paused to have a good look for a sentry using shadow, but there didn't seem to be one, which suggested that my stunt had worked and really thinned down the police left behind on guard duty. I was standing feeling just slightly smug about this when I heard the jeeps coming back. I started to run again, this time toward more primitive rain forest which began just beyond the swimming pool and carried on, with few interruptions, all the way up to the border with Thailand. That sprint to safe cover took all of a minute, and I fell into it, using a handy traveler's palm to keep me on my feet.

The swimming pool was near and still floodlit, though there was no one using it and the surrounding terrace was empty. It was a big pool, at least a hundred feet long, and the deep end nearest me missed most of the light. I was beginning to think about a final dash for that ramp and my room when a figure emerged from an area of darkness directly under it, a man in uniform. He began a slow walk down beside the water toward me. I didn't think he had heard anything—this was just his assigned beat and he was patrolling it. He was a compact Malay, a little bored and probably nursing the idea that back toward the shadows he might risk a quick drag at a cigarette. I heard jeep noise again and he must have heard it, too, but didn't seem disturbed.

I considered tackling him. If I was clever enough in the ap-proach run, I might manage total surprise and be able to chuck him in the pool, but with those jeeps arriving back at the hotel entrance this would probably mean a hue-and-cry following me to my room, which was the last thing I wanted. I willed him to

25

go away. Instead he brought out a pack and matches, taking his time, looking all around before he struck flame.

There were voices. I attributed them to police reinforcements. So did the man on the terrace. He dropped the cigarette and stepped on it, swinging around. Policemen on duty don't often go off into shouts of laughter. They don't usually have young girls with them, either. I looked up toward the deck. At least a dozen guests were on it, making their way toward the ramp. Even before they came into the bright light and I could see the champagne bottles, I could hear they were pretty lit. This was a move out from a suite party.

I watched with a kind of dawning of hope even before there was any real reason for this. I welcomed the row. If nothing else, it was providing a diversion, and it was certainly focusing a policeman's attention. The Malay stood staring as though suddenly faced with a situation that hadn't been in any of his textbooks. He wanted to get in touch with HQ for help, but hadn't been issued a two-way pocket radio.

It was an entirely Oriental party, not a European in it, yet those girls and boys, before they were even down the ramp, had started to behave like luxury-sodden Westerners in a wife-swapping movie. The Malays are great party-givers themselves, but not this kind of party, and two or three of the girls were countrywomen of the policeman. He was shocked to the very fibers of his being, not by vice, but by the fact that it was imported vice. He was a man raised in strict disciplines and to a strong sense of new ethnic identity, forced to watch the big money among his own people taking to alien dissipations as though this was the liberation they had all been waiting for.

I was a bit shocked myself. I'd seen a few illustrations of this kind before, but none so highly colored. While the policeman continued to stare, I moved just a little closer toward the top of the pool.

Someone had brought a transistor and found Hong Kong, which offers South Asia's noisiest stations. Two of the girls started to sway like trained snakes. A man pulled off his dinner jacket and shirt and dived into the pool. It was the shallow end and I thought he'd killed himself, but he came up, seeming a little surprised. A Chinese girl unzipped her cheongsam, wriggled her arms free, shook the sheath down her body until it was a little silk heap on concrete. She hadn't been wearing anything underneath. She kicked off her slippers, looking like a lithe boy not yet fully equipped. One of the men grabbed at her arm as she turned toward the pool. Another girl behind him screamed, aiming a champagne bottle at his skull, but missed her target. Glass splintered over a large area of terrace. There was a screeching that wasn't just fun noise.

Whatever his orders in relation to the guests may have been, no policeman with riot training could stand by in neutral watching all this. He saw before him a simple charge-sheet case of assault with bottle with intent to do bodily harm, however that may be put in Malay. He began to walk down beside the pool, with one hand on the holster of his Luger, purposeful and, to me, impressive.

He was spotted. Two men and a girl went into the pool, presumably to escape the law. Laughter was loud through splashing, but the cop wasn't deterred by any threat of ridicule. He had his duty. I didn't envy him. A moment later he was under attack from two of the girls, who apparently had the cute idea of getting that gun from its holster. The men kept clear, one more going into the water.

No one noticed me at the deep end. I could have put on a diving display without an audience, but all I did was slide in. Then I went under and down, all of ten feet to the bottom, my eyes open, seeing a dull glow ahead beyond brownish gloom. I swam, keeping in touch with tiling by my toes. It was quite a long swim and the first pair of legs I saw were female. I avoided these and also two sets of black trousers, making for a ladder I had noted. I reached out for bars and gripped them before suddenly pulling myself up.

My terrace was away from the action and I walked along this, unlike Lot's wife in that I didn't look back. If any of the shouting was being directed at me I didn't acknowledge this, and I didn't think it was. No one could have seen my face or even my profile, just the dripping back of a man opting out of a party that had become female-dominated. It was a dinner-jacketed back, too. On the ramp I kept staring toward the building.

My room was six down, the ones before it all dark. I had switched off air-conditioning and left sliding doors open a foot or two, but a security-minded maid had closed them again and flicked down the lock. Two more dark walls of glass brought me to one where light blazed.

This was where the party had been. The panels were open. I went into a chaos suggesting a burglar raid except for the dirty glasses, crossed to the door, and opened this very carefully. All luxury hotels are overstaffed with maids likely to come popping out from a service cupboard at any hour, but no one disturbed my passage to another door which accepted my key.

I didn't switch on light, but went straight into the bathroom, a windowless inside job ventilated by fans that came on automatically when you closed the door. Safely in there with the whining about me, I had light in which to strip. I ran hot water in the tub and dropped everything in as I emptied pockets and peeled off. Then I padded out into the dark for pajamas under a pillow, carrying wet shoes to push these tidily out of sight under the bedcover. A grope about in my suitcase located two hangers and I took them, along with the pajamas, back into the bathroom. I showered, standing on my clothes like a washerwoman in a stream, then hung everything up on a couple of swing-out chromium bars provided. My bottom half was clothed in brightly printed nylon before I turned around to look in the mirror over the washbasin.

What I saw was a shock. The jungle had marked me, not by welts from its mosquitoes, but with a long thorn tear I hadn't even felt when it happened. The cut was quite deep and pool water had started it oozing blood again. I dabbed with a face cloth and cold water, and while I was at it the ventilator whine stopped.

The mirror showed a face beyond my shoulder. A man was standing in the open door with the bathroom light full on him. He was short even for a Malay, with a squarish face and small eyes, wearing a dinner jacket but still not contriving to look at all like a playboy. He didn't look friendly, either.

3 🙿

I turned around. The man seemed almost as interested in my cheek as I had been.

"You have a job in this place which entitles you to a pass key?"

"Yes," he said. "Inspector Kadok of the Selangor Security Police."

I had already guessed as much. He didn't look the type to be intimidated by a performance of the outraged hotel guest, so I just waited for his lead-off. This came after he'd had a good look at my laundry.

"You've only just got back here, Mr. Harris?"

"About half an hour ago."

"Much less, I think."

Which meant he had visited my room earlier.

His English was competent. If having to deal with Europeans had once made him slightly uneasy, he had long since been emancipated from this by "Merdeka," which is how the Malays label their national sovereignty. The word means *freedom.*

"Quite a washing," the Inspector said.

"Routine."

"Indeed? You wash suits every night?"

"It's a drip-dry age. And you get in the habit when you live alone."

"I see. Is that a thorn tear on your cheek?"

"Fingernails."

He turned. "I'll wait for you out here if you want to put on a dressing gown."

"I was going to bed."

"Later, perhaps."

I put on the pajama top. The Inspector had switched on the center fixture, which was bright. He had also drawn curtains over the glass wall. I hate glaring light, but it was obvious he used it for all interrogations. He was sitting on one corner of the long sofa and looked comfortable. All the chairs were opposite him; I could only choose the angle. I wanted a drink. There was a bottle in my suitcase, but I didn't get it out.

"You claim to have been visiting a lady, Mr. Harris?"

"Yes."

"She was responsible for your cheek?"

"We had a slight misunderstanding."

"Her name?"

"You expect me to tell you that?"

"Yes. I am a police officer. You weren't in this room fifteen minutes ago. I have reason to believe you were outside the hotel. Were you?"

"Not within the last hour or so."

"You were seen going out onto the hotel terrace through a sliding door from that bar off the gaming room."

"Then I should have been seen coming back in through it again."

"You were not."

"I can't help that."

"I suggest you did not come back into the hotel."

"You can suggest what you like. I always take cover in a gun battle. The nearest cover. That was the hotel. There was considerable excitement. It's not surprising I wasn't noticed."

"You made contact with the lady during the excitement?"

"No. We fixed the appointment earlier. I just kept it."

31

"I think you're lying, Mr. Harris."

"I'm sorry you think that."

He sat there looking at me. I had the sensation of skating over the thinnest ice. At any moment it could crack, plunging me into freezing water. Possibly the worst part of these minutes was not having a clue as to what had happened to Li Feng Tsu, though I was beginning to get the feeling that if he had been killed, or even nicked, the police just wouldn't have dared to issue the kind of sedation to hotel guests which had got them back into their holiday escape mood so quickly. But how do you gloss over a good five minutes of solid small-arms fire followed by a few later outbursts? You can't just turn up Muzak volume.

There was another factor. I just couldn't believe that the assassin, given those almost perfect conditions, would have botched the job. It was out of character. I thought of swimming lessons years ago, the basic technique of the crawl acquired in just two of them, and by a five-year-old. It had been like that ever since, skills picked up with an almost casual ease and then perfected to a high-gloss finish. These natural aptitudes would certainly apply in the sport of putting a bullet smack into the middle of a target.

"You had better put on some clothes, Mr. Harris. If you have any that aren't hanging over the tub."

"Does this mean an official interrogation?"

"It means that I would like to have a tape of your answers to my questions and the machine is in the temporary office I have here."

"In that case, I want to get in touch with my Kuala Lumpur lawyer."

There was a flick of resistance to this suggestion in Kadok's eyes. "These are routine inquiries only. We have questioned other guests."

"And told them to be suitably dressed just in case it became necessary to whip them off quietly to headquarters in K.L.?"

He didn't like that. "You refuse to come?"

"You'll need to use force to get me out of this room. And if you try that, I'll make a helluva noise."

He stood. "It is very foolish to obstruct the police!"

"All I want are my legal rights."

He got up and walked past me to the door, where he turned. "Your sleep will be well guarded. Perhaps the morning will see you more reasonable?"

I had no comment.

"Was the woman Mrs. Nivalahannanda?"

"Ask her," I said.

He went out. The door clicked.

At the washbasin again, I squeezed out toothpaste and then let battery-powered brushes get to work on my teeth. A heavy feeling in my stomach was psychosomatic in origin. I hadn't been very clever and knew it. When I had finished in the bathroom I put out all the lights and padded over to the wall of curtains, lifting an edge. A man was sitting in the chair I could use for breakfast out on the deck in morning sunshine. He had his Luger on the table beside him. He was the Malay who had been morally so deeply disturbed down by the pool, a man with plenty to think about. I doubted that he would go to sleep on duty.

I have never gone in for any kind of sedative tablets at night, believing that it's better in the long run to let your worries keep you awake. That way you may find a solution to them. Doped you won't. The bathroom door was open and the tub echoed a steady dripping. The maid had switched on air-conditioning and the room was comfortable enough, but I had the feeling of being in a sealed box, and my Scots blood was already resenting what I was going to have to pay for a horrible night.

The phone had one of those gentle bells meant to spare the nerves of well-heeled patrons suffering from hangover. Light came through floral curtains. My watch said 9:15. I lifted the handpiece slowly, a man expecting bad news.

"Mr. Harris?"

"Who are you?"

"Mrs. Nivalahannanda."

"Oh."

"I make a point of always having breakfast with my lovers. Do you like bacon and eggs?"

"What?"

"I said, do you like bacon and eggs?"

"Well, yes."

"I'll order. You remember the room number?"

"Actually, I don't."

"Twenty-seven."

"Of course."

"In about twenty minutes?"

The line went dead.

I got out of bed wondering what the hell you wear to breakfast in her room with a woman you haven't slept with. A certain formality seemed indicated. I took Courtelle trousers and a jacket out of my suitcase and considered my shirts, choosing one that had seemed too bright a blue in Glasgow but appeared to have faded under tropic sun. I went into the bathroom to shave and shower, finding my laundry quite dry.

I didn't open the curtains until I had dressed. The deck was empty. A moment later I found the corridor empty, too, but it would have been foolish to assume from this that the police had quietly withdrawn during the night.

Twenty-seven was in my wing, on my floor and my side of the building. I could have got to it along the deck, but it was the wrong occasion for that. I knocked.

If Mrs. Nivalahannanda always looked like this in the morning, I couldn't see how her marriage had failed. Breakfast had already arrived and was set out on a glass top pulled up to the settee. She was sitting behind the table wearing the kind of pajama suit some women go shopping in, bright, floppy-bottomed, with what seemed to be a chiffon fluff at the neck. She had pulled back black hair from her face and tied it with a ribbon, which somehow put an even stronger accent on good boning than the pagoda earrings.

"Don't just stand there. Come in and shut the door."

She wasn't smiling. She had no reason to.

"Did that cop . . . ?"

"Yes," she said.

"It never entered my head he would."

"Didn't it? You forget, perhaps, that I'm a divorced woman. To a Malay policeman that means I rate little better than a whore."

"I'm sorry."

"It's so nice of you to apologize."

The windows to the deck were closed, but the view through them was splendid. I looked at it.

"Sit down. Shall I pour your coffee?"

"Thanks."

She lifted a silver lid. "Please help yourself."

It was something to do, though the egg was slippery and I had difficulty in getting it on the plate. I was having second thoughts about Ranya as a wife. It was an exciting face all right, but also a strong one. And there was a complete lack of Oriental pliancy in her manner which I could see Mr. Nivalahannanda finding a bit hard to take before breakfast. She was inspecting me again as she had done in the gaming room downstairs, but this time the verdict was unfavorable.

"Toast?"

"Thanks."

We might have been doing this for ten years.

"Did that policeman ring you?"

She shook her head. "No. He paid me a personal visit."

"Good Lord!"

"I've explained, I have no status. I should be used to it by now, but I'm not. It stays unpleasant."

"How could he know?"

35

"That I'm divorced? From the barman. The police would naturally be interested in me after that half-hour I had with Li Feng Tsu. I went back to finish my drink, but you'd gone. There was no one to talk to but the barman. He'd already heard my life story, so I asked him what he knew about yours. He didn't know a thing at first, but two banknotes changed that."

She didn't believe in tips, just bribes. She cracked a piece of toast with sharp white teeth, chewed, then swallowed.

"You were quite modest about yourself, Mr. Harris."

I broke the yolk of my egg. It was runny and spilled out all over the plate.

"What were you doing last night during the time that interests the police so much?"

"What did you say to the Inspector?"

"That I'd been entertaining you for most of the later evening. I couldn't remember exactly how long. But the memory of you was still very fresh. He had a look at the bed for evidence. I'd been in it for some time, alone. I've always been a very restless sleeper."

"Why did you alibi me?"

She smiled for the first time since I'd closed the door. "I left the bar downstairs with the feeling that you'd be a useful man to have a hold over. Perhaps you'll be able to help me fit into my new life?"

I've always been billed for everything later, never a free handout.

"You haven't told me what you were doing outside the hotel, Mr. Harris."

"I'm Paul at any girl's breakfast. I was having a walk in the gardens when the firing started."

"So?"

"The action cut me off from the hotel. For quite some time. After that, all I was trying to do was get back into this building again without being identified. I don't like answering police questions."

36

"I'm sure you don't. What did you see out there?"

"Nothing much."

"You saw something that would interest the police a lot. And you're not going to tell them about it."

No wonder she owned restaurants and bus companies via a proxy husband. She was beginning to make me really nervous. At the same time, and even while trying to eat a splashed egg, I was extremely conscious of her body below the neck. That Javanese carved head somehow seemed to have an existence totally separate from the rest of her. The rest of her was a positive invitation to an explorer. It was quite some time since I had felt this particular excitement along with my first cup of post-waking coffee.

She was looking at me like a trained mind-reader.

"How did you get that gash on your cheek?"

The Inspector hadn't probed her about this, which was something.

"From a thorn."

"These are still allowed to grow in the hotel gardens?"

"At the edges."

"Where you were hiding?"

"I was using shadow."

"To watch for Li Feng Tsu as he went back to the helicopter?"

I didn't like the implications of that at all. "I have no interest in Li Feng Tsu. I took cover from bullets. They were flying about. Target area seemed vague. How did the police explain all that firing to the frightened guests?"

She smiled again. "Of course you wouldn't know about that, would you? We were told that one of the guards thought he heard something in the woods and let off two rounds. Others followed. It had all been a mistake. Only a monkey."

An assassination attempt was being smothered in terms of the press and public, and not a word about all that wasted ammunition would appear in the papers. Kuala Lumpur hasn't got as firm a control over the news media as Lee Kuan Yew down in neighboring Singapore, but the government up here can still clamp down when it wants to. And if one of the bullets meant for Li had hit someone else and he didn't happen to be important, there would be no publicity about that either. I could be fairly certain now that the Chinese Minister was both alive and well.

"Do you think it was only a monkey?" Ranya asked.

"Probably."

"Plenty of people in Malaysia still hate Red China. One of them might have wanted very much to kill Li. This would have been an ideal place to do it."

I shook my head. "It wasn't a scheduled stop. He came here on sudden impulse. I don't see how an assassin could ever have known he was going to."

"Unless he was at that banquet last night in Kuala Lumpur which is reported in this morning's paper. Someone must have suggested that Li might like to see some gambling. There would be talk about it. Also, they drink a lot at these parties. Li holds it well, but I'd say he was half drunk when he was with me."

"You mean the assassin just jumped in a car and drove like mad to get to this mountain?"

"So you believe with me that there was an assassin?"

"We're merely discussing your theory!"

"Of course. Yes, I think he might have done that. Why not? There was plenty of time for the police to get here before the helicopter. They must have had only a late tip-off, too."

Ranya reached out for a cigarette packet. She had eaten nothing but that piece of toast. Her lighter had too much flame. She adjusted this, then said: "It would be interesting to know whether the police have found a dead monkey."

When I got back to my room the bed had been made and the place tidied. Inspector Kadok was sitting on the sofa. He didn't ask me if I'd enjoyed my breakfast. There had been plenty of

time for him to have another good look around and I was quite
sure he had done this. Colleagues had probably also had a good
look around the two-room flat I keep in Kuala Lumpur. The
idea of a search warrant really has gone right out of fashion, and
the Inspector once again failed to apologize for his uninvited
presence in accommodation I was paying for. He didn't waste
any time in verbal skirmishing either.

"I understand you're just back from England, Mr. Harris?"

"Scotland. I only passed through London."

"A business trip?"

"All my trips are for business. I never travel any distance for
pleasure."

"Which is why you find this place to your liking?"

"It's not to my liking at all. I came up here to get away from
a K.L. hung with flags."

"You don't approve of the Chinese Minister's visit?"

"I don't find it particularly meaningful."

I reached down under the bedcover for my suitcase. My
evening shoes weren't quite where I had left them. I set the
case on the bed and went into the bathroom, emptying hangers
and coming back with an armful of clothes. These I started to
pack. I put in the shoes, too. I lifted the phone and told the desk
to get my bill ready.

"A short visit," Kadok said.

"I have to get back to work."

"In Kuala Lumpur?"

"Briefly. Then Singapore."

"You are a Malaysian subject."

I looked at him. "Which means you could call in my passport
and hold it?"

"Yes."

"Try it," I suggested.

I knew damn well he wouldn't try it, firstly because he had
no grounds at all yet for taking my passport from me and sec-
ondly because the Inspector was bound to have found out by

this time that I was capable of making a loud noise in some embarrassing places, like the summer palace of my co-director in the oil business, Tunku Batim Salong, Prince of the Blood. He was having to suppress a lot of his zeal this morning, which made him angry. He didn't like Europeans who had gone native as a matter of business policy; if he had his way we'd all be bundled out of the country. He was a Malaya-for-the-Malaysians man. There are a lot of them; they represent a growing threat to free enterprise.

The phone rang.

"I'm ready," Ranya said.

"All right. Have them take your bags down to the lobby. I'll have the Ford at the door in about ten minutes."

Kadok was staring at me. "The woman goes with you?"

"Yes. It's a big thing. After all these lonely years, two people have found each other."

A Thai lady executive's luggage looked more like she was emigrating for good than traveling on business. There were nine pieces, not counting an outsize handbag and a jewel case. I spent ten minutes packing the stuff, wondering what she had paid in air freight coming down from Bangkok. As we drove off I couldn't see any sign at all of police on guard duty.

Ranya was smoking again. She was at least a pack-and-a-half-a-day girl, which threatened to undermine my shaky resolution only to use cigars and cheroots and to ration them. For travel she was wearing a green trouser suit in nylon with a kind of sleeveless bolero jacket over a white shirt. Pinned on the V of the shirt was a day brooch the size of a soup spoon showing off what might be called a happy marriage between heavy-carat diamonds and pearls, these latter the real South Sea thing, not Mikimoto cultured, plump and as rosy as the second night of love. From the way she kept the jewel case tucked under her legs I guessed that it was pretty tightly packed with the kind of capital asset which even a Thai girl can contrive to remove from the jurisdiction of an ex-husband.

The morning views were magnificent, but the driver couldn't risk glancing at them and Ranya didn't seem interested. I had the feeling she had now written off Malaysia and was already directing her thoughts toward Singapore. In this I was wrong. She was directing her thoughts toward me.

"Are you a millionaire?" she asked.

I pulled the car around a sharp-angled double turn, tires squealing.

"Depends on the currency. In Malay dollars, probably. U.S. dollars, no. Pounds sterling, a long way from it."

"You mean your assets are buried in your companies?"

She'd hit the right word for it in respect to one of my companies, its assets now permanently interred on the banks of the bonny river Clyde in Scotland, with no hope at all of resurrection. Even in a good year any reminders of that shipyard were depressive, but in the middle of a recession they brought thoughts not too far from the suicidal. I had nightmares in which everything I had built up out here was slowly but surely siphoned away back to the Old Country to help support a welfare state.

"When I was paying my bill," Ranya said, "there was a man at reception in a terrible rage. He said someone had stolen his car and wrecked it."

"Oh?"

"A new Volvo, apparently. You didn't borrow a car last night?"

"Why should I? I have this job."

"I was wondering if it could have been part of your plan to get back into the hotel."

"Drive round it, you mean?"

"No. Distract police attention from the building."

A couple more sharp bends demanded all of my attention.

When we were past them into a hundred-yard straight, I said:

"Did you enjoy your time with Li last night?"

"It was an experience."

"The small talk sounded a bit formal at the start."

"He relaxed later."

"Is a visit to Peking now a possibility?"

"Yes. It must be very beautiful."

"It's been completely ruined by a lot of horrible new buildings for bureaucrats."

"You know China well?"

"I know it as a man desperately anxious to get out again during most of his stay. And I didn't think I was going to make it."

"What were you doing?"

"Selling engines."

"Sounds innocent enough."

"That's what I thought, until I got there."

"All this may account for the police interest in you now?"

I didn't like that trend either. The rear mirror showed a car tailing us and another behind it. They weren't jeeps, but the police have other vehicles.

"All Li's personal bodyguard were at least six inches taller than he," Ranya said.

"So?"

"Broad, too. Good protection against bullets. Except when he was climbing up steps into the helicopter. That's when Li was shot at."

"The police say he wasn't shot at."

"The jungle would give the killer perfect cover," Ranya said, as though she hadn't heard me.

"Li is alive and well."

"Lucky. What did you see, Paul?"

"Nothing!"

"If you saw nothing, why are you hiding behind a woman?"

"I am not hiding behind a woman! You'd be poor cover."

"But the best you've got at the moment."

"Look, I'm driving you to your hotel in K.L. out of the kindness of my heart!"

"Really?"

"There's also the fact that you're very good-looking."

"You can buy good-looking women anywhere."

"I don't use my money for sex!"

"How foolish of you. There seem to be cars following us."

I hadn't seen her look back.

"It's one-way traffic down this stretch. Controlled by lights."

I didn't think this accounted for the chain of cars now behind the Ford. There had been no suggestion of a convoy building up at the hotel entrance.

"I think I have been very foolish to try to help you, Paul. After all, I'm a stranger in this country. And a woman. The police could do what they like."

"Meaning what?"

"I need some kind of protection."

"I'll see they don't arrest you."

"That's not what's worrying me. They could put other obstacles in my way. In matters of business. Preventing me opening a restaurant, for instance."

"You think it might help if it was known some of my money was involved in your scheme?"

"I do, yes."

"I've never been interested in the catering trade. Also, I don't react to blackmail. No matter how gentle. So if it would ease your conscience any, get in touch with the police from your K.L. hotel. You'll have Kadok in your room again in no time at all."

Ranya said nothing. We reached the intersection with the highway, the light green for us, but there was no sign at all of the man in a little wooden box whose job it was to control the traffic flow. There were, however, what appeared to be two roadmen, though I doubted if the palms of their hands carried work blisters from spades. Both looked at us—young for the job, I thought—but neither gave any sign at all of interest, having received instructions not to by two-way radio. I turned into the main road, blinkers flashing, accelerating hard. The other cars were most of them returning to the capital, too.

Rent-a-cars get a lot of abuse. On a fast though still twisting surface I put the Ford through a mini-trial, and I must say she responded nicely. These days the difference between a family car and the so-called sports models is mainly a matter of body styling. The springs on this job could have been tightened up a bit, but she cornered reasonably and after the first controlled skid I decided I could risk these again from time to time. Ranya's comment on all this wasn't verbal; she just fastened her safety belt.

I was traveling fast because I wanted buildings and people around me and there is something unassailable about a man sitting at his own desk with the trappings of respectable enterprise all about him, a secretary on call and a personal assistant available by intercom. An Inspector is much more likely to be polite in these surroundings than in a hotel room. Also, I wanted to clear up any business waiting for me in K.L. and then catch a flight to Singapore.

When we reached a long straight leading out of the foothills, there was no following car in sight. Ranya paid me a compliment, her first.

"You could drive the getaway car for bank robbers."

4 🦁

Maria, my secretary, now runs the K.L. office of Harris and Company. Bahadur, my personal assistant, tries to fight this, but I don't. She is a large woman who sits pulled in tight to her desk, looking as though she is about to overlay the electric typewriter. She lifted her head as I came in. There was no smile.

"Nice of you to show up before lunch, Mr. Harris. I wonder if in future you'd tell me when you're going to take a midweek holiday? It's embarrassing not knowing. Especially when it's the police asking."

"They've been here?"

"No. I wouldn't have minded that. It was one o'clock this morning. At home. My husband took the call. It was a bit of a shock to him. You know what he's like. Schoolteachers have to watch their position. He wants me to give up working here and get a respectable job."

"What did they ask you?"

"What I knew of your plans."

"You said?"

"That you rarely told me about them. What I think they really wanted was to find out whether I'd booked an international flight for you under an assumed name for use with a false passport."

"I'm sorry you were troubled, Maria."

"Oh, I don't mind. It's just my husband who worries about who calls up at one A.M. Tamils are a jumpy lot. Me, I don't give one damn for these Malay police."

Earlier she hadn't given one damn for the British police either. As a Eurasian, Maria was a social neutral. She had once given me her views on this, which were simple: no society had ever accepted her, so she accepted no society. Born in Malaya under the British, she had changed her passport when the great day of Merdeka dawned, with no more sense of loyalty toward the new authority issuing it than she had felt for the old one. I believe she really is immune to any kind of national feeling. She can watch the follies of the country in which she lives with the same dispassionate detachment she keeps for the follies of other countries, a resident whose heritage is such a race mixture it would exhaust her to untangle it and define herself, so she doesn't try. At times I envy her. For my part, I worry about Malaysia as a federation with bad cracks in it and I'm deeply concerned about Singapore's chances of surviving as a separate city-state. I'm also pretty uneasy about where Britain is going and wonder whether the Common Market is going to starve out Scotland, which it rather looks as though it may. I even feel responsible for America sometimes and have to restrain myself from writing the U.S. President with free advice on how to conduct Far Eastern foreign policy. My trouble is that I just can't shake off a tendency to feel responsible. The really happy people are the ones who let others feel responsible for them.

"I'm afraid I've got bad news," Maria said. "Mr. Lindquist is dying."

"*What?* Why the hell didn't you tell me sooner?"

"I was getting round to it, Mr. Harris. So much has happened in the last twelve hours. He's had a heart attack."

Probably I shouldn't have been anything like as shocked as I was. Sven Lindquist had recently celebrated his eighty-seventh birthday with a monster party, reaching an age at which no one can really complain about being cut down, but he had always seemed inoculated against ordinary mortality, a mountain of a man built to endure forever, and with no mental symptoms of senility at all. The last time I'd seen him he was just as interested in making money as I'm sure he had been sixty-five years earlier.

"When did this happen, Maria?"

"Yesterday afternoon, apparently. He was in his office in the morning. Mr. Lung has flown up here to see you about it."

My secretary's sequence of priorities made some kind of sense to her, but little to me.

"And where is Mr. Lung?" I asked politely.

"He was in your office until half an hour ago. Has been since nine thirty. He seems to be under some strain. Very jumpy. He went out without saying when he'd be back. Probably to some bar."

"You've no idea which bar?"

"I do *not.*"

Maria is a total abstainer on principle and Bahadur won't even touch a beer on account of his Sikh religion. At times the office feels like a branch of the national temperance union, and even in the privacy of my own cell within it I've got out of the habit of keeping alcohol to offer business associates, something that Lung must have discovered for himself after opening all the unlocked cupboards. The general manager of Hok Lin Shipping, of which I am principal shareholder though not board chairman, needs his regular gins to counteract the tensions of his job. In fact, he drinks more than any other Chinese I know, but without any damage as yet apparent to his general efficiency. He's a very efficient man indeed, not prone to panic, and if he had flown up here as the personal bearer of the sad news about Sven it could only mean one thing: that the imminent death of one of my co-directors on the board of Hok Lin was producing a crisis situation down in Singapore that Lung simply couldn't risk discussing over the phone.

I didn't have to guess what the crisis was about and went along to my office to think it over. Lung had been my choice. I had been supported on the board at the time by Sven, with old Hok himself a neutral in the matter, but with the other two Chinese directors bitterly opposed to my nominee. The most I've ever had in the company is a forty-percent holding, which, with Sven's thirty percent, gave a couple of Europeans comfortable control. Originally we were the Lindquist, Harris and Hok Lin Shipping Company, but, as well as that being a mouthful, it became policy to operate under a Chinese name and we peeled off the first two at the time we went public with a share issue to raise money.

This reshuffle altered personal holdings in the firm, mine dropping to twenty-five percent, Sven's to twenty, with another twenty between the three Chinese directors, leaving thirty-five for the general public. This meant that Sven and I no longer had total control, but we weren't worried about that, for Hok Lin himself, who wasn't really too interested in the business and had only come into it because he had been my father's friend, always voted the way we wanted. The other two directors didn't, quite often. One of these was Tsing Tai Tai, a grand-nephew of Tsing Tung, the patent-medicine king who had made his pile out of an aphrodisiac called New Sun Tonic. The other was Wen King, a so-called merchant banker whose funds came from sources no one inquired into too closely.

Tsing Tai Tai rather fancied himself as a financial whiz kid. He was in control of the aphrodisiac business now, and this was still booming, New Sun Tonic selling all the way from Hong Kong to New Delhi, and I had long suspected that he and Wen might be planning between them to get a much bigger stake in Hok Lin Shipping. They could do this by proxy buying in London of our issue shares, and for some time I had been keeping

48

as sharp an eye as I could from this distance on any dealings in these.

I stared at the clean sheet of blotting paper Maria fitted into a pad on my desk much more often than was necessary in order to remind me how little work I did in that office. Sven's death was going to mean a very real shift in the balance of power on the board of Hok Lin Shipping, particularly in view of the fact that I was certain his widow would inherit all the old man's holdings. This thought didn't make me too happy. Sven's first wife had been a charmer from Copenhagen who shared all those early struggles to make his first million and then died just after her husband's seventy-fourth birthday. We all thought that would be that, Sven remaining a respected widower looked after by his houseboys, but we underestimated the old man, for nine months later he remarried, this time an Englishwoman, the widow of a civil servant who had lived in near penury all her days and hadn't liked this much. Sven had no son, just five daughters, who now all lived in Europe and had received hand-some settlements when they married—by my guess, more or less out of the picture in Papa's will. Mrs. Jane Lindquist would be very much in the picture, for he had doted on her, and I was almost certain that the twenty percent in Hok Lin would be part of her legacy.

I can't pretend that I'm too fond of Sven's second wife. It isn't just that I had great affection for Karen Lindquist, her predecessor, but Jane has so much charm it makes me uneasy. She puts it on with her makeup in the morning and it covers everything except her eyes, which are like pebbles newly washed by a high spring tide, shining but dead cold. At fifty-one she could be taken for thirty-nine, a highly durable British blonde, and I believed that once she had fought down her grief she would start to lay plans to have the best years of her life still ahead, these years to be supported by as much available ready cash as possible. It seemed very likely indeed that she would sell her holdings fast to anyone offering ten new English pence more than the current market price.

The trouble was that I just wasn't in a position at the moment to make that offer. A year earlier I had used all available reserves to buy out two partners in Johore Diesels, which was now completely mine, something I was proud of, and the last thing I wanted to do was to give bankers a hold over that company by raising a loan on it. The diesel-engine business is a much more stable proposition in our area than shipping, particularly since I am still managing to keep costs quite comfortably below that of my Japanese rivals, and look like going on being able to do this. In Southeast Asia it's a great feeling not to be losing a commercial battle to the men in Tokyo.

I knew who would have the ready for Jane's holdings: Tsing Tai Tai and Wen, either together or separately. In fact, I could see them already on tiptoe now for a quick dash in with an offer the moment Sven's funeral was over.

Maria's voice came out of the intercom. "Phone from Singapore for you, Mr. Harris."

I identified the caller from a spasm of coughing before he spoke. It was Tsing Tai Tai, third generation in the virility business.

"Paul? Had you heard about Sven?"

"Yes. Just."

"I have the saddest news. He's dead."

"Oh."

There was a pause for me to recover.

"We can be glad it was quick. His wife says he didn't suffer."

He sounded like an undertaker about to start a sales pitch for polished mahogany instead of plain pine.

"The funeral is on Saturday, Paul. Will you get down for it?"

"Of course."

"I'll tell the others." Again a pause. "What are we going to do without Sven?"

The answer to that could be go Chinese fast.

50

"See you," I said, and hung up.

I sat thinking about Sven Lindquist. In some ways he had been an old bastard, the kind of man who, if you turned to him in time of trouble, would give you good advice, a glass of firewater, but no money. He had never played an off-color commercial trick on me, possibly because I had never given him the chance. I liked his sense of humor, which was rowdy, and his laugh from it, which was rowdier, but the man's greatest appeal was his bigness, physical and financial. If he ever made a small deal in his life, it was before my time and probably before my father's too; all of the gambles I had seen were huge, some of them preposterous in concept and doomed to failure, but a big percentage so shrewdly conceived that they came off. It was really Sven who got the idea for a shipping company to replace lost Dutch trading rights in the vast Indonesian waters, and we went into the business at a tricky time, which nonetheless turned out to be the right time, just as the old man had said it would be.

The door opened and Lung came in. He was looking troubled and, as he always did in this state, intelligent.

"If Maria was listening on the line, you already know about Sven," I said.

He nodded. Lung is a slight man with a head a size too big for his body, horn-rimmed spectacles, and good teeth. If he has vices other than an addiction to gin, he hasn't confessed them to me and I haven't heard rumors.

There was no need to beat about the bush. "What's been happening in the last few days to bring you haring up here?"

He shook his head. "It's not a matter of the last few days. I wish you'd come straight to Singapore. This thing's been going on for months. I think it killed the old man."

"Eh?"

"I tried to get you on the phone. When I couldn't I decided to tell Mr. Lindquist. I shouldn't have done. I kept forgetting he was so old. And it put him in a towering rage. That brought on the attack." Lung was looking very troubled indeed.

"Go on."

"Tsing and Wen between them have seven percent of the London issue through proxy buying. They've been doing it by small deals over a year."

"This came from Jeremy?"

He nodded. "In your personal code. I deciphered like you told me to."

No one else besides Lung has a key to that code in Singapore and only Bahadur in Kuala Lumpur. Jeremy, my cousin, was once our agent in London, but resigned a couple of years ago, retained by me privately on a commission basis for jobs like this.

I worked things out and didn't need pencil and paper to do it. If Tsing could now get hold of Jane's shares, these, plus his own and Wen's, plus seven percent more in London would give the two Chinese forty percent of Hok Lin. Further, if they could contrive to swing a British investment trust which had bought fifteen percent of the London issue to their way of thinking, they would have virtual administrative control. My appointee now sitting opposite would certainly get the sack and I would have to take a back seat.

Lung's chin was down on his chest. He had one leg across the other knee and stared at a shining calf shoe, periodically waggling this. Then, as though he couldn't stop an involuntary movement any other way, he put out a hand and held the foot still. At the moment he didn't look managerial caliber at all, a man under tensions that weren't far from proving too much for him. In fact he was a brilliant administrator and could absorb and retain for instant mental reference an incredible range of the minutiae of our operation, but he was just no good at all at the kind of company in-fighting which had suddenly flared down in Singapore.

The reason for this was simple. The Chinese upper-echelon man is only very rarely a solitary who has got to the top unaided by anything more than his own drive and determination. Usually the tycoon is the top figure on a huge supporting pyramid of family connections—and family in the widest tribal sense, cousins and second cousins all ready, in any kind of stress, to put first the survival of the clan.

Lung had none of this underpinning at all, a trained-engineer refugee from Shanghai who had arrived in Hong Kong penniless, without a hope of a job in his profession. He had worked as a coolie, then as a waiter in a tourist hotel, saving enough money to take himself over to Borneo, where he had acquired a corner of the lumbering trade. He had returned to Hong Kong with some capital, enough to set up a minute factory manufacturing engine components, which expanded until he was employing thirty men and was able to approach me with an offer to supply a part for my standard heavy-duty diesel manufactured in Johore. This was the start of a contact between us which led to Lung's selling his factory and coming to Singapore as general manager of Hok Lin Shipping, but functioning in this role without a seat on the board.

All he brought with him were two suitcases. There were stories that his entire family had been wiped out in a Shanghai purge, but if this was so, he never talked about it. I suppose in a way the man's utter solitariness had appealed to me, that plus dogged Chinese determination and astonishing industry. It had seemed to me that in Hok Lin he would have a ready-made pyramid giving the support that would allow the release of his energies. He would also be my man all the way. To a degree this had happened, but I hadn't foreseen that his solitary state would make him a kind of pariah among his fellow countrymen. It wasn't just that he was my appointee more or less forced on two of our directors; much more than this, he was a man totally outside standard Chinese patterns and therefore suspect. His abilities only aroused barely controlled animosity.

I had never told Lung that I would keep him on, whatever happened to his job in Hok Lin, and I didn't intend to. You don't get the best out of a man by telling him there is a pillow waiting underneath if he falls off a ladder. At the same time, I had never expected from him something he couldn't give in the kind of crisis that had suddenly hit us, an ability to face it out on his own. He just couldn't do it. He had come haring up to fetch me, totally out of his depth and wallowing. He was frightened. He also believed that he had helped to kill an old man.

I tried to take his mind off that by discussing the new situation, with special reference to the widow's part in it.

"I'd hoped you'd get to Mrs. Lindquist first," Lung said.

"Instead you think Tsing is already in there offering consolation and advice?"

"I'm sure."

"Until the will is probated, she can do nothing about selling those shares."

"But supposing Tsing and Wen get some kind of interim authority to act on her behalf? It can be done. It would give them effective control of the board right away."

"Not without those investment-trust holdings."

"Their man in London is probably working on that now."

"Then we'll get our man in London working against them. It's the kind of job Jeremy likes. Since he's found out about that proxy buying, he must know the broker who organized it. The chances are the same broker is being used to influence the trust."

"It may be too late," Lung said, waggling his foot again.

"It's never too late for a fight. And we've got the company books on our side."

"Profits were down last year. Way down."

"Everyone's profits were down last year. The point is we're still in the black. Comfortably."

"Our shares dropped eleven pence yesterday on the London exchange."

"Part of a general slide?"

"Yes."

"Then to hell with that."

But I was worried. The trust's accountants might decide that this was the moment, on a falling market, to get out of a Far East share that might fall further. Also, if my guesses were right, there were buyers waiting: Tsing and Wen, probably willing to make a deal at a price above the quotation.

I switched on the intercom.

"Maria, book me a call to London, will you? When you've done that, get two seats on the next flight to Singapore."

"Yes, Mr. Harris. I was just going to let you know you have a visitor."

"Who?"

"An Inspector Kadok."

"Where is he?"

"Right here."

"Just a minute, Maria."

I switched off. Lung was staring. I did nothing about his curiosity, suggesting that he wait for me in Bahadur's office. When he had left by a door to the corridor, I sat alone for a minute thinking that I could have done without Kadok as an addition to my problems this morning.

The Inspector came in without offering any hint of that deference to my work scene that I'd hoped for; we might have been back in a hotel bedroom. He sat down without being invited to, a man obviously in need of a six-week crash course on police relations with the public. His business suit didn't really fit him any better than the dinner jacket. Out of uniform he would always be wearing an indifferent disguise.

"So you leave for Singapore on the next flight?" he said.

Intercoms have a lot to be said against them. I made a mental note to have one of our storerooms converted into a waiting area with hard chairs. I watched Kadok fumbling in his pocket. He produced a length of what looked like black silk ribbon. Then I recognized it.

"We found this evening tie in the hotel grounds, Mr. Harris."

55

"The place is already getting quite a name for its strip parties."

He looked at me. "This was picked up twenty feet back in the jungle. I don't think people take off their clothes in there. A long way from the swimming pool. But not very far from where the helicopter was sitting."

He continued to stare at me.

"As a matter of fact, I ordered a search for this. We didn't find an evening tie in your luggage when we checked it. Have you lost one?"

"I don't know. I haven't been back to my flat here to unpack."

"I see. No doubt it would have troubled you to find that you'd lost your tie?"

It would have, but I hoped this didn't show in my face. I now had a policeman riding on my back who wasn't going to be easy to shake off. I wondered if he had come here with authorization to stop my going to Singapore. Once down there I'd have to be extradited if they decided they wanted me, and this with much red tape. Aggressive tactics seemed indicated.

"Who was killed up on that mountain, Inspector?"

It was pleasant to see that this really startled him. He said nothing.

I went on: "Or was wounded? And you're keeping that quiet, having given it out to hotel guests that the firing had all been a mistake. A jumpy sentry disturbed by a monkey. Are the police investigating the death of a monkey?"

He took a moment over his answer. When it came, it was official jargon.

"We are investigating abnormal circumstances surrounding the unscheduled visit of a Chinese Minister of State to a hill resort."

For a man whose native language isn't English, that was a pretty good effort.

"Not a handout likely to satisfy a newspaper reporter, Inspector."

56

At the mention of the press, his face, pretty expressionless on the whole, showed anger. Even a nominal adherence to democratic principles can be trying for the men whose job it is to maintain law and order.

Maria's voice reached us. I could tell she was positively goaded by curiosity. "I've got you on the four-twenty flight, Mr. Harris. Two seats. Only it has been delayed for forty minutes. Li Feng Tsu leaves the airport at four and they're closing down the runways until his plane has cleared. It'll be five before your takeoff. Will that be all right?"

"Fine," I said, switching her off.

She wouldn't dare switch on again—the box makes a slight hissing when activated.

"How long do you mean to be in Singapore, Mr. Harris?"

"At least a week. A business matter has come up that will take time to sort out. My home is really down there now, as you know."

He stood. "Perhaps you should change nationality once again."

A nasty crack, but I just took it. I could see that he had decided, for reasons of his own, to postpone a third degree with my black tie as the centerpiece. Also, silk doesn't take fingerprints too well.

Lung and I were in the back seat of the rent-a-car with Bahadur up front as chauffeur. My assistant in K.L. hates to have to do jobs of this kind, which he considers beneath his dignity. He sat in white-turbaned dignity showing a chiseled profile set in cold reserve, interpreting the silence between Lung and me as a decision not to discuss business in his presence. The affairs of Hok Lin have nothing to do with him anyway, and perhaps he resented this, too. He's an ambitious young man.

At ten to five the airport was showing signs of a VIP's recent departure—hordes of policemen still about, most of them on the point of getting into their jeeps. There was a feeling that the whole area had been under tight security only minutes earlier and not all the guns were yet tucked away. We went into reception to check out my still unpacked suitcase. I turned to Bahadur.

"I've got a job for you to do back at the office."

"I was going home when I'd turned in the car," he said, like a clock watcher.

"I want a complete check with Pridol in Bangkok on a woman called Ranya Nivalahannanda. You'd better get out your notebook and write the name down. The spelling is tricky. But Pridol should have heard of her if she's what she claims to be, which is the owner of a restaurant and a divorcee. She says her ex-husband is the cousin of a prince. There's just a possibility that she left Thailand because she had to. Check on that as well. Also her political connections, if any. When you hear from Pridol again, ring me. It doesn't matter if it's in the middle of the night."

He took down the spelling I gave him, looking displeased, then left us, an impressive figure under the turban in an uncrushable suit, slim, tall, and taking himself far too seriously as usual. Lung watched him go as though he found something slightly intimidating about my Sikh assistant. I could understand the feeling. I get it too, sometimes.

The flight wasn't half full and we settled in seats at the back, Lung at once fastening his belt. Some years ago his plane went into a takeoff skid at Tai Kak airport and he has hated flying ever since. I don't like it much myself and didn't plan to use the time we were airborne for any business discussion. Squeezed down into one of those seats they have the impudence to advertise as designed for the human contours by an orthopedic surgeon, I tend to find myself thinking about death, far more conscious than usual of it waiting there somewhere ahead. When we hit air pockets it suddenly doesn't seem all that far ahead, either. I have to fly a good deal and it is high time I became blasé about the whole thing, but I haven't yet.

58

We had a last-minute passenger who only just made it before the door clanged and the NO SMOKING sign glowed. I turned my head to see Ranya coming down the aisle looking like a girl who has never hurried for anything. She was still in the green trouser suit, and all she carried was the jewel box, which must have made up most of her baggage-weight allowance. The rest of her stuff would have gone by rail—the plane wasn't equipped to carry freight.

She saw me and after a fractional hesitation I got the kind of cool nod a good-looking woman keeps for an acquaintanceship which is going to be allowed to lapse. There was an aisle seat beside Lung, but she went on up the plane. It was the first time I'd had an uninterrupted view of her walking away. She was good from that angle, too.

5

When it became obvious that I was going to have to spend too much time in Singapore to make living in a hotel an economic proposition, I looked for somewhere reasonable to live and was bitterly disappointed. Every drop of Scots blood was shocked by rentals demanded for two-room flatlets, and when I kept asking for something cheaper the agent finally took me to a house out in the country off the road to Changi. It was a good way off the road, too, up a rutted track through a patch of neglected rubber, and hadn't been lived in for some time. This seemed surprising on a crowded island until I saw the house. It was big, built by an escapist towkay with security at the forefront of his mind, so that outside it was practically windowless and looked rather like a badly baked cake covered with thick chocolate icing. Inside there was no plumbing, crumble, and a ghost.

The ghost was of a previous tenant who had hanged himself from the one central tree in a courtyard featuring a great deal of virulent green moss. I had a look at the tree and could see why the poor man had done it. It was a large growth with nude limbs, no bark, just a kind of skin, many branches like the many arms of Shiva lifted up toward a lofty dusting of leaves. One particularly obscene arm was just asking for a rope to be tossed over it and knotted, and I had the feeling that during one of the occasional depressions resulting from contemporary commerce I just mightn't be able to resist a really pressing invitation, so I said no to the place even though it could have been made really cute for a hundred thousand dollars.

After that I went hunting in the slums, and without the assistance of a property dealer. What did actually come to my aid was a business need that was a direct result of increasing overhead in the junk side of my operations. With the advent of Hok Lin Shipping I had gradually cut down on these picturesque vessels and now had only twelve left, all based in Singapore, which was handy for the Dyak crews, who could fly straight home on leave from the international airport. Trading profits were dropping from the usual wage-cost spiral and I decided that it would pay me to eliminate a middleman's cut with my own ship-chandler's business for servicing these craft. Actually, I'd always wanted a ship-chandler's business, fascinated by these marine junkshops smelling of tarred cordage and new canvas, with all kinds of gear hanging from the roof. We stocked spare components for our own diesels used to power the boats and even had spare electric motors for operating capstans and loading booms. There was a whole bay devoted to chains of assorted sizes, another to fenders, and we had a grocery section catering to Dyak tastes, which gave off its own unique smell.

The building I found to contain the great cave that housed all this backed onto the Singapore River in an area which even the most imaginative real-estate men hadn't yet started to develop as a residential district. I wasn't really nervous that any of them ever would, either, for the river does stink—sometimes a high stink, sometimes muted, but always there, so that what I had to pay for four floors on a narrow street frontage with a rear entrance from the river was considerably less than the price of a small villa in one of the more airy suburbs, and this even after alterations.

The architect I brought in was shocked. He got the idea in the

61

end, which was to hollow out the first two floors to give us a vastly high-ceilinged shop, the next level converted into an apartment for the shopkeeper plus another small one for my servant, and above that my rooms, which were a duplex, bedrooms below with the living room built on what had been the old flat roof. I had the new top construction camouflaged with a mock Chinese frontage to the street side, but behind that windowless façade was almost brutal modernity, with glass walls and a roof terrace. The potted plants in my lofty garden don't do too well, probably because everyone forgets to feed them, but the Hong Kong wicker outdoor furniture is elegant. You get used to the smell.

My new home gave me the feeling I was keeping in touch with the dwindling exotic side of my enterprises. Power junks under the Harris house flag chugged upriver and then nudged through a mass of barges right up to the back door for refits. I could entertain my captains and occasionally the rest of the crews as well, though I kept the social side rationed, for a Dyak with drink taken is unpredictable.

It was all very democratic and contemporary, remote from old colonialist traditions, and when surviving sahibs and their wives visited and we sat out under the tropic sunset you noticed them starting to sniff with the first martini. Not too many came back. Actually, I've never been on any of the important Singapore dinner lists, and am not likely to be, despite the fact that I can claim to be third-generation local, which in this city is equivalent to having ancestors who came over first-class on the *Mayflower*. This just isn't the place for a man with social ambitions to live. You can get a car down the narrow street to the shop frontage, but there is no place to park it, which doesn't worry me since I don't own one anymore, just rent or use taxis, a convert to the new ecology morality. Now if the world cools or gets hotter from excess carbon monoxide in the atmosphere, I've got a relatively clear conscience.

The apartment is more or less what I wanted, but I still get the feeling sometimes that it hasn't much to do with me, even when I see my clothes hanging in a cupboard. The two lower-floor bedrooms have their own bathrooms, one rose pink, the other green, both with waste pipes going down the back of the building into the river. I use the green one. From the hall a teak spiral stair with an iron grille railing goes up to the living room, forty feet by twenty-five, with a small kitchenette off it tucked into the windowless façade. The big room is done in white, the creation of an émigré Yugoslav with a black beard. He wanted me to promise never to use anything but white flowers, but I've broken free and I bought an imitation sang-de-boeuf vase three feet high which sits in an alcove establishing the owner's identity. The sofas and chairs are all dead-white washable plastic, while white transparent curtains put a haze between virginal pallor and the roof garden.

All Chinese must sleep sometime, but in my neighborhood they've worked out a shift system for this, to keep at bay the quiet that reminds them of death. I once came home at four in the morning to find a party of six kids all around the age of seven playing marbles two doors down from mine on the wooden boards over the storm drain. Local mealtimes tend to be highly flexible, too, and it's not uncommon for the big eating session of the day to start at 1:30 A.M. and go on for another hour, with all the family, including baby, pitching in. Transistors are on around the clock, turned up full. On the upper floors I'm elevated above all this din; it's just there all the time like a continuous tape, something you'd miss if it were turned off, giving the feeling that your favorite bar was somehow losing its character.

Tong Tsun, who handles the ship chandling, keeps variable business hours. On occasions when his newish wife's cooking hasn't agreed with him I've known him to put up the shop shutters at ten P.M., forcing me to get out a key to let myself through a wooden hatch in them, but usually you can count on reception functioning until about two in the morning. Tong, in spite of a personal history on the grim side, is a jovial character in love with the human race, or at least his own race. He has two gold teeth up front and no fingers at all on his right hand, just a thumb. He has a tendency to stand rubbing the stumps against the palm of his good hand as though he hoped regular massage might make new fingers sprout.

I can only guess at his age, but until three years ago he was headman of a predominantly Chinese village up in Kedah, toward the Thai border, where he made the serious mistake of deciding to stand firm against a rump of the Red guerrillas who nearly won the civil war in Malaya twenty years ago. Tong was running a shop there also, the village store, from which he refused to supply the guerrillas or pay tribute, this in spite of many warnings that he had better change his political convictions or else. Not only did he disregard threats, but sent out return messages of defiance, telling the blackmailers to go to hell. They brought hell to him. One night during a thunderstorm they attacked the village after having cut phone wires to it, blowing up the police station on the outskirts with the policeman and family inside. Tong was hauled out of bed, along with his wife, and taken to adjacent rubber, where the wife was tied to a tree and used for bayonet practice while he was held to watch. The poor woman didn't die for a long time. At the end, or near it, Tong went berserk and got away. After that he emigrated south to Singapore, and who could blame him?

He seems to have no bitterness at all about the past. Life is violent, it always has been and always will be, and you survive in it by chance, each day a gift to be used for many things, especially good eating. His absences from the shop are usually accounted for by his being in a restaurant three doors along, his new wife being, in his own words, a bitch of a cook. She is little more than a girl, but already running to fat, with a wobble for a walk, and spends a lot of time complaining about having thrown away her young life on a man who can't begin to appreciate what she has to offer. She does this at a high-pitched yell, which appears to be their only home life. I sometimes hear

64

them at it as I climb the stairs, though naturally enough Tong is usually down below. In the shop he continually has green tea brewing and entertains his cronies. I often stop for chats, and though my Cantonese has always been passable, he has done a lot to improve my vocabulary in esoteric speech areas.

Tong is really highly symbolic of the Chinese will to survive as a race first and as individuals second. It's a fine balance: they have no illusions about the importance of a man as a separate entity within the mass, and yet they respect that entity. You are you, and this matters. As a people, they hit on this idea about five millennia before Jean-Paul Sartre.

I was pretty certain that my shopman thought me an idiot. I had the money to live in a big house with a first-class cook in the kitchen, but instead I had chosen three weirdly decorated rooms at the top of a moldering building, my only servant an old man who couldn't fry a chicken. He never said this, innately courteous despite a remarkably obscene tongue, but I frequently caught him directing toward me a heavily ironic stare.

The man was a natural shopkeeper. Within six months of taking over he knew all there is to know about ship chandling, and practically his only excursions far from our street were to haggle down the wholesale prices we paid for stock. He kept his accounts in English for my benefit, and these were careful, detailed, and seemed to allow no room for squeeze at all, though I knew he was getting this, since cooking the books is a national art. What I paid him was adequate. What he paid himself from my money covered the cost of eating out a lot, as well as jade and gold ornaments for a discontented wife.

Tong wasn't in the shop when I arrived from the airport, just his assistant, a youth with pimples who in a less scientific age would have been called "simple." The boy was paid minimum rates for the job and as a special concession was allowed to sleep in a cubbyhole under the racks for sail canvas. He also ate with the Tongs, apparently impervious to Mrs. Tong's culinary failures. He was using a straw broom when I walked past, doing the job slowly, as though he had been at it for a long time. My greeting got a grin of recognition. I didn't bother to ask where his master was. The boy wouldn't know.

No sound came from the Tongs' apartment as I climbed past it, though there was an old man snoring in the rooms opposite. I put a key in my door, flicked on lights, realizing at once that Chong, my sleeping houseboy, was still adhering to established domestic routines. One of these was to open all the windows daily 'just when the stink from the river was at its worst under noonday heat, closing them again in half an hour to capture this, then switching on the air-conditioning, which ought to have filtered away the smell, but didn't. Also, as though out to ruin me by electric bills, my help invariably turned the dial to maximum, which meant that mine was probably the only home in Singapore in which you needed to wear a double cashmere to keep your teeth from chattering.

The rooms were now more than just chilly; after my absence in Europe they simply refused to acknowledge me at all. Upstairs my oxblood vase had disappeared. Either my decorator had sneaked back in here to chuck the thing in the river or Chong had broken it. I looked at the room with a world traveler's eye, deciding that the white lampshades were too much and I wasn't going to live with them.

Out on the roof terrace half the plants were dead, with not a flower among the survivors. I sat down to gaze at Singapore by night and got up again quickly from cushions sodden by a midday shower. An open glass panel was taking the goosepimples out of the atmosphere in the living room and I went back in to pour a whisky, taking this to the plastic sofa.

Homecomings oughtn't to be like this. The family man returns from a business trip to welcoming arms and at least twenty minutes of noise before the kids start devaluing his presents. I get back to a personalized foretaste of the coming new ice age.

The phone rang. I have an unlisted number which few know.

It was too soon to hear from Bahadur. I let the thing ring. Chong's answering service while I was away would certainly have contributed toward the sharp decline in my social life. The old man grabs the instrument and then, without letting the earpiece near his ear, shouts: "No home!" He then slams the receiver back on its hook. Only those who really love me try again later.

I reached out for the hand-set. A man said:

"You take your time."

I knew the voice. It was my old contact in the Singapore police, Chief Superintendent Kang these days, and a power on the island, though I can remember when he was running around in shorts as a fledgling detective sergeant.

"Nice of you to ring so soon to welcome me home," I said. "But if you want a free meal you're not getting it tonight. I'm frying up bacon and eggs and then going to bed."

"You're going to see me."

"Why?"

"Because I'm coming round."

"I don't like the police coming to my home. Even in this area the neighbors notice."

"I'll be there in twenty minutes. And I won't be in uniform."

"Make it tomorrow sometime, Kang. I'm tired."

"No!"

He hung up. I went out into the kitchenette, which is straight from *Homes and Gardens* down to the ornamental ceramic tiling, suggesting at once that no good food could possibly emerge from all the sterility, as it certainly doesn't in my flat. The refrigerator offered ice cubes, no bacon, no eggs. Behind a Formica panel I found a tin of ravioli, the really meaty kind that makes the man in the television ad smack his lips. When I'd warmed it I didn't smack mine.

It wasn't worth putting on the dishwasher for one plate, so I left this for Chong to deal with in the morning, going back to my whisky and staying with it for five minutes before the bell rang. I had to go downstairs to open the door and Kang was looking impatient by the time I reached him.

It always amazes me how young he keeps, presumably under stress the whole time in his exacting role, but thriving on it, a well-integrated man whose uniforms are impeccable and civilian clothes superbly tailored. He is compact and polished, with black hair greased down onto his skull. It was the first time he had been in my new residence; we usually meet in restaurants with me picking up the tab. At the top of the circular stairs he paused, staring.

"My God! What's all this?"

"Hilton Gothic," I said. "You get used to it."

"It's a long way from that planter's bungalow in K.L."

"I'm in a new phase. Sit down. Whisky?"

He nodded. It seemed to take him some time to decide which chair to choose. I get the same feeling often. While my back was still turned he said:

"Paul, in some ways I wish you hadn't come back to this city."

"I know that."

I went over with his glass. He was looking up. For the first time I noticed just the slightest hint of bags under his eyes.

"You go to Europe more often these days. Ever thought of staying there?"

"Not unless I'm deported."

"That could happen."

I sat down with my own refreshed glass. "What do you want with me?"

"We keep a pretty close liaison with the Malaysian police. This evening I had twenty minutes on a scrambled line with an Inspector Kadok in Kuala Lumpur."

"He suggested you keep me under surveillance?"

"He knows I do that anyway. The idea was that you might talk to me. Of your own free will. If I brought out the thumbscrews."

He smiled. It was somehow a tired smile.

"You have nothing on me, Kang."

68

"Oh? There's a file, quite plump, which if brought to the attention of the right person down here could see you declared an undesirable alien."

"Try that on me and I'll fight."

"It wouldn't do you much good. Your position is a bit precarious. To survive, you need friends in the right places. I want to stay your friend."

Kang and I have crossed swords a few times, but he has never used this particular technique with me. I didn't like it. He wasn't liking it either. There were pressures on him.

"How much does your friendship cost?"

He stared toward the door to the kitchenette. "It comes cheap enough. Just the truth about what you saw up at the casino last night."

I asked a polite question. "Is it Li Feng Tsu you're worried about?"

He nodded. "We get him after Bangkok and Rangoon. For a three-day stay. It's a long time to be responsible for his security. And that's my job. Which is why, if you know anything that might be important, I have to know it, too." He looked at me again. "Kadok's a bit of a bully. It's not the best technique to use with you."

"Blackmail is better?"

"I think so. Paul, there is one thing that isn't forgotten down here. Your late partner turned out to be one of the cleverest double agents operating in these parts since World War II. And he wasn't only your partner, he lived in your house."

I felt myself stiffening up. My voice was too loud. "You know damn well how that came about! Menzies was my father's friend and lawyer. I practically inherited him. He was dug into Harris and Company while I was still in short trousers. And he fooled you, too. You'd worked with him for years. Let me point out that I was the one who exposed him in the end."

"Yes. But it took you years to do it."

The Superintendent was a dirty fighter when he had to be.

He had set out to build up my anger, knowing damn well how I can flare and blow my top. Then suddenly he offered that bogus sedative, a police confidence.

"In case you didn't know, Paul, Li Feng Tsu *was* shot at up on that mountain."

I hadn't time to prepare a performance of startled surprise and the one I put up wasn't too good. It didn't fool Kang.

"You weren't with that woman in her room," he told me. "So where were you?"

My return of service wobbled a bit, but it was still in. "Li wasn't hit?"

"No. You didn't actually see what happened?"

I let that go.

He served again. "But you did hear what was going on? From close range?"

"I heard a lot of gunfire. So did all the other guests."

Advantage Harris. You could just see Kang walking back up the court to spin about suddenly and deliver a ball designed to break my nerve.

"It was *not* an assassination attempt," he said.

He got what he had planned, my real surprise. After just a moment I said:

"Some kind of practice?"

"Not quite. The man who shot at Li could easily have killed him. He chose not to."

"Which makes no sense to me. Where did the bullets go?"

"They smacked into the helicopter each side of the open door. One to the right, the other left. They ricocheted, but the marks are there. Each six inches away from the door and exactly parallel. The work of a trained marksman. Further, he fired when Li was entirely unprotected on those steps, his head on a level with the first shot. The second could have got him in the back."

"He might have been hit by the ricochet."

"That was a risk they decided to take."

70

"Who's 'they'?"

Kang didn't answer that. He asked me another question.

"I take it that while all this was going on you were sharing the gunman's cover?"

I said nothing.

He stared at me. "That's Kadok's deduction. Reasonable enough since they found your tie not eight feet from trampled grass where the gunman had been standing. In my younger days I've arrested men on much flimsier evidence. It's a sign you're getting on when you start thinking about what is going to stand up to a very smart lawyer in court. The kind *you*'d hire. Which is why Kadok had to let you wander off like this."

"Hand me over to you, you mean."

"In a way. I feel a little sorry for Kadok, hamstrung by that statement about firing at a monkey. What could he charge you with? Loitering?"

I laughed. Kang didn't.

"Situations of this kind are professionally painful," he said.

"I'll bet."

Kang emptied his glass and put it down on a handy table, a signal for a refill, but I didn't react at once.

I was very uneasy. There are political tensions between Malaysia and Singapore at times, but these have small effect on the liaison between the police, as he'd said. Kang meant to take up where Kadok had left off. He was going to sit here gnawing at me until he got at least more of the truth than I had served to his colleague. There were a number of reasons why I could afford to let him have some of the facts, the chief one being that off-duty he was my friend. We had known each other a long time and on occasion I had been useful to him, just as he had been to me. There was a bond of sorts between us even under stress and when we were in opposition. But I didn't like his mood tonight. His usual easy manner was now a very thin quilt indeed laid over a hard grimness. There was a lot more on his mind than what I had been up to.

"I was not in that patch of jungle when the first shots were fired," I said.

He gave me his complete attention. "Where were you?"

"On a path that ran along beside it. Above a ravine."

"What were you doing there?"

"Getting some fresh air."

"You decided on this walk after the arrival of the helicopter?"

"I decided on it after Li Feng Tsu had pinched my girl for the evening."

"The Thai woman?"

"That's right. I found her attractive. So did Li."

"How long were you out before the shooting?"

"Perhaps half an hour. Maybe more. I sat down on a seat to smoke a cheroot. I heard those two shots, then war broke out."

"But you could see nothing?"

"Kang, there was at least a hundred yards of jungle between me and the action."

"What did you do during the firing?"

"Went into the jungle for cover. I had a feeling someone might come down the path."

"Did anyone?"

Our eyes met and held.

"Yes. The gunman."

"You saw him?"

I nodded. "Just for a moment. A figure running past. There was a screen of leaves."

"You did nothing to stop him?"

"I don't chase assassins carrying automatic rifles when I haven't even a penknife in my pocket. I wouldn't be here if I had."

"You saw his face?"

"Not really. Young. A youth, I'd say."

"Where did he go?"

"Into the jungle again, behind a summerhouse. Smack into it."

72

"He used the path to speed his getaway?"

"That's it."

"What did you do after he'd gone?"

"What would you expect me to do? Come out of the woods and run up toward the hotel shouting for the guards? I had a strong feeling they'd be pretty trigger happy. Strict neutrality seemed called for. I decided to preserve it by going through the woods and making myself scarce. All that gunfire had nothing to do with me. But I could see the trouble I'd have convincing the police of this. You've just defined my position out here yourself: it's precarious. Believe me, I'm aware of that all the time. And my one idea then was to get back into the hotel as quickly as possible to mix with the other guests. The best way to do this was to go through the woods. Things then developed into a rather hectic chase, but I made it to my room."

"It's a pretty lame story, Paul."

"The truth often is."

"Had you any plans to report what you had seen?"

"Yes. To you. I was going to let you handle it."

He took a deep breath. "Am I to take that as a compliment?"

"You can if you like."

"The matter is not within my jurisdiction."

"That's a formality if there ever was one. Why are you so interested?"

"I'm interested in its bearing on Li Feng Tsu's safety while he is here in Singapore."

"Quite. And I've told *you*. Kadok doesn't have to worry about Li anymore."

"Describe this man you saw. What was he wearing?"

"Some kind of jungle camouflage. I suppose you could say it was a guerrilla uniform. Also a floppy hat pulled down about the face."

"Chinese, of course?"

"Yes."

"You saw him well enough to be sure he wasn't a Malay?"

"Well enough for that."

"Yet you couldn't identify him in a parade?"

"I'd hate to have to try."

He stared at me. "Paul, you could really be booked as an accessory after the fact."

"What fact? Officially, nothing happened."

Kang got up then, swung around, and went over to the windows. I had left one of the glass panels open and he pushed aside gauze curtains to go out on the terrace, apparently to commune with the stars, leaving me in a brightly lit room with a sense of sin.

I refilled his glass and took it out to him. The Superintendent was standing by the balustrade, which was mock Chinese rococo to tie in with the front façade. He was gazing out over a city in which he had a vital role. It had always seemed to me he did a pretty good job in urban circumstances as difficult as New York's. Down under all those lights was a mass concentration of forces, both political and criminal, in opposition to him, yet you could walk those streets at night with a considerably smaller chance of being mugged or kidnapped than had been the case five years ago. This is certainly progress in a period which doesn't have too much of this sort of progress to report. A good part of the trend was Kang's doing. Perhaps the most remarkable thing about the man was that, though a hard nut, he hadn't lost compassion, but I couldn't risk testing that compassion to its limits, not at the moment. I knew too well that he would break me if I made this an unavoidable part of his duty, doing it without any of the malice it is so fashionable these days to attribute to policemen. If Kang is a pig, then I'm all for pigs. Also, we had shared many a good belly laugh. I liked the man a lot, a feeling I kept coupled to a watchful respect.

"Here's your drink," I said.

He took the glass without looking at it. "I wish to hell Li Feng Tsu had stayed in Peking."

"I'm sure our Prime Minister wishes the same thing. In spite of the splendid speech he'll make at the banquet."

Kang put his drink on the flat top of the balustrade. "Five hundred of my policemen will be assigned to look after one man for three days. I can't afford five hundred men, or fifty, on any one job for one day."

"I got the impression that Li travels with his own security force."

"They didn't come between him and that gunman. The trained man with the telescopic sight always gets his chance if he's patient. No matter how many men we use."

"You think there's going to be an assassination attempt in this city?"

"There could be."

"The same people who were behind the man up at the casino?"

"Yes."

"Why didn't they finish the job when they had the chance?"

"Locale and timing were wrong. That was a demonstration. A shot across Li's bows. Telling him to alter the course he's been on so far during this tour."

"I don't think I get you."

He turned to me then. "It's not important that you should. But there's one thing you had better understand. If I find out that you've been holding out on me over this identification, I'll come down on you like a pile-driver."

6

Kang's unveiled threat was something of a punch in the stomach. I was conscious of his tensions held in check by only the thinnest of bulkheads and this already bulging from pressure. I'd never seen him like this, drawn tight, and making no real effort to conceal strain.

The city's neon gave the sky a reddish tinge, almost lurid. I thought about what the killing of Li Feng Tsu in these streets might mean. Singapore is now the real focal point for the whole of non-Communist Chinese life, far more important than either Hong Kong or Formosa. On this little island Lee Kuan Yew is trying to create something rather like the old doges' Venice, a city-state which will serve as a mart for the whole of Southeast Asia. To do this effectively, he has to keep clear of alignments with either Mao dogma or Western free-enterprise dogma. Lee aims at a kind of socialism which makes active use of capitalists, and that's all right with me—I'll go along with almost anything that will keep me active. But the snag in all this is that the Prime Minister still hasn't got a really united community behind him, and a strong sense of new nationhood, though emerging, is still under threat from certain quarters. The local Communists are in aggressive opposition both to Lee personally and to his policies, just waiting for their chance to make full use of any sudden emergency.

He also lacks full support in an area where he might seem to have a right to expect it, the local moneyed power group. A considerable number of these gentlemen continue with their almost traditional policy of sitting on the fence, watching developments from this perch while they secretly try to secure themselves against all eventualities by cash backhanders to Peking. Topping off these factors operating against Lee is the terrific emotional appeal to all Chinese of the emergent strong mother country. Plenty of Singapore citizens with fat share portfolios in capitalism want to go on living where they can retain these while at the same time celebrating with firecrackers each strategic victory by the Peking Politburo.

I believe that Lee is a very brave man, not even much frightened of the label of *dictator* which a fair percentage of the locals and almost all Western liberals pin on him. I think he sees clearly that democracy is in fact a luxury by-product of economic growth and that until you've got that growth, and the wealth from it, you just can't afford the luxury. Democratic trimmings mean nothing to empty bellies. Not one single nation with the bulk of its population below the poverty line is now moving toward the future with a political system based on the sanctity of the individual's rights. Prosperity alone allows for personal freedoms to emerge in due course.

This is only a businessman's thinking, of course, to be dismissed as such by the enlightened, and my motivations are suspect, the main one being that I don't want the shambles to happen where I live because if it did I'd be swept right out of the picture. If Lee goes, it will be the shambles here all right. And the assassination of a Peking Politburo man in Singapore could light a fuse for a big explosion.

I asked Kang a question which had been at the back of my

mind for some time. "Who do you think was behind that shooting on the mountain?"

"Lum Ping," he said at once.

For a moment I thought he was trying to be funny. Lum Ping is the Red guerrilla leader who came very near to taking over Malaya during the civil war back in the early fifties. He is still the nominal commander of a rump of revolutionaries who continue to hide out in jungle country up north, though these days their activities are confined to minor, if still vicious, sorties against outlying settlements like my shopkeeper's little village. The whole movement would almost certainly have been completely wiped out by this time but for continuing moral and material support from Peking.

I sat down on a damp cushion. "Are you saying that Lum wants to bite off the hand that feeds him?"

Kang turned. "The hand isn't going to feed him anymore. That's what Li Feng Tsu's goodwill mission here means."

"*What?*"

"Europe seems to have dulled your perception of local developments, Paul. Haven't you been reading any of Li's speeches?"

"No."

"You should have. They're a plain statement of change of policy in Peking. The new realism. Red China is postponing its takeover of these parts for a couple of decades in return for having been accepted in the U.N. and other places. The supply switch to local revolutionary movements has been switched off. Click, like that. If you're a guerrilla, you've had it. And you don't like it. Particularly Lum Ping doesn't like it."

"But he must be a pensioner by this time, an old man?"

"He isn't, you know. He was young during the Emergency. He's only fifty-three now. And a tough nut. He could have another twenty years of political usefulness if he got the chance. But he isn't getting that chance, at least not supported by Peking. They've written him off."

"Are you suggesting that Lum is now taking up some kind of personal vendetta against them, starting with Li?"

"Why not?"

"I'll tell you why not, Kang. It's not Marxism. They're trained to accept the twistings and the double-crossing. Even when this means their bodies on the sacrificial altar."

"Lum isn't the kind to let himself be put on any sacrificial altar. Remember, he damn nearly won out here. He was nearly the ruler of Malaya. He sees himself as one of the Red mythological figures. Like old man Ho Chi Minh. Or Che Guevara. Only he's not interested in getting on posters after he's dead. He plans to stay in the picture alive, Peking or no Peking. Those two bullets so neatly placed by the door of a helicopter were an announcement that he doesn't mean to bow out. And you can be certain that Li got the message and that it was sent on to Peking by him."

"Is this guesswork or have you evidence?"

"Some evidence, a lot of deduction. I've told you, Paul, that the gunman could have killed Li with no trouble at all. He didn't because that wasn't his job. What the gunman was doing was punctuating a note that I'm sure Li had already received, telling him that he'd better rewrite those speeches planned for Bangkok and Rangoon and here about China's new fraternal policy toward existing governments in these parts. Li knew who had fired those shots as he got into the cabin."

"Did he say anything to Malaysian security?"

"Not a word. Kadok says he was perfectly controlled, showed no sign of shock at all."

"You don't expect Li to be recalled to China?"

"No. He'll continue with the tour. And there will be no change in the tone of his speeches. Peking's reaction to threats from any quarter is to thrust out its jaw. If they've decided to write off Lum, he'll stay written off."

"As one of their trainees, he must surely know that."

"Of course he does. But these days there's another big brother out here. Russia. Who look as though they'll soon have the world's biggest fleet. An alternative supply source for Lum, provided he can demonstrate very clearly that he's still a force to be reckoned with. Paul, if Lum can kill Li Feng Tsu in this town, it will be a double demonstration to the Russians: one, that he can still do what he likes in this area when he sets his mind to it, and, two, that he can also function as an *urban* guerrilla, the new thing. And a very necessary new thing. During the Emergency Lum was never really effective in the towns and cities. That's why he lost."

A policeman was letting me have a look at his nightmare. In many ways it was also mine. Up until two or three years ago the Russians were simply hamstrung in anything they tried to do out here by a lines-of-communication problem. Almost overnight this has changed. Their fleet has arrived. We're very conscious of it steaming around in the Indian Ocean. Moscow isn't just in the process of filling the vacuum left by British naval withdrawal, she has done it. If Lum Ping could sell himself to the Russians as the guerrilla leader with the future, he could be supplied from the sea and in a big way. From having been little more than a bandit in hiding he could soon enough be leading a heavily supported revolutionary movement.

It would be the kind of set-up the Russians like, difficult to prove even by air reconnaissance that they were pouring in arms and specialists to Lum, for along that indented island-spattered coast from Penang to the Isthmus of Kra are hundreds of small harbors where powered junks, acting as feeders from the Russian ships, could unload almost without risk. It wouldn't take long, either, for a revitalized revolutionary movement to establish areas in which it couldn't be challenged. It is wild country on both sides of the Thai border, thinly populated for Asia, hills, jungle, and whole districts that haven't yet been properly mapped.

For a long time now there has been evidence that the Rus-

80

sians want a base in Southeast Asia. They tried to get one via Ho Chi Minh in Vietnam, but the old man wasn't having any: he took their supplies, but rejected their advisors, fighting his own war. A Russian foothold, or even toehold, on that long peninsula which has the Indian Ocean on one side and the South China Sea on the other would give them a most useful move in the continuous chess game played against the Peking Politburo.

I looked up at Kang. "Do you think the Russians would ever be persuaded that a Peking-trained Mao Marxist could switch his allegiance?"

"Yes," Kang said. "For one thing, I don't think he is a Mao Marxist. For another, Lum knows that the alternative for him is oblivion. Peking-trained, all right, but he also went to Moscow at the end of World War II to study guerrilla tactics. He was there for a year. He even speaks Russian quite well. He's the kind of Marxist who would probably have been eliminated if he'd been in China. Mao and Chou don't trust these Russian-orientated men. Lum's last visit to Peking may not have been too much of a success. There have been rumors that it wasn't."

"You think he's been waiting for twenty years for his time to come around again?"

"I do. And his Peking courses have taught him one thing. Patience. Now is his last chance. He won't get another. It could be that even if he kills Li, Moscow won't back him. In that case, he's finished."

"What about local Chinese support for Lum?"

Kang made a sound that might have been a laugh. "Li Feng Tsu has just made it plain that this is no longer necessary. Local businessmen are having this burden removed from them. And are they happy about it! Lum won't get another penny from those pockets unless he can scare their owners, in spite of Peking, by getting his revolutionary operation swinging again. If he can do that, the money will start clinking toward him again. We'll then have the interesting situation of local Chinese money helping to support a Russian-backed uprising."

After a moment I said: "The brain reels."

"Mine suffers from a permanent headache."

"Come inside, I'll get you another drink."

"Not inside. It's just occurred to me that your living room could have been bugged while you were away. It's becoming very popular. Also phone-tapping."

"Were you thinking of having mine wired to your HQ?"

"I can get what I want out of you, Paul, without listening to boring tapes."

I took his glass away for the refill. When I came back, he was still at the balustrade.

"You think Lum is going to use the same assassin here in Singapore?" I asked.

"Yes."

"Why?"

"Intuition. Plus the fact that he has obviously been specially trained for the job. Probably at the Johore camp the guerrillas set up recently. The Malaysian army are looking for it, but they haven't found it yet."

"You think Lum is there?"

"No. He's here in Singapore. Has been for some years, as a respected businessman."

"That sounds like a wild guess."

"It's a reasonable deduction. We used to manage to keep a man with them up in the jungle. The flow of new recruits from here was small but steady, and we infiltrated them. From this we know that Lum left his hideout to go to Peking on a course in 1960. He never went back to the hideout."

"He could be dead?"

"Take it from me, he isn't. He has a certain unmistakable style. The myth figure's style, like a trade mark. Not easy to copy, and it appears in all his orders. Those orders are being issued from this city. We have evidence of that. It's logical that they should be. He is now an urban guerrilla."

Kang drained his glass.

"Even if you think you can't identify that gunman, Paul, I still want you in the office to look at some photographs. You mustn't be seen coming to the building. You'll be picked up by a closed van at the corner of Bukit Timah Road and Putang Street at ten fifteen. We don't meet in public. It's best that we aren't seen together just now."

"I have no part in all this."

"So you say. That Thai woman with whom both Li and you have been so closely associated recently has taken a room in the hotel where the Peking party have booked a whole floor. Did she tell you where she was staying?"

"No."

"It's the Orient Palace. Room two-seventeen."

"Thanks."

"I wouldn't get in touch with her if I were you. Good night."

"I'll see you down to the shop."

"Don't bother. I came by your back door. And it was wide open. Is that locked at night?"

"Yes. My storekeeper does it when he shutters the shop."

"Don't be careless about security, Paul. In your case it isn't wise."

After that warning I locked Kang out of my flat and then climbed back up to watch him leave by the river entrance. There was no sign of a police launch hanging about anywhere waiting for him—nothing but the barges of the river people who use moorings all along the backs of these buildings. I have an understanding with the bargees that they always leave open to my ramp a passage wide enough to take one of the Harris junks. The arrangement is maintained by occasional donations to their favorite charity, which is themselves.

They're a tough crowd, water gypsies who live on their craft, tied up here while they wait to be towed away for the next load. Their boats can be up to a hundred feet long, pot-bellied and cavernous-looking when empty, with the tiny living accommodation crowded into the stern under an arched awning. Cooking is done on deck in charcoal braziers, and most of the rest of their living too, the river used for everything, the bargees contriving to avoid Singapore's new public-health regulations. No one knows why they don't all die of cholera. I could smell fifty suppers frying down below, all of them fish. There was one small sampan moving, and though I couldn't see her very well, the figure at the stern oar appeared to be an old woman with arthritis, each dip painful to her. She was probably a peddler of reject vegetables from the city market; the bargees seem to get all their supplies from these floating shops, and it wouldn't surprise me if some of those water-borne housewives never step on dry land from one year's end to another. What I do know for certain is that they visit each other's boats a lot. I've sat on my terrace trying to do some work through a matrons' tea party going on down below and the Cantonese din was unbelievable.

The old woman recovered from her rheumatics at startling speed, giving the stern oar three sharp, deep flips which sent her sampan scudding in toward my ramp. Kang was ready to catch the boat's bow and spin it around again. He jumped in, at once disappearing under the small bow awning that might have been erected just to give him cover. I watched the craft move out into the main flow, then down it.

The Superintendent had certainly gone to great pains not to be seen contacting me. I didn't know whether to be flattered or insulted.

I was nearly asleep over the financial section of the *Straits Times* when Bahadur finally called in from Kuala Lumpur. He tends to sound bored on a phone line and is always cryptic.

"The woman Nivalahannanda owns the Ponchana restaurant in Bangkok, all right. She was divorced from her husband two years ago. Pridol says she's not to be blamed for doing that. Seems he knows her personally. Eats in her place. Do you want a physical-appearance check?"

"Don't bother. Anything else?"

"She flew south four days ago. Telling no one she was going to. Her husband is angry. He's about to bring an action against her in the Thai courts for illegally smuggling out of the country a considerable portion of their joint assets. He claims he owns her jewelry, that she only held it on loan as a capital asset and got out with a quarter of a million U.S. dollars' worth of stones, a lot of them unset."

I'd only seen a selection of the set ones and you had to allow for the exaggerated claims of an ex-husband starting a court action, but there was also that Swiss account. Ranya could afford to abandon her restaurant and bus companies, out in the wide world with reasonable protection against its bitter winds. I wondered why she had tried to blackmail me to back her new enterprise, but not for long: it's good business to use someone else's money instead of your own on a highly speculative deal.

The buzzer sounded from my front door. I said good night to Bahadur and went down the stairs. My visitor was Tong, just back from eating well three doors along. He was apologetic about no welcome home and said I should have sent a telegram, presumably so that he could have arranged a firecracker display from the roof as I got out of the taxi.

I took him upstairs and gave him a beer—he never touches anything stronger. We sat down and gossiped. He smokes Javanese cigarettes, which are the world's worst, and even with the glass door to the terrace open I began to feel as though I was being fumigated.

During my absence the price of copra had fallen and the price of diesel oil gone up, which meant reduced junk-trading profits. In the last fortnight two of the boats had come around here after unloading for engine replacements. There had been a huge party with one of the crews which had spread all over the building, I hoped not up to my quarters. Tong's wife believed she was pregnant and was making a fuss about that, but he was sure it was a false alarm. He didn't really want to be a father again at his age—he had four sons and three daughters scattered around Malaysia and that was enough for any man. Anyway, Lan Nin would make a terrible mother. He didn't believe he could stand it. His stomach was troubling him again. He prodded his abdomen with the maimed hand to show me where the pain was concentrated, but he was trying a new formula from the herbalist, ground snakeskin and turmeric plus a mystery ingredient, and already there was some improvement. He asked me if I was also constipated.

Somehow with Tong opposite me, life seemed to swing back onto a reasonably even keel again, despite all the things I had on my mind. He has a broad face with a bad skin the texture of cracked shoeleather, but his smile reveals beautifully balanced teeth without a visible filling. The gold crowns don't count; they're assets placed so that every time you grin at yourself in a mirror you know you've got something to fall back on.

I didn't get to bed until one fifteen. On his way out Tong used the Cantonese word for *friend*, which sounds as though it has warm laughter through it, or did from him. I closed the door with the feeling that my world wasn't too bad.

7

Kang's office is in a block with a huge basement garage, handy when you want to have someone smuggled up to you without the world knowing. The building is the newest thing for our climate, with permanent angled screens down the façade to keep out glare, which means that not much color survives inside, the tone mostly gray. The Superintendent also has a gray steel desk with filing cabinets to match, and the framed picture of his parents at their golden wedding celebration is gray, too. He gave me a mug of coffee and we settled to photographs, needing a desk light to see them.

It was an odd rogues' gallery, not the usual front and side on the same print, but mostly snaps obviously taken by micro-camera when the subject was very much unaware of what was happening. In a lot of them enlarging hadn't helped detail and there was a tendency to have the subject overpowered by shadow suggesting jungle even when this wasn't obvious in the background. None of the faces were of criminal types, if there is such a thing; most were highly intelligent-looking and I knew there was a sizable percentage of university degrees among the batch.

Kang had been doing a good deal of selecting among his

pictures, apparently eliminating the too old or the jailed. He shoved another over toward me.

"That one?"

"No."

"Or this?"

"No."

"Paul, are you really trying?"

"Look, I warned you I wouldn't be able to help on this."

He leaned back in his chair, groped for a cigarette on the desk, lit it, and then stared at me. A policeman can make a highly effective use of silence and after a full minute of Kang's a section of my conscience was starting to squirm. Also, he has that rare combination, a logical brain which can also be switched suddenly onto an almost totally intuitive approach, with the result that you can never be quite sure in what gear he is operating. He does this quick change when he's relaxing, too. I've heard him setting out an idea with a simple clarity that would have done credit to a very good lawyer, only to flip over into what amounted to pure fantasy, the man romping away down this new path with all the zest of a slightly half-witted butterfly collector. I found this terribly disconcerting; having dinner with him became at times like eating out with a schizophrenic. Also, it wasn't always the wine that started up the fantasy; sometimes just to fool me he did the butterfly-hunting sober and started getting coldly logical over the brandy which followed wine and pre-food whisky. A formidable man, and at his most formidable now. In these moments, as in others, the bond of affection between us was stretched near to snapping.

I watched him groping in a drawer. He produced another photograph and shoved it over. It could have been one of the blown-up micro-snaps he had eliminated earlier because of the subject's years, a man probably in his forties somewhere, though I couldn't even be sure of that because of the blurring. It wasn't full-face; the man had turned his head just as the button clicked, the result a half-profile but with features undefined.

"Means nothing to me," I said.

"That's Lum Ping. Taken in 1959. The only picture we have of him. He didn't allow cameras in his camps. He was to stay the faceless myth figure. Micro-cameras weren't as good then as they are now, either."

"Who took this?"

"One of my men. He got the picture out, but didn't get out himself. Lum had him shot. His intelligence service was remarkable. We never got a man in who lasted more than three months."

"Your infiltrators were shot?"

Kang nodded. "They died in raids. That's Lum's method with traitors. A bullet in the back of the head during some action. Not always in the back of the head, either. It kept the rest from feeling that their security had been penetrated. As a leader Lum is fussy about small detail."

"Why show me this?" I asked.

He fished in the drawer again, this time producing a large square of cardboard, again a blow-up, but with a very different background: no blur of jungle, a city pavement in bright sunlight. Here again the man was turning, as though into a building. I knew him very well. It was Lung, the general manager of Hok Lin Shipping.

"Put them side by side," Kang said.

I did this.

"Well?"

"Look at them. *Look* at them!"

After a moment I asked: "Are you suggesting a resemblance?"

"Allow for nearly thirteen years and better feeding. Possibly some plastic surgery."

I took a deep breath. "All I can say, Kang, is that if you're as desperate as this, all your leads must have gone stone dead. These are two different people."

"Say two different identities and I'd agree with you. Lum has a new identity. Completely new."

The Superintendent had been overworking himself to near breaking point. What I felt was a kind of pity, nothing else. I tried to be reasonable.

"I can see certain similarities, but they're racial. I'd say you could make this comparison using the faces of a thousand local businessmen."

"That's just about what I have done! And these two faces, side by side, say something that the others didn't."

"You expect me to agree with you?"

"No. You haven't the trained eye."

My sudden anger kicked out words. "It could be that I haven't your imagination!"

His cigarette had gone out in an ash tray. He lit another, inhaling. He sat back with the smoke dribbling slowly out of his nostrils as though he had forced it into every crevice of his lungs.

"What do you really know about your man Lung's background?"

"Oh, hell, Kang, don't you think I investigate the people who work for me? And down to the fine print of their past histories? There are sometimes things I overlook because it's policy, but I *know* about them. I know that one of my directors, who doesn't need naming to you, got where he is on a great pile of shady property deals, any one of which could have landed him in jail if he hadn't been lucky. I don't particularly like having this connection with the man, but he was wished on me, and he's useful. He's an important member of a big tribe and his cousins bring us business."

"We're talking about Lung!"

"All right. Lung was working at his job as a trained engineer in Shanghai when he was accused of bourgeois revisionism and

90

sentenced to six months on the city sewage farm to learn the dignity of manual labor. When that stint was over, he was sent to Canton on a building job, but more re-creative coolie work was threatening, this time helping to move a mountain, using only wicker baskets and spades. He decided to get out. He came the hard way to Hong Kong: swimming. You know the route. Six of his party were swept out by the currents and drowned. Lung just made it, along with three others. I talked to two of those others. They didn't seem like Red agents to me and they certainly didn't think Lung was. In Hong Kong they all worked as the coolies they'd left China to escape becoming. I checked the fight Lung had to get on his feet again. I don't think the Reds would have subjected one of their own to what he had to go through."

"They might have done just that," Kang said.

I tried to keep calm.

"You know why you've picked on him? It's the old Chinese thing. Any man who hasn't got a host of relations is suspect. Lung's up against that in our company, too. Remember, I brought him down here. I picked him out and brought him."

"You don't think he could have picked you out? Who made the first contact?"

"He did. He had something to sell!"

"Quite. You know, Paul, even among all those refugees in Hong Kong you'll find very few who haven't some relations there, people who got out before them or have always lived in the British territories. Lung had none at all."

"You've been checking?"

"Yes."

"If this is your stated case, it's about the feeblest I've ever heard."

"It is not my stated case. But before I tell you more, let's look at things from Lum Ping's angle. After it had been decided that he would be more useful back in the world than up in the mountains, his new career had to be carefully plotted. This was certainly done in Peking. Without doubt he went there, to be fitted out with his new identity. His cover had to be good, very good. It had also to be achieved slowly, in a natural-seeming manner. Before any contact at all was made in the Singapore target area, he had to be established elsewhere, and well established, his new identity a straight pointer to his caliber potential."

Kang's phrase reeked of a top executive's refresher course.

"The company into which Lum would infiltrate had to be carefully chosen. It had to offer him two things: a chance to get in a position of authority at some speed, plus an opportunity to make quite a bit of money on the side when he got there. The Reds like to add to their funds from all sources. They're always short of foreign currency."

"Lung earns a good salary with Hok Lin, but that's all he takes out of us!"

"Please don't interrupt! For reasons I've just mentioned, a completely Chinese firm wouldn't suit him. The stranger coming in wouldn't be likely to get on quickly inside it. So it had to be a business with a strong tie-in to European interests, preferably a company with local Europeans as the real power. Again, a purely European business wouldn't have served because a Chinese would have been up against another kind of race barrier there. The firm they were looking for had to be one that had achieved a compromise for this time and place—one foot in each camp, you might say. Like your company, Paul. And there aren't too many of them, you'll agree?"

"I agree. The only thing wrong with your theory is that Lung is not a face-lifted Lum Ping!"

Kang stayed calm. I sat waiting for him to trot out that old theory about how a man changing his identity is always propelled toward choosing a new name that has euphonious links with his old one, but the policeman didn't do this, just continued with mechanistic reasoning that sounded as though a top-floor computer bank had worked it all out for him in detail.

And that could well be the way these conclusions had been reached. They seemed to have peeled away the human element altogether, discarding it as irrelevant, turning out a chrome-polished assessment.

"I'm sure contacting you was skillfully done," Kang said. "What you saw was a little engineering concern in Hong Kong struggling to survive by manufacturing small parts of a kind you could use and, more important, get cheaply. Like everyone else, you're very cost conscious. Why not avail yourself of cheap Chinese labor?"

"Which makes me once removed from a sweat-shop proprietor. Don't forget I got Lung to wind up his business and come down here. And the men he was employing in Hong Kong now have jobs in my Johore factory. I seem to be employing quite a troop of Red agents. You said something just now about Lum wanting to make money on the side if he could. Well, he can't with us. Bills of lading for all our ships are very carefully inspected here at head office. I do spot checks myself."

"I'm sure you do. But I think you've forgotten one thing. Your ships go from port to port in Indonesia—very small ports, most of them."

"That's right. We're running tramps. But head office knows exactly what they're loading and unloading, even in those very small ports."

"You're sure?"

"Of course!"

"Look at this, then."

"Not *another* photograph?"

"They make useful police evidence. Not easy to fake for the expert eye, either. I don't think you'll feel that one is a fake."

I took the postcard-size piece of cardboard. It was a glossy print that might have been of a local tourist attraction, but instead showed our oldest ship, the *Kao Ming*. She is scheduled for scrapping in Formosa the moment her replacement arrives from that yard of mine on the Clyde, two thousand two hundred tons gross, twelve knots maximum on a couple of pre-World War II diesels that keep putting her into drydock for emergency patch-ups. She's very far from being our flagship, an antique with center superstructure and a tall black funnel dating from her coal-burning days, this now serving mainly to provide a large area for the company colors, which are green, yellow, and heliotrope stripes suggested to me by one of our sunsets.

There was something very wrong with her in this photograph. The *Kao Ming* hasn't been converted for carrying standardized steel containers, serving out her now very limited time on the copra pick-up routes which require a vessel of shallow draft to get up rivers to the small ports. She loads by old-type boom derricks and cargo nets, not powered for the heavy lifts at all, yet in this picture she carried two metal containers for'ard plus another aft, these on top of the hatches and surrounded by wooden crates of assorted sizes, some of them very large.

I stared down at the picture, conscious of Kang staring at me. He knew what I was thinking. A deck cargo of this kind would knock the ship's trim to hell, this plus the fact that she was down in the water to well over Plimsoll line. It wasn't difficult to imagine what the helm reaction would be on a shallow-draft craft loaded down like this.

I asked my question without looking at the man on the other side of the desk. "Where was this taken?"

"At Bontang in East Borneo. By one of my men."

"What was your man doing so far from home?"

"On a special mission for me."

"You mean you were checking up on Hok Lin ships?"

"Yes."

One of his intuitive ideas which this time had paid off, from his point of view.

"How did your man get on to the *Kao Ming?*"

"He tracked the ship from Bandjermasin. She picked up that deck cargo at Bontang, crane-loaded from an oil-company dock.

She off-loaded the stuff at another company dock near Paloe in the Celebes. Then she sailed for Onan to pick up more copra. I don't think you'll find that deck cargo entered on any of your bills of lading."

"How long ago?"

"Three months."

"You've been sitting on this?"

"For further evidence. Which I haven't got so far."

"So you can't prove these deck cargoes are a regular thing?"

"No. I don't have an unlimited expense account for jobs of this kind and my man had to be recalled. But I think you'll find when you investigate that this wasn't an isolated case."

Kang wasn't smiling at me, but he was still pleased with his timing during this interview. I had a cold feeling in my stomach. If the *Kao Ming* had made the passage down the Straits of Makassar with that deck load, she had done it with more than her trim gone, so top-heavy she could have rolled over and sunk in a gale. It was a monstrous thing for her Chinese captain to have permitted. Other things were involved besides the risk to her crew. Insurance was one of them. Our cover simply wouldn't stretch to manic loading of this kind. And if Lloyds got wind of the fact that Hok Lin was playing this kind of game, they'd move in to break us, and quite right, too.

"Your idea is that this overloading has been a regular thing? With other ships of ours?"

"If it hasn't been, it's remarkable that my man just happened to hit it with the *Kao Ming*. This has been a carefully planned business, Paul. At the big places like Bandjermasin everything is nicely in order, your ships carrying the usual copra and small stuff. The extra cargoes were loaded in the little places and carried to other little places. Wouldn't you say private deals arranged by the ships' skippers and local agents? I don't think, though, that they could have risked doing it without knowing that they had the backing of someone with authority here in your Singapore offices. They needed that cover. I'd say that the skippers and crew got their cut, but the real money went into a pocket in this city. I'll leave you to guess which pocket. Personally, I don't have to."

I didn't say anything. After a moment Kang continued chipping away.

"A profitable sideline for the man running it. From what I can see, three of your ships seem suitable for this special trade and have probably been used. For how long is anyone's guess, of course. Perhaps a couple of years? Since soon after Lung took over?"

I wanted to tell Kang to shut up, that he didn't have to spell everything out, and he must have sensed this, for he got up suddenly and walked over to one of those long windows with a restricted view. I sat on with my black thoughts.

The man running this would have his take completely immune to tax, and from the look of all that stuff piled on the holds, it would be a huge take, too. As manager, Lung pays fairly frequent visits to the major ports we use and a good few of the minor ones as well. If Kang's man had stumbled on this as the result of just one sortie from Singapore, it was remarkable that the company's manager hadn't run into it too.

"I'll investigate this, Kang."

He didn't turn. "I'm sure you will. Only go at it gently. We don't want to frighten our bird off. And you're not to leave Singapore."

"I may have to."

"You're *not* to leave this city! If you do, you may find you can't get back in again. And I don't want you descending on Hok Lin offices like a whirlwind, either. If Lung has the least hint we're on to him, he'll slip away. And there are plenty of places he could go from which he could continue with his big plans. If things work out as he plans, he won't be needing his little nest with you any longer. I want him kept in Singapore. This is vital. Once he gets on the mainland across the Johore Straits, we've lost him. And Kuala Lumpur won't be able to pick him up."

96

"You don't have any doubts that Lung is your man?"

"Would you if you were a policeman?"

"I just don't know."

"Let me tell you something. I've been after Lum Ping for years. It dates from the time when Singapore and Malaya were one country. I was certain he'd move down here. It was the natural base for him. And he's here, all right. Has been for years. Laughing at us, sure he was safe. So confident he took the big risk of working this racket. He's probably been laying in a store of Czech guns on his side profits from Hok Lin."

Kang was certainly heaping it on. I could only hope he was enjoying the process. I was sitting in a chair feeling physically sick. I could have done with a shot of the whisky I knew he kept for people who looked likely to pass out in his office.

I remembered Lung traveling down with me on the plane, apparently worried by Tsing and Wen's bid for a majority holding in the company and what this was likely to mean to his job. He had been my man all the way, the Chinese with no relations. If he *was* Lum, and when the news of this broke I was going to have the nastiest hour of my life facing the board of Hok Lin. The only way to save the company from the ensuing scandal would be to offer up a sacrificial victim, and the only candidate for this was me. Even old Hok was going to move in from his neutral stance to support his Chinese co-directors—he couldn't do anything else in the circumstances. And all I could do would be bow out, taking what price I could get for my holdings from a couple of smiling buyers. I would be writing my own commercial obituary in Singapore. As if all this wasn't enough, there was also Kang's reaction when he found out what I had been keeping from him. He had promised to use a pile-driver on me, and he would. Now that I was facing the imminent prospect of it, I knew just how much I didn't want to be exiled back to Scotland.

"Can I have a print of this photograph?" I asked.

Kang came back across the room. "You'll get one through the

mails later. Meantime, as I said, I don't want you to start any obvious investigation in the Hok Lin offices."

"Are you suggesting that I just go back to my flat and sit there waiting?"

"No. I've got a very active role for you."

"I shudder to think what that's likely to be."

He sat down. "I want you to watch Lung."

"You mean tail him all the time? Like a divorce detective? He's likely to recognize me through my disguises."

"I'm not being funny, Paul."

"Neither am I. And I still don't believe that Lung is Lum Ping. Your evidence is neat, but it's all circumstantial. You have no real proof."

"I admit that. But on the strength of the circumstantial evidence, would you say that I ought to keep Lung covered?"

He had a point. I nodded.

"I'm glad you see it my way," Kang said politely. "Let's forget about Lung for a moment and just look at Lum Ping. If, as I believe, Lum is about to prove his new power as an urban guerrilla by trying to assassinate Li Feng Tsu, then he is going to be using the whole of his organization in this city to bring off the job. He'll have to. He knows what he's up against: a massive guard of my forces. He also knows that we're scared as hell of what could happen here if there was any attempt on Li's life. It's my bet that Lum has his men out now trying to probe every plan we've laid to protect Li, where policemen are to be stationed, in what depth they're to be deployed, all that kind of thing. In an operation as big as this, it's impossible for the police to keep total security about all their plans. There will be leaks. Lum's scouts will be on to these. They will have to report back to HQ, where Lum will be."

"I see. My job is to watch Lung just in case he's who you think he is?"

"Yes."

"Sounds simple. Except that Lung has always lived in a downtown hotel and it's going to seem a bit odd if I suddenly take a room in it down the corridor from him. I suppose I could say I've decided to have my flat painted. Incidentally, you must have searched his room in that hotel a few times. Find anything?"

"No. We didn't expect to."

"Any sign of his scouts reporting to him there?"

"It's a big hotel, which makes ideal cover. And we've had to make damn certain he didn't begin to suspect he was watched. A lot of the time he hasn't been covered. He uses that Cortina of his erratically. Sometimes he takes it to the office, but more often he doesn't. There are days he doesn't use it at all. We couldn't risk a tail on his car."

"What about girl friends?"

"Doesn't seem to have any. Goes to a brothel sometimes, always the same one. But not regularly, by any means. The mama running it is very much in our hands. We also tailed his secretary. A dead end. She lives quietly with her parents and is nobody's sex symbol."

"In other words, Lung leads a normal bachelor life and you haven't been able to find a thing out of the ordinary in his patterns."

"That's quite true." Kang was being so reasonable it made me nervous. "Don't get the idea that I've got all my eggs in one basket in this matter. I'd be a fool if I did. I simply want Lung covered all the time before and during Li's visit, and you're the only man who can do that without raising his suspicions."

"Eh? How?"

"By keeping Lung in your flat."

I stared at him. "You don't think it would seem the least odd if I set up house with my general manager?"

"I'm hoping you can come up with a reason to have Lung live with you for a few days, beginning with the twenty-four hours before Li Feng Tsu flies in from Rangoon."

"Well, I can't. Lung would think it weird in the extreme, and quite right, too."

"Even if you had chosen to deal with a company crisis that way?"

"What do you mean?"

"By that time you'll have received this postcard of the overloaded ship. What could be more natural than that you should want to deal with this matter very privately indeed, and out of Hok Lin offices? Lung is your man. You've always trusted him. Much more, perhaps, than some of your co-directors?"

"You have something there."

"The fact that you wanted to have him help you deal with this business in a very quiet way would be right on the line of your relationship. You could give it out in your offices that Lung was away on a sudden business trip on which you'd sent him."

"If he *is* Lum, I wonder if he'd be fooled."

"If he is Lum, he's going to be a mighty worried man that you've discovered his side racket just at a time when he has so much else on his mind. I think he is going to want to watch *you*. You'll find he'll pack his suitcase like a shot and come over. Remember, he's adaptable. Used to shifting headquarters fast and often. He'll see at once that your building could be a very convenient operations center. It's in a crowded Chinese quarter, people come in and out of your shop the whole time. I'm sure you don't know who half of them are."

"My shopkeeper does."

"You have that river entrance. I walked in and out of it and no one saw me."

I thought about the company power struggle that had been about to start. It all seemed highly irrelevant now, though I could still make use of it with Lung. I had no intention of telling Kang this.

"All right, I'll do it."

After a moment the Superintendent said: "You won't be sorry you've helped me."

100

What he meant was I'd be damned sorry if I didn't.

"I still think you're on to a complete red herring with this, Kang."

"That may well be. But at least a flank I'm worried about will be covered. And I won't need to waste men watching Lung. A couple keeping an eye on the building should do."

"How do I get in touch with you when I've got the urban-guerrilla high command all assembled in my spare bedroom?"

Kang didn't like my tone. "You'll have a small two-way radio on a special frequency."

It suddenly got dark in the room, the lamp on the desk making a pool of light in sudden gloom. Even with that protective screening down the front of the building, the sound of the flurry storm reached us, a lashing of wind. It was a sumatra, one of those flare-ups of turbulence that reach us from the Indian Ocean. They feel like the beginning of a hurricane and up in K.L. used to roar through my old bungalow, catching loose shutters to bang them, dropping the air temperature as much as ten degrees and sending down driving sheets of rain which in minutes convert wide drainage culverts into frothing streams in spate.

The Superintendent turned his head to look out of the window.

"This is a good time to get you away from here. The storm will clear the streets."

"Your van wasn't too comfortable transport."

"I'll send you in one of our special taxis this time. Where to?"

"My office. I haven't reported there since I got back."

"Paul, I want you to play this thing my way and all the way."

"When have I ever not when you've insisted as forcefully as this morning? I'm not forgetting you hold the trump card. But one day I'm going to get it from you. For good. So you'll never be able to wave it at me again."

Kang didn't smile. I wasn't smiling, either.

I got wet between the door of the bogus taxi I didn't have to pay for and the steps up into the building containing the head offices of the Hok Lin Shipping Company. The pavements had been swept clean of pedestrians, and cars splashed along the bund slowly, wipers not able to keep pace with the assault of water. But there were already signs of the sky clearing, a lightening in the west and some color. In ten minutes the sun would be out, and not long after that the dripping would stop, everything steaming, Singapore's humidity at a peak. I shook myself like a dog in the vestibule and then walked across the lobby to a telephone booth that was a wonderful specimen of carved mahogany Victoriana. A servant answered the ringing and, sounding rather like Chong, told me that the master was not available. I asked to speak to another member of the Hok Lin family. It apparently took him a long time to find one, for it was more than five minutes before a breathless voice said:

"Sally Loyang here. I'm so sorry, I was at the other side of the house. Who's that?"

"Paul Harris."

"Paul! How lovely. It's ages since I saw you. When did you get back from Europe?"

"About a week ago. Sally, I was wondering if I could come to see your grandfather."

"I'm afraid he isn't here."

That surprised me. Old Hok never goes anywhere these days, or at least not any great distance from home.

"He's in K.L.," Sally said.

She was actually Sheh Loh Loyang, but had become Sally by her own wish early on. Even her grandfather uses it.

"Granddad was up at my graduation and stayed on."

"So you finally made it? How many years has it taken?"

"Don't be nasty. Only six. And I'm now a Master of Arts with honors."

"What class honors?"

"Well, third. But there were only a few firsts and not many

seconds either. The exams were terrible this year. Everyone's saying so."

"And what are you going to do with a third-class honors degree?"

She laughed. "Rest for six months. I'm exhausted."

"Sally, does your grandfather know about Sven Lindquist?"

"Yes. That's why I made him stay up north. I only got back today. I think he felt it terribly. He's over eighty himself and is beginning to talk about that, you know. He's with my uncle. The one the family pensioned off with a rubber estate because he was no good at anything."

I knew the uncle. When a Chinese is bad at business, he really is bad. It's a rare occurrence, but a unique phenomenon when it happens. Sally's relative couldn't even collect the latex that dripped out of his trees. But he was a merry remittance man and just might be what old Hok needed to take his mind off yet another of those intimations of mortality which come in thick and fast to the aged.

"Your grandfather won't be down to Lindquist's funeral, then?"

"That's the trouble, he insists on being there. I tried to make him see there was no point in it, but he just wouldn't listen. A car's going up for him the day before. I think I'll go with it. I'd have stayed on up there, too, but I had to see a boy friend who's off to Hong Kong. Also, Mother's been feeling neglected again. She hadn't the strength to come up to my graduation. Can you imagine?"

Sally has always been remarkably candid to me, and I suspect to many others, about moderately intimate details of her family patterns, which may be why some of them don't seem to care for me too much. Certainly her mum doesn't. She's an early widow quite rich enough to find herself a new husband if she bothered to get off her backside and hunt for one, but she is as attached to a hammock as an ante-bellum Southern belle. Every now and then she does get out of the thing to fly up to Hong

Kong, where she has relations, usually dragging Sally with her, which might be one reason why the daughter hasn't been too glittering academically, though I didn't think so.

"Why don't you just come out here anyway, Paul? Have lunch?"

"Sorry, but I've got to pretend to be a businessman for an hour or so. See you."

"At the funeral," Sally said. "That's a dismal thought. Bye."

The building's self-operated lift squeaked as it crept upward, an aged installation due for replacement, like a number of our ships.

We have a suite looking out over the harbor, the reception area the size of a ballroom but now chopped up by seven-foot-high frosted-glass partitions so that you can't see the view as you go in and neither can the typing pool from their machines. The public is held back by a long counter that might have come from a nineteenth-century wonder bar, only we don't have much public, really, not being in the passenger trade. At both ends of the counter are arches leading into high-ceilinged passages, one way for the directors' private rooms, the other for lesser executives. I insisted on keeping the huge ceiling fans which look like props from outmoded aircraft. They're rarely used these days, though I sometimes switch on the one in my room just to work up a bit of nostalgia for the lost days of colonialism.

I punched a bell instead of going straight to my office, and the girl who emerged from one of the cubicles was the secretary I had shared with Lindquist, now presumably mine alone, though that mightn't be for long. She is tall for a Chinese and has recently switched from mini-cheongsams to floor-length ones which give her the look of being ready for the cocktail party we never give. The girl is an urban sophisticate, as polished as a New York career woman, and considers any kind of excitement vulgar, which made her agitation now a decided surprise.

104

"Oh, Mr. Harris! Everyone's been wondering when you'd come in!"

Chronic with all my secretaries.

"I was delayed. I'd like to see Mr. Lung in my office. Will you ask him to come in?"

"I can't! I mean, he isn't here. Perhaps . . . Mr. Tsing will explain. There's been trouble. One of our ships. Mr. Tsing will want to tell you about it."

I decided to let Mr. Tsing do that and went along the corridor. My room has kept its view, through a vast sheet of plate glass. As well as the old fan, it has a great deal of mahogany paneling, this aged almost to the tone of black syrup. The desk is so big that if you put a mattress on it it would serve as a double bed. The chairs are scuffed, buttoned dark-brown leather that holds the smell of cigar smoke. At times I can kid myself that I'm an 1890 taipan, but never for long.

Tsing Tai Tai came in. He was breathless, too, as though the office had suddenly been swept by contagious asthma. My co-director is running to weight somewhat and makes up for a lack of height by bounce, his steps elasticized. He's a natty dresser, but his tropic suits always seem made for his last year's figure, and therefore under strain. His eyes protrude slightly, but the rest of his face is unremarkable, black hair pomaded down like Kang's, neat ears streamlined in against his head.

"Paul! I'm so glad you're back."

"What's this about one of our ships?"

"It's sunk."

"Eh?"

"We heard just an hour ago. It was late last night."

"Which ship?"

"The *Chai Ming.*"

A twenty-five-hundred-tonner. And old.

"What about her crew?"

"We think they're safe but are not sure. She ran on a rock."

"Where?"

"Off the west coast of Sumatra. Near Pagai island. That's one of the Mentawei group."

"What the hell was she doing there? We don't trade with the Mentaweis."

"We don't know that yet, either. Lung has gone to find out."

"He's *what?*"

Tsing was watching me, his eyes narrower even than normal. "He's our manager. He thought he ought to go and see for himself. Is there anything wrong in that?"

"When did he leave?"

"The office, you mean? About half past nine. There was a flight to Padang at ten thirty. He got a seat on it."

"How does Lung plan to get to the Mentaweis from Padang?"

"He said something about a hire flight. Or a boat."

You could go almost anywhere from Padang by charter flight or boat. I went to a wall map of our trading area, pulling the thing down full length from its container, staring at it. Lung would have something like two hundred miles south to travel from the Sumatra port to South Pagai, if that really was his destination.

"Didn't you want Lung to go, Paul?"

I turned. "I'd have sent someone else. Do you know whether the ship sank in deep water? Or is it still on rocks?"

Tsing shook his head. "The captain's cable doesn't say."

"When was our last signal from the *Chai Ming* itself?"

"About twenty-four hours ago. She was leaving Benkoelen to load copra offshore at Moekomoeko. Pagai was more or less on her route."

"I'd say just forty miles off it if she was hugging the Sumatra coast as she should have been doing on that run."

"The weather was stormy. Perhaps she was making for deep water."

"I wonder."

"Is something troubling you, Paul?"

"Yes, Tai. The loss of one of our ships. It was troubling you when you came in."

"I know. But, after all, we've got to look at it this way. We're covered. And she's one of our oldest. If there was no loss of life . . ."

His words dribbled off under my stare. I was damn near to saying that we mightn't find ourselves covered after a Lloyds inquiry. He found a flat case streamlined not to bulge his jacket pocket and took out a cigarette, tapping the end of this on etched silver like a twenties gigolo. A gold lighter flared. I was conscious in those seconds that Tsing loved me about as much as I love him, which isn't too much. I had the thought then that if that photograph in Kang's office had suggested a resemblance to Tsing, this would have come near to making me a happy man. But Tsing just looked like himself, a too plump thirty-eight born to money which he was busily increasing.

My co-director put aside shipwrecks and turned to the sad matter of Lindquist's funeral, but I couldn't turn with him and got rid of the man. After another half-hour I decided that the offices could do without me and were probably planning to anyway, so I went out without telling my secretary where I could be found. I got into a legitimate taxi this time and asked to be taken to Raffles Hotel.

Raffles is a hangover from the past, which may be why I like it. It retains tone, approached via a few palms outside, and because it hasn't proved easy to air-condition, when you get in you find huge white ceiling fans still turning, stirring up tepid drafts. It also has good food and at night you can dine out in the open court under stars. The Japanese would have pulled it down to erect twenty floors, as they have done with the beautiful old Imperial, the only building in Tokyo that was worth looking at, but fortunately Singapore still seems to be hanging on to at least some of its traditions. But it wasn't the hotel's atmosphere I was after this morning, just its telephones. These are in a nice row of old-fashioned soundproof booths instead of those hooded jobs which force you to share your neighbor's love life while you're trying to get through to Manila.

I went into one, shut the door, and, without bothering about dialing, asked the operator for police headquarters. She took me seriously and I was through to Kang in half a minute. He was sounding like the senior man he is, a bit distant, as though he hadn't wanted or expected to hear from me for some time.

"What is it, Paul?"

"The bird has flown."

He didn't ask what bird, just held silence for seconds.

"When?"

"While we chatted."

"Where are you phoning from?"

"Raffles booth. Safe."

"Know where he's gone?"

"Yes. Padang."

I told him about our sunk ship, giving it as my opinion that an unauthorized deck cargo might well have contributed to this disaster. That should have interested him, but it didn't seem to, as though one of our ships sinking was something to be expected. All he said was:

"He could go anywhere from Padang."

"Where do you think he's gone?"

"To a new operations center. Probably in Johore. He can still keep in touch with Singapore from there. But he must have discovered we were watching him. One of my men boobed. I'll find out which one." He sounded grim.

"Look, Kang, it could well be that Lung was sent to Padang at speed to block the threat that I might go myself. One of my co-directors could have believed that he had less to fear from Lung's investigation of the sinking than from mine."

"I see. You believe one of your directors is in this cargo racket with Lung?"

"That is *not* what I said!"

"You find it very hard, Paul, to admit that you've made a massive error in judgment."

I counted up to three and then said in reasonable tones: "There's an afternoon flight to Padang. My suggestion is that I be on it."

"No."

"Kang, even if I don't quite accept your assessment of Lung, I'll take him under my wing and bring him back here."

"I doubt if he'll be available for you to take under your wing."

"I'll find him and I can bring him back. Your men wouldn't have the authorization to do that, not without extradition proceedings."

"No!"

"You've got your needle stuck in a groove!"

"You're not leaving Singapore."

I hung up on him, angry.

8 🦎

I went into the quieter bar of the hotel and sat in a corner with a small whisky and a lot of water, alone with my thoughts. These did nothing for my day. The barman's day had just started after a late night and he didn't want to talk. No one came in or out. It was peaceful, but I didn't get caught up in the atmosphere and after ten minutes rose and went back to the phones.

Maria in Kuala Lumpur sounded as maternal as ever. I asked if I was lucky and had struck one of those times when Bahadur was in the office. My northern secretary drew in her breath audibly.

"Mr. Harris! If you're suggesting that when you're away we all play around here . . . !"

"I'm not suggesting anything. *Is* Bahadur there?"

"Certainly." Her triumph vibrated down the wire. "I'll put him on."

That left me with half a minute in which to build up a picture of my personal assistant sweating away at his desk with his jacket hung over the back of his chair. I've yet to see him with his jacket off in the office.

"Yes, Mr. Harris?"

After three years we still don't use first names—it's the vestigial British in me. I use his surname without the polite prefix and he gives me the prefix because I'm the boss, often with reluctance. Bahadur's voice sounded cool. It usually does. His English is interesting—he never stumbles in it, he might have been brought up bilingual, and yet somehow there is an accent. It isn't a British accent, or American, or that Welsh whining which for some reason the whole of India adopted. It's just Bahadur's own. In moments of excitement he can become tonally rather thin and high, but he's conscious of this and usually manages to check the tendency.

"I want you to pack a bag for travel. You're going to Sumatra. Been there before?"

"No."

"Malay will get you by and you may have a use for your Cantonese, too."

He hates to use his Cantonese. I gave him a summary of the situation about the wreck, but this did not include any of Kang's suspicions and he didn't ask me why I wanted a man from my independent company to run a parallel investigation to the Hok Lin manager's official one. Bahadur rarely asks silly questions. All he said was:

"I don't know too much about ships."

"What interests me is whether she was carrying a deck cargo."

"How do I find that out if she's sunk?"

"Take a diver with you. In a hired boat."

"From Padang?"

"Yes. It shouldn't be hard to find one. The place is a base for oil companies prospecting. Bribe one of their men away for the weekend. And maximum discretion in everything you do. It's important that Mr. Lung doesn't know you're in the area. He may remember you from K.L. Would you remember him?"

"Yes."

"It's possible that you won't see any sign of him."

"I don't understand."

"He may not be in the area. Padang or the Mentaweis."

"Are you saying he's run for it with your shipping company's cashbox?"

That boy is too bright.

"It's not a question of the cashbox. Get over there quickly, Bahadur. A flight from K.L. even if you have to change in Sumatra. I don't want you coming down here en route. When you get back, ring me. I may want to arrange a meeting which we'll keep private. Perhaps in Johore. But go back to K.L. Get in touch with me first from there."

I didn't irritate my assistant by asking whether he had the picture. He had it all right, plus fifty percent more added by himself. I authorized him to draw two thousand dollars in cash from Maria, who runs the office finances. She was going to hate paying it out.

I came out of my booth to find that one further along was in use, by a girl. She had her back to me, but I recognized the back. It was Ranya's. At my tap she turned, irritated by a pre-lunch attempt to pick her up. Her expression didn't change much when she saw who it was. I made a signal toward the nearby bar, and after a moment, reluctantly, she nodded.

I bought malts and carried the glasses to a table in the corner myself, sitting to face the door. She came in wearing another Bangkok *Vogue* outfit, not trousers this time but a tube sheath from ankle to neck, lemon-colored silk that should have been all wrong for her skin but wasn't. Today's accessories were mostly just semi-precious moonstones set in wrought Thai silver, only a platinum watch being indiscreet about its diamonds. She must have put that pigskin loot case in her hotel safe, for she wasn't carrying it. I stood and bowed.

"How delightful," Ranya said, without a smile. "Why do you have an unlisted phone?"

"When that bell rings you know it can only be a friend. You've been trying to get me?"

"Yes."

112

She sat down. If the woman didn't quite have beauty, she didn't need it. Her face had stayed stamped on a sheet in my mind and this refreshment of the picture brought no disillusion at all.

"I thought you were living in one of the glossy places."

"I am. But who told you?"

"I have a friend who knows everything."

She wasn't too interested in my friends. After a moment she said: "I thought I'd better have a look at this hotel. And it interests me. It has character. I want something like this for my restaurant."

"I know where I can get you a junkload of old ceiling fans. Have you started to look for a property?"

She nodded. "This morning. Which is why I wanted your advice. All the agencies are most discouraging. I was phoning another firm just now they told me about at the desk here. That was a blank, too. None of them have anything to show me."

"Singapore is packed out. I had to move to a slum."

"But I'm not interested in being in the city. That's what I've been telling them. Something miles outside, even."

"You can only go twenty miles one way and much less the other. Are you thinking of a roadhouse?"

"No, no! A place of character. With a view of the sea if possible."

I thought about that stucco-iced cake where the poor man hanged himself. It didn't have a view of anything except one obscene tree, and half a mile of approach road would have to be completely resurfaced, but it could be made quaint, all right. The haunting would be an added attraction. Ranya was very interested indeed. She got out a notebook with a gold pencil and wrote down the name of the agency which couldn't get rid of the place. After that she was nicer to me.

"You'd have to spend thousands," I warned.

"Of course."

If you have plenty of the right ice there's no trouble about collateral for a bank loan, though maybe the news that her ex-spouse was suing for the jewelry would be a bit of a shock. I didn't think she knew yet. The news had come to me hot from Bangkok, and it wasn't my place to tell her. Also, if I did, it might put back into her head those earlier ideas about a bit of ladylike blackmail to raise capital. She appeared to have forgotten all about this, which, if true, was a real advance in our relationship.

I suggested lunch where we were and she accepted. The courtyard was still damp from the sumatra, so we went into the dining room, where the service was relaxed without being too slow. Ranya wanted an Australian Angus fillet steak with green salad and I had the same. We shared a bottle of Beaujolais, which somehow in this hotel never tastes as it does in many of the others, as though it was far from home and pretty sick about that. During the meal I was very conscious of Ranya's hands; these kept up a restless movement as though for a long time now they hadn't found the right things to rest on.

We had coffee at the table and when the bill arrived she reached for it. I thought for a moment she was one of those still rare girls really determined to play hostess in a public place, but it wasn't that—she was just engaged in a cost check-up.

She put the slip back on its plate. "Not cheap. But you wouldn't expect this place to be. Eating at the Singapore Ponchana won't cost you so much. At least for the first six months. I keep my prices down at the start."

"And when the carpark is full every night?"

She smiled. "Items start wriggling upward. Like leeches looking for holes in clothing."

It was a horrible image of inflation.

"For how long do you expect to lose money?"

"At least a year. But what does that matter with all the other years to come?"

I left a bigger tip than our modest meal rated and Ranya

noted this, too, awarding me a couple of demerits for unnecessary extravagance.

Outside the hotel I put her in a taxi in which she was bound for a real-estate office and after that out into the country if she could get hold of the keys to a ruin. I stood waiting for the doorman to whistle me up another cab, just able to see through the screen of palms and shrubs which makes a poor bid to screen Raffles from the noisy world beyond. In the shade a man was sitting on a motor scooter resting. He was wearing a white helmet and goggles. Either this man, or another remarkably like him, had been waiting among parked cars, also on a scooter, when I left the company offices to come here. During that taxi drive I hadn't checked to see if I had a tail, but it seemed now that I did, and not a very highly trained one. Singapore is of course full of young men on motor scooters wearing crash helmets, but very few of them are goggled, as eye protection is not really needed in a city with a tropic climate.

It looked as though Kang had assigned one of the newest recruits in his plainclothes service to the job of checking on my movements, which in a way was rather insulting. It did seem a pity, too, that the Superintendent, with his problem of a manpower shortage, should be wasting stretched resources on me. I thought of phoning him about this, but decided not to. After all, snoopers have to get their basic training somehow and I was prepared to be a kindly quarry. When I looked back from the taxi taking me home, there were the crash helmet and goggles tucked not too neatly into the early afternoon traffic.

Tong was at the back of the shop, brooding over a teapot, when I passed through. He gave me a wave of the hand, but the settled gloom on his face didn't lift. He was having wife trouble again, a refugee from upstairs.

I put my key in the lock, but before I could turn it the door opened and there was Chong. The old man must have been crouched waiting, like the serf he isn't. He had served me his

115

usual indifferent breakfast, but could still be slightly haunted by a total failure to welcome me home the previous evening. There was now an unnatural smile on his skull face.

"Tuan, you eat?"

"Yes, thanks."

"Tuan, no need eatee all day outside."

"You been taking cooking lessons?"

"Okay, you wanchee, I do."

"I no wanchee. Relax. Any phone calls?"

The smile went. He shook his head.

The apartment hadn't had time to get chilly after Chong's airing. I went to the control dial for the air-conditioning and turned it to low. My staff had been housecleaning. There was a shine on things. I went up the stairs to find flowers. He had been out to the market to get them—cannas, the cheapest, but still flowers. He had followed me up.

"That's nice, Chong. I'm going to have some color in here."

"Tuan?"

"Too much white. We need a bit of gaiety. What happened to my vase? The one over there?"

"She no good."

"I like she. If you've got it away in a cupboard, bring it out again."

"Okay. Tea?"

"No, thanks."

"Beer?"

"Well . . . yes."

This was service. I might have been back in Raffles.

The glass was only half empty when the phone rang. I reached out for a perfect connection with the other side of the world. Jeremy sounded a bit grumpy. It was about eleven at night in London.

"Your message boy has been running around until his feet hurt," he said.

For a time Jeremy stooged in espionage, but that must have

hurt his feet, too, for he gave it up and returned to importing Hong Kong's less desirable products. He sees himself as a man about the City. I don't. However, he has his uses and what amounts to a pension from me because I'm foolishly sentimental about relations.

"What's your news?"

"Bad," he said. "I'll read you an item from 'Dealer's' column in the financial section of today's *Citizen*. It's on you."

I don't often get publicity in London, preferring not to.

"Ready?" he asked.

"If you mean am I sitting comfortably, yes."

" 'Paul Harris, Singapore's runabout tycoon, seems to have run into sudden trouble with his Hok Lin Shipping Company, whose shares have been dipping badly, and apparently with reason. Profits are off and competition in what had been an almost exclusive trading area has sharpened, with two Chinese companies and one based in Tokyo now operating rival fleets of tramps in Indonesian waters. There are rumors, too, that the Dutch are contemplating a return to an area once dominated by their vessels. In addition, the long-established British Far Eastern companies are probing in those waters. The ancient and out-of-date vessels of the Hok Lin fleet, bought at near scrap prices and hastily reconditioned, are gradually being replaced from Harris's own Scottish yard on the Clyde, but the process is a slow one, complicated by shipyard obsolescence and a capital shortage for modernization which is forcing Harris to run this company at a big loss even when he is his own customer. The Hok Lin prospects don't look too bright at the moment, with a sharp cut in the next dividend a virtual certainty, and Far Eastern-born British expatriate Harris may well be having sleepless nights just now.' "

"The rat," I said. "Whoever he is."

"Everyone in the City reads 'Dealer.' Any idea who his Singapore correspondent might be?"

"No. Journalism isn't my world. Particularly this kind of journalism."

"It might pay you to make a few contacts. For a better press. Can you authorize me to issue a quick denial on misrepresentation of fact for tomorrow's *Citizen?* There's still a chance of getting it in if I phone right away."

I thought about that, then said: "The big news here is that one of our ships has just sunk."

"Oh, God! That'll take another twenty pence off your shares!"

"Which someone wants."

"I didn't hear that, Paul."

"This is being manipulated. I'd say, from this end."

"My deduction, too."

"It's something I'll have to handle myself. Here."

"May I make a suggestion? Don't start playing around carelessly with press correspondents. They have the power to cut your throat. Neatly."

"This doesn't concern the press."

"So you've no denial for me?"

"None that would have the solid ring of truth."

"Paul, this could hurt you. Especially if you have any ideas of raising more money in London."

"I'll go to the Argentine when I next want to do that."

"I saw about Lindquist's death. Has that led to in-fighting at Hok Lin?"

I was cautious. "How could it, since I control the company?"

"What about Lindquist's holdings? Do they go to his widow?"

"I think so."

"She might want to unload for cash."

"A bit early for that. The will won't be probated for months."

"There's something else," Jeremy said.

I could guess what was coming and tensed for it.

"I haven't been able to find out much about planning at the Excelsior Trust. I mean whether or not they're going to suddenly unload their Hok Lin shares. But from the looks of things here I'd say it's very much on the cards. After this 'Dealer' para, the news of your sunk ship could push them to a decision. If they think you're on a real slide, they'll sell before they have to take a big investment loss. They held Hok Lin for income and they won't like that talk about a dividend cut."

"This is just your opinion, Jeremy?"

"You can call it an informed guess. What will you do if Excelsior sells?"

"Buy up their holding."

"You have the cash to do that?"

"Of course."

I had practically no cash at all. And the only way I was going to be able to raise enough for those Excelsior holdings was by allowing a bank a mortgage on my one remaining sound asset, the Johore diesel factory. Even the thought of doing this hurt. But there was no alternative.

"Paul, how are things with you, really?"

"In spite of 'Dealer,' our company prospects are excellent."

"This is just a sticky patch?"

"Yes. A year from now our profit margin will be very sound again. Which is why I want those Excelsior shares if they come on the market."

"So that proxy buying by your directors doesn't mean a battle for control of the company? Just a little private dirty work?"

Damn Jeremy!

"They want bigger holdings because they see how good our prospects are."

He didn't believe me. There was an expensive pause on the line to London, then his voice again.

"Do you know what's really kept you solvent all these years? Something I've watched and found bloody near marvelous. Just one thing."

"And what's that?"

"Luck."

Any businessman who denies the luck factor in his affairs is a fool, and I've certainly had a fair issue.

"The fates are still with you, Paul. One day they're going to turn around and kick you in the teeth." Jeremy sounded almost bitter. "Excelsior's brokers are Gascoigne and Peebles."

I very nearly let out a long, sharp sigh of relief. This was more than I had dared hoped for, even though it had seemed a distinct possibility, for Michael Gascoigne had floated the London issue of shares in Hok Lin for us. He has also been my personal broker for years, as well as a friend.

"If Excelsior sells, you can do a private deal through Gascoigne to buy," Jeremy said, pointing up the picture for me. "All you need is a slight inducement over the current market price. See what I mean about your bloody luck?"

"Thanks for digging this up."

"I'll expect to be remembered with a bonus," my cousin said.

There is nothing like a fairly pretentious public funeral to bring out the latent hypocrisy in all of us. At Sven Lindquist's I had the feeling that the pomp of his send-off would have produced a thundering laugh from the old man. There were representatives from practically every section of the community—government, civil service, banking, other business houses, his bridge club, and the water-polo team to whom he had given their largest cup. Dress was sober and demeanor solemn and we moved without much chat up toward steps and an open door from which flowed organ music. If Sven had ever entered this building it could only have been for a wedding now and then, plus other unavoidable occasions like this one. That he was being buried an Anglican would almost certainly have surprised him, but probably his widow had distant connections with the communion, and on the whole it is obliging, geared to take even the ungodly under its umbrella in sudden emergencies, like death.

I passed beneath the entrance arch in a little clump of people, most of whom I knew by sight but no more, at once looking around for a pew near the back. Kang was already in one, tucked well along it toward the stonework. I was surprised. It had never occurred to me that Sven was the type to buy even a top policeman meals. They must have had other contacts. I moved in from the aisle to join my friend, who didn't look too pleased about this.

I whispered: "Do you agree with the author of Lindquist's obituary that this funeral marks the end of an era?"

Kang looked at me. "*Yours* will," he said.

Organ music swelled, just slightly off pitch, as though our recent high humidity had got at the reeds. A considerable number of the women were wearing hats of the kind we don't see often in Singapore, kept in the back of cupboards for weddings and funerals, with detachable trimmings for either event. The general settling took all of ten minutes, during which Kang and I stared at stained glass gifted by long since departed empire builders.

I can't say that what I felt was deep grief. I had been fond of the old man, but this was now more than just slightly conditioned by the thought that if he had really had my interests close to his heart he wouldn't have landed me with the current mess at Hok Lin. It would have been so easy for him merely to leave Jane the income from his holdings for her lifetime, which I was damn sure he hadn't. The lady was not the mother of his scattered family or the companion of most of his years in the Orient, but just someone who had nipped in for the last chapter. It could be, I suppose, that in spite of his advanced years Sven had resolutely never thought about what could happen when he was gone, in this like so many of us.

The widow's processional up the aisle was a distinct shock. She made it leaning heavily on the arm of that avowed Taoist, Tsing Tai Tai, with on her right Wen King, who wore the expression of a man who simply refuses to believe that death ever comes to merchant bankers. Behind the principals came Hok

Lin looking pretty near to immortality himself and also leaning on an arm, Sally's. It was a long time since I'd seen her in a dress; normally it was trousers, and this one, a flower-printed cotton, wasn't anything like mourning. Her face was half hidden under a floppy-brimmed hat that would have been all right for a garden party, her concern all for her grandfather. She was just slightly awkward about adjusting her pace to his and looked up suddenly while altering step. She's not really a pretty girl, but her face seems full of character which her actual living has always appeared to me to deny. Old Hok spoiled her atrociously, of course. She could get anything out of him she wanted and she had wanted a lot, including a grandfatherly tolerance of an outstandingly undistinguished academic career.

While we were still all on our feet out of respect for the chief mourners, Kang leaned toward me. "Why have they left you out?" he asked.

The actual service didn't go on for very long. There was no eulogy, possibly because the officiating priest simply couldn't bring himself to hold up to us Sven's lifetime in the Far East as a shining example of a man operating always within the Christian ethic. He neither praised nor damned, an admirable neutrality in the circumstances. There was one hymn, which it seemed likely Jane had demanded, and the congregation tackled this with the kind of zest you often get at these ceremonies, as though it gave them the needed relief of being able to proclaim their own survival. During it I had an uninterrupted view through a channel between heads to Hok's.

I had known the old man all my life. He had been a friend of my father's both in business matters and out of them. He had also been a student at the London School of Economics back in those days before that institution had started to churn out Keynesian socialists, not to mention Marxist ones. I wasn't sure what England had given Hok beyond an ability to make a precise and tidy use of the world's international language, for his ability to survive violent change with his personal affairs remarkably intact was a very Chinese thing. He had steered a careful course throughout the Japanese occupation, neither a collaborator nor a resister, and there was a rumor that a couple of years before Pearl Harbor he had converted a sizable portion of his assets into gold bars which he then buried under the rubber trees of one of his plantations. If the story was true it must have hurt him not to be earning a return on his capital during those years, but it had meant that he emerged with the immediately available means to take an active part in the reconstruction. This had been a very active part indeed, and he was now certainly a millionaire in almost any currency you'd care to mention except perhaps Russian rubles.

I loved him for a very simple reason. When I suddenly had no family at all in these parts he offered me his, a free pass into the Hok tribe. It wasn't just a gesture, either. He meant it. I could come and go in that household as a son might, and I often did, swimming in the largest private pool on the island, having meals with the family, or just sitting on the terrace in the sun with the old man himself. When Sven and I formed the shipping company Hok had allowed us to use his name even though by that time he was virtually retired himself, agreeing to be nominal chairman when that became wise policy, and I was pretty sure this was more as a kind of memorial to my father than anything else. If I went to him for advice he gave it, and with all the old shrewdness, but if I didn't he never fussed me. I could have gone to him for the money I needed to buy the Excelsior holdings and got it, too, but I was damned if I'd do that.

We all stood again while Jane came down the aisle with her two financial bodyguards. By the time I got outside the church she was being driven off in Tsing's Cadillac, which was being closely followed by Wen King's Bentley, but Hok was engaged in the laborious process of being helped into his Mercedes by Sally and the chauffeur. Kang had lost me quickly, heading for police transport. I went over to Hok's car. One of its back doors was still open. Hok saw me coming and held out his hand, saying in English:

"Good you're back, my boy."

"How are you?"

"Old. Creaking."

"I hear you've been whizzing about the country."

"Well, Sally's graduation was something I really never expected to live to see. I felt I must go up for it."

"Sorry you had to come back to this."

"Sven had a good run, like me. When are you coming to see us?"

"Maybe this afternoon."

"Do that. You look thin. We'll feed you."

"I'm fine."

"You need a decent house, a woman, and a cook."

"Will you get them for me?"

Sally climbed in the opposite door.

"What about her for the woman?" Hok asked. "She needs an older man to settle her down."

"Too much of a generation gap."

"There's no such thing among Chinese. You should have been born one."

"I'll ask for that before my next reincarnation."

I shut the door, watched the car move off, then walked through midday heat to a restaurant and brooded over two courses. After them I went to keep a two-thirty appointment with my Singapore banker. His name is Alec Macintyre and he comes from Milngavie, a plush suburb of Glasgow in which he might still be living, for all that foreign parts have changed him. Twice a week he plays golf and two evenings bridge. He drives a conservative car and keeps to a tight circle of conservative friends, none of them natives. He must have been brought up a Presbyterian, but somewhere early on switched faiths from God to Mammon, remaining a zealous convert ever since. I sat on the wrong side of a desk at a considerable disadvantage not

124

only from this but also because Alec knows all about my Clyde shipyard and precisely what its deficit was last year. It took hard work and damn near sweat to convince him that Johore Diesels wasn't going the same way, in spite of the books, but I left that office no longer the sole owner of my one viable company and in a black rage against the men who had reduced me to this condition.

In anger I tend to go theatrical, aware of this even while I'm at it, but not able to stop myself. I went back to the Hok Lin suite and sat in my room for ten minutes without doing a thing, but anger stayed. I picked up the phone and rang the widow's house, where the call was received by a servant who had muted his voice for mourning. When Tsing arrived at the instrument he was practically whispering.

"There will be an emergency directors' meeting here in my office in half an hour," I said. "Mr. Hok won't be able to attend, but I'm deputizing for him."

"I'm sorry, Paul, but that's impossible!"

"I'll expect you and Mr. Wen."

It took them three quarters of an hour and they came in practically side by side, looking like men used to doing the summoning but still uneasy behind a slapped-on dignity. I asked them to sit down and was at once pompous.

"Gentlemen, even if I hadn't had a detailed report from my London agent about your proxy buying of Hok Lin shares, I'd have suspected something curious was up from your devoted attention to Sven's widow."

I got the effect I wanted, both of them bolt upright in their chairs.

"I think I've taken the necessary steps to meet a takeover bid within my own company. My London broker now has my instructions to do a private deal with Excelsior Trust should they decide to sell our holdings. He has also been instructed to top any outside price that may be offered. Your price, gentlemen. Interesting situation, isn't it? Directors bidding against each other to raise the price of their own shares. In the matter of Mrs. Lindquist's interest in Hok Lin, let me remind you that probate on a deceased director's holdings can take a long time. In this case I'll see that it takes a very long time, possibly even a year or two. By then there will have been an upturn in our trading profits, as both of you know very well, with a parallel upturn in the price of Hok Lin stock on the open market. This is going to make the buying out of Mrs. Lindquist much more expensive. It might be a good idea to get her to agree now on a fixed price before probate. This, of course, would require the cooperation of all of us. You see my point?"

They saw it, all right.

"There is another matter. Neither of you is executive director here, which means that you have nothing to do with the day-to-day running of the company. Mr. Wen clearly understands this. But it appears, Mr. Tsing, that you do not."

"What do you mean?"

"You took it on yourself to order our general manager over to Sumatra without making the slightest attempt to contact me as executive director."

"I didn't know where you were!"

"If you'd picked up a phone, you could have found out in ten minutes."

"It was an emergency situation!"

"I prefer to deal with those myself. I think in the interests of efficiency at boardroom level it would be a good idea if you resigned your directorship."

The heir to sexual-potency money was staring. He looked as though he was considering the feasibility of hiring a thug to do me in.

"You may want to retain your holdings with us as an investment," I suggested. "It isn't, after all, a good time to sell."

"No!" Wen appeared to have exploded. "You can't do this, Harris!"

"Why not? Doesn't a majority holding do the talking?"

126

The merchant banker got up. He was wheezing slightly. His English reverted to its root stock, pidgin.

"We fix you good, see? Our money come out what you do, eh? Flat on face you go."

"I think not, Mr. Wen. Block selling by former directors would certainly depress the market value of our shares, but this would give me the opportunity to make it plain to other interested parties here in Singapore just what a bargain they'd get in buying them. The new buyers could be our new directors. In spite of that talk in London, we're not in any trouble, as you both know very well or you wouldn't be so hard at it trying to get control."

Wen sat down again, as though suddenly realizing that I hadn't asked for *his* resignation. A wedge driven between this unholy pair began to take effect at speed.

I looked at Tsing. "You gave 'Dealer' that tip-off for his article?"

Tsing's mouth opened, but for a good three seconds no sound came out of it.

"I . . . I don't know what you're talking about."

"I'm not suggesting you made direct contact with the man who writes that column. No need. Just a little careless talk at a party. You go to so many parties."

Wen stared at a colleague, his act of shocked innocence one of the worst I've seen. I wanted to be rid of them both. I was weary suddenly, anger no longer sustaining.

9

Some years ago Hok built his tribal fortress seven miles outside the city limits on the road to Changi. It is set in five expensive acres and decked out with tidied-up palms and casuarinas under which winds a drive of polished asphalt. The view is splendid, out over the Straits to the first of Indonesia's myriad islands which carry on east for three thousand miles, but the trouble is you can't see a thing from the house itself, at least not the lower floor. Security demanded an inner perimeter wall fifteen feet high topped off with broken bottles set in concrete. There's a gateway with a hatch in it and you're inspected before being allowed through. The house is also equipped with every burglar alarm I'd ever heard of and some I hadn't, not to mention a private wire to the nearest police station.

It's not really that Hok Lin is a nervous type, but when you're building a fort—and a high percentage of the local Chinese very rich live in them—you might as well make a good job of it. If civil war ever breaks out in Singapore, I know where I'm going. I reckon the Hok homestead could stand up to a three-month siege, provided the howling mob didn't get hold of a bulldozer. And we'd never run out of water with a good two hundred thousand gallons of it in the monster pool. We probably wouldn't run out of champagne, either. It's the only thing Hok has been allowed to drink since his prostate operation, and he buys it by the dozen-case loads, though with an unfortunate emphasis on the pink kind.

Usually I come to the house knowing that I'm going to be sucked into a family party that can get a bit exhausting after a few hours but which nonetheless fills a basic need in my life. This afternoon I came feeling like an angel of death.

A houseboy let me in. Behind austere walls Chinese imagination had run riot. The thirty-room mansion had a decorative façade plastered all over with pink stucco. The gardens, mostly artificial rock grottoes, were at the back. An entrance court was almost entirely dedicated to reinforced concrete, which is one way of keeping down the weeds. The few plants in pots didn't look any healthier than mine up on a roof. Screening the reception area from the pool was another wall, this one only ten feet high and running all the way up to the house like a stone knife thrust into the building's vitals. The wall had one small opening, this rounded, and attention was sucked through to vivid color beyond, the pool tiled in electric blue.

The Hoks did a great deal of their living out on the terraces surrounding that water and I could hear them at it now. I went through the round hole to see at least a dozen of them in the water and more than this sunning themselves on pads. Not all of this crowd lived here, but they all dropped in often and catering was on the scale of a small hotel. A female child of about seven with a protruding stomach hurled herself, dripping, at me.

"Paul! You to swim now?"

It was a family rule that everyone practiced their English on me and I paid for what I ate and drank with conversation lessons.

"Maybe later."

She took my hand, possessive, totally secure in her walled world. Then we both waited to watch her nineteen-year-old brother go off the high board on a tower. He took his time about this, bouncing, showing off physique, and the actual dive came as a bit of an anticlimax, starting out a perfect swallow but deteriorating, with legs curving in toward the spine. He surfaced, angry at himself, tossing back longish hair, a perfectionist like most of his family. The boy was the first Hok to my knowledge to study medicine, his future practice within the tribe ready-made and waiting when he qualified. The little girl beside me did nothing for her brother's ego by jeering at him. She then released my hand, to crouch at the edge of the pool like a mini athletic coach, shrieking her unwanted advice.

I walked on up the terracing toward the chair where the ruler of all this was enthroned, on the way passing Sally in the water practicing a backstroke.

"Come and sit by me, Paul. Get him a lime juice."

A handmaiden brought me the drink, ice clinking.

"Were you in the office today?"

"Yes. For a bit. Long enough to sack a director without your authorization. I've come for your rebuke."

After just a moment Hok asked quietly: "Which director?"

"Tsing."

"I see. Well, perhaps he's the one we can most easily afford to lose."

"That's my feeling, too."

"What did he do?"

"Sent Lung off to investigate that sunk ship without consulting me. Though he knew I was back and where to get me."

"You've been away for some time, Paul."

"You're saying it's not surprising Tsing took on an executive role in the company?"

"I'm not saying anything of the kind. It's your company, as it always has been. And now that Sven is dead it's the right time for you to take on the chairmanship. I'll stay on the board as a name. That's all I am these days anyway."

"I'll always come running to you for guidance."

130

"The senile make poor guides."

"You'll never be that."

"Paul, I can feel my brain slipping notches as the weeks go by. Part of the disintegration process. As yet I'm still conscious of what's happening. Perhaps I'll be more comfortable when I no longer am."

I didn't like to hear the old realist talking like this, particularly as what he said was the truth, something he had faced and assessed. When the time came I wanted him to die comfortably, not from a broken heart.

Sally pulled herself out of the pool and came over. "You've given up swimming, Paul?"

"Yes, my rheumatics."

She flopped down on a pad, on her stomach. "Oil me, someone," she said in Cantonese.

Sally tucked her head into her arms, waiting for service. All her life she had rated it, as the old man's favorite. I knew that Hok had tried to conceal his special feeling for a granddaughter who had never known her father, but his efforts to do this had fooled no one. A cousin came over and oiled Sally's back. I didn't hear the girl being thanked for the job.

"There's the sunset beginning," Hok said. "Soon we'll have a glass of champagne. But first I'll take my walk. One of my rituals."

"I'll come with you."

"No, Paul, I . . ."

Sally spoke without lifting her head. "He likes to do it on his own. Let him."

I stayed in my chair. Hok Lin used only one of his sticks; this was part of the discipline. He wobbled on the terrace, moving very slowly.

After a moment I asked: "Where does he go?"

Sally moved a leg. "Round the pool. Once. Soon he won't be able to. I hate to think of it. I hope I don't live to be old. I hope . . ."

I didn't prompt her. My heart was thudding. Hok Lin was creeping along past the young of his clan. None of them joined him, as though ordered not to. The splashing went on and the shouts.

"Sally?"

"Mm?"

"I taught you to swim. Who taught you to shoot?"

For a moment she didn't move. Then very slowly she turned over on one side. She lay still then. I saw eyes that seemed to have screens over them. There was no hostility in her look, and no fear either. Toward me she was in neutral. And this was the real thing. Our relationship, easy and casual-seeming, was a sham from her side. The world she lived in had no room for people of my kind. I didn't mind that so much. What frightened me was that perhaps it didn't really have room for her grandfather either.

I don't know whether she was conscious then of the old man hobbling along not fifty yards from us. I was. And I was equally conscious of something else: that I was quite helpless. I had overrated myself, believing that somehow I could deal all on my own with this time bomb ticking away to the moment when it would explode in a little world. But I could do nothing. If she was frightened now, there would be some hope still, but there was nothing in her face to suggest fear.

There was no one within hearing range. She could have said anything to me then, even if it was only a question to find out how I knew. I expected this. She had a right to be curious. She didn't seem to be. I said the only thing I could find to say, an admission of defeat.

"Sally, get out of Singapore. Now. Fast."

She reacted to that. A nod, as though it was something simple she could accept. She got up, remembering to collect her towel, and went off into the house without looking at me again.

The old man had reached the bottom of the pool. I ought to leave now, going straight to Kang, but I sat on. I had to wait to drink a glass of champagne with Hok Lin while above us wild color flared for twenty minutes before dark sucked it all away.

My driver was sprawled along the front seat, using paid time to catch up on some sleep. He looked as though he needed it and he woke with reluctance, like a man who spends his days skidding near the verge of total exhaustion, never getting enough rest and probably not enough food, either.

"Police headquarters," I said.

We turned out of the drive into the highway, the old car's lights bad. There seemed to be more glow from the dash. The driver's head had been shaved, leaving a black stubble. I caught glimpses of his face in the mirror, small-featured, almost simian. He might have been a captured creature staring out at a larger world forever beyond his reach. We grow used to these faces in the Orient, the deprived whose lives are separated from ours by the seemingly bottomless chasm of circumstance. When we talk to them it is across this abyss, like Victorians to their servants. I didn't try to talk to my driver.

I was riding toward Kang's anger. From it he might well take steps that would destroy my life in Singapore. I ought to be frightened, and probably would be in his office, but now I sat like a man coming from dental extractions under Novocain, given a time of numb reprieve before the pain flared.

My driver had accelerated to nearly forty even though his lights barely showed the road for five yards ahead. He seemed to be running on side lights alone, probably to ease the strain on an ailing battery. Traffic was thin in our lane. Nothing had passed us for some time, though there were cars coming from the city, commuters belting home late, some of them not bothering to dim their lights for a glowworm, sweeping down behind swelling explosions of white glare.

We turned into a long straight. An approaching car swung out for a pass, its lights showing the vehicle it was leaving behind. This was a contractor's truck, a heavy-duty vehicle with a power hoist apparently on overtime taking away red clay from some excavation for a new skyscraper. I got a glimpse of a great mound of the stuff behind the driver's cabin. The truck driver flickered his headlights at us.

"What's that for?" I asked.

"Not know, tuan."

My driver braked. Worn tires didn't have too much traction even on a dry surface. We swerved. The truck did more than that, suddenly dousing headlights and swinging over into our lane, front wheels mounting a grass verge before the drainage ditch. There it stopped, a looming obstacle. In a wild bid to get around the monster, my driver yanked down on his wheel and, like a fool, accelerated hard. I could feel tires going into a skid even before hot rubber screeched. All I could do was brace for impact.

This was a clattering bang. My head smacked into the cushions behind, then all of me was catapulted toward the driver's seat. My hands pushed my head over the top of this. The driver was sliding down over the wheel, out cold from crashing into the windshield. There was a roaring as red clay poured down on the car roof. It felt like being under a waterfall.

The door beside me had sprung. I got out through it, chary of another avalanche. I was shaking like a fever victim. The driver's door had jammed and I started to kick at it. The truck loomed up like a sea wall on the other side of the taxi, more of its load threatening a slide. There was no sign of the man who had been at its wheel. I couldn't believe that anyone up in that high cabin had been hurt; the truck hadn't even moved from the impact.

There was a smell of petrol. The taxi's exhaust would still be very hot. I had literally to pull the car's front door off its hinges, rusting metal scraping on asphalt. There was no blood on the driver's face, just a bump at the front of a shaven skull. I lifted the man out, no more weight to him than a ten-year-old, and carried him well up the verge, out of range if there was an explosion, laying him down on grass. I was straightening when I saw lights in our lane. The car was coming fast, giving no sign of braking for a pile-up.

I looked back at the taxi. There was now a figure standing by it. The cab door of the truck was open. The man inspecting the wreckage, shown clearly by increasing white glare, was a uniformed policeman. I yelled at him, but he paid no attention, just walked out behind the truck into the up lane and stood there as though ready to direct traffic past a pile-up. It made no sense. There could be a police car parked beyond the truck, but I certainly hadn't heard it arrive.

An alarm klaxon under my skull went off when I saw heads at two of the windows of the car slithering to a stop. They weren't faces, just heads masked by nylon stockings. The act of drawing on that mesh serves as a kind of symbolic release of the bestial.

I swung around toward the drainage ditch, but had to jump over the man I had laid on the verge, one foot skidding on the grass beyond him. I didn't fall, but it took a moment to get balance and one of the masks had got across the ditch and was waiting for me. I turned back toward the other man still in the road. He hadn't a gun, but was ready for unarmed combat, professional, covering me like a forward in a rugby line-up. I went straight for him. He stiffened to use a chop on the first punch I threw. I jackknifed my body down, putting my head in his stomach. The man's breath exploded, but reflexes still brought hammer blows on my shoulders. I went flat on asphalt. The mask was down, too, a couple of yards away, on his back. He flipped over and without trying to get up writhed toward me for an ankle hold, a snake's head with nylon sucked into the hole of a mouth.

It wasn't a contest between two. A kick in the groin reminded me of that. I balled up from the agony. A second kick got me in the chest, just below my head. I saw a hand with a cosh in it.

I opened my eyes, but shut them quickly. My throat was full of vomit. I rolled over on my stomach and pulled myself to the edge of something hands had found. I was very sick, making a noise like a child with whooping cough. When it was over I managed to get onto my back again. Wherever I might be, it felt as cold as a Scottish winter. I couldn't stop shivering. Light was a red pulse against eyelids and there was a war going on in veins, my heart on violently increased revs.

After some minutes I tested sight again and this time the light didn't seem anything like so glaring. It was coming from a camper's gas lamp hissing on a table. I was in a bed placed about four feet from this and well out in the middle of a room. The mattress gave to my slightest movement and seemed to be a luxury job straight from a Hilton. Some kind of coverlet was twisted about my legs, mostly down by my ankles. I was wearing underpants, nothing else, not even my watch. On the table were a glass of water, a box I couldn't see into, and a hypo-dermic syringe.

I sat up. It took a bit of doing, especially getting my legs free of that coverlet. The impulse to just lie down again was very strong indeed, but another impulse was stronger: I had to uri-nate somewhere.

There were two doors, one shut, the other open. Beyond the open one, light glinted off what looked as though it might be a chemical water closet. I tested my legs. Knees were a bit pulpy, but muscles were functioning and the only thing wrong with my walk was that my brain wasn't sending down the right signals, which meant quite a bit of heaving about. At one point I went teetering off to one side like a soft-shoe dancer who has lost balance. But I got there. Not only was there a chemical W.C. but also a table on which sat white enameled basin and jug with beside these a neat little heap of beautifully clean hand towels. I used all the conveniences provided, grateful for them, and began to feel a bit better even though I almost toppled forward into the basin while sloshing water on my face. There was a bucket for dirty water but no basket for used towels, so I left mine scrunched up on the table like a napkin after a formal dinner. Then I went to hang on to a door jamb and have a look about my quarters.

Giddiness was easing, replaced by a tight steel band that came around from the top of my spine to the front of my head. This was unpleasant but easier to live with, and I became moderately observant again, even able to look at the light without suffering.

My captors hadn't thrown me into a cellar, which was something. Also, this place had been carefully prepared for the reception of its prisoner and with some curious touches of near-luxury, like that bed and the portable plumbing behind me. All the enameled objects were brand-new, as though they had come straight from a hardware store catering to remote estates whose owners were too mean to provide modern amenities for their managers. I had the feeling, too, that I was in a room that had once been a bedroom, and on an upper floor, though I had no means of checking on this. But the ceiling was high and the place spacious. I had seen rooms like this in now abandoned old Chinese houses on distant up-country estates, which brought the thought, and I didn't like it, that I might no longer be on Singapore island. I didn't like, either, the strong hints about me that I was in for a lengthy stay.

If this was the case, I was going to have to do most of my living on that bed. There was one chair beside the table with the lamp, nothing else. A large expanse of floor was covered in moldering brown linoleum, swollen into almost balloon blisters in places by damp. The walls had once been green, but most of the paint had flaked off, leaving huge areas of tobacco-colored stain edged by growths of active fungi. There were remains of period electric light fixtures and quite a large hole in the ceiling where plaster had come down, along with a wide-bladed fan. Two windows were shuttered and the shutters had heavy planks nailed across to keep me from guessing the time of day by light changes outside.

I made the gesture of testing the other door, expecting to find this locked, which it was, though not by a key, for the hole was blocked by some kind of plastic filler. I set off across that rolling flooring toward the table, making steadier progress this time, suddenly very interested in what I found in the box by the syringe. There had originally been twelve ampules; five were used, seven waiting, presumably to round off my course. There was some information about the drug on the lid, but this was in Chinese, which I have never had the time to learn to read and never will. I did what seemed to me the right thing, piercing each ampule with the syringe needle like sausages in a frying pan, then reversing the box to make certain that all that liquid ran out.

My efforts had left me feeling like an Olympic athlete at the end of a record three miles, and I just made the bed again, climbing onto it from the side where I hadn't been sick. For about twenty minutes I just lay not thinking about anything at all. Then the old habit reasserted itself.

I could have been kidnapped for money. It's still moderately big business in these parts, and most Chinese taipans continue to live in fear of the sudden snatch, followed by ransom notes to frantic relatives demanding huge sums—hence their fortified houses and discreetly armored Mercedes. With one or two exceptions, however, the men operating these enterprises have steered clear of Europeans. It may be that we're not rich enough or it has been found that our relations don't care enough. In my case, certainly, there wasn't a single available relative who could be rendered sleepless from terror. They wouldn't get much out of my banker; all he'd do would be move in to run Johore Diesels as an executor until I could be presumed dead in law. Up in K.L., Maria, who might be fond of me in her way, had access to the office cash but no really big money. She could mourn but not pay up. Professional kidnappers investigate intended victims pretty carefully as part of normal market research, and I didn't think I'd have passed their tests.

Somebody, somewhere, could hate me. The name of Tsing Tai Tai came into my mind in panic headline lettering. Motivation was there. In my office he had looked as though he would enjoy seeing me struck dead. And if I was out of the picture for an indefinite period he might put up a fight to keep his old position in Hok Lin Shipping while continuing his dirty work in London to gain financial control of the company. He could also afford to hire half the thugs in Singapore if he wanted to, but somehow kidnapping just didn't bear the Tsing seal; I couldn't believe he had the cold nerve to see something like that through to the end. Cornered, he might employ an assassin, but not kidnappers. And anyway I didn't have him cornered at all, just angered, for New Sun Tonic continued its success story in his favor and always would.

I was certain I had not been tailed to the Hok homestead because I'd taken sound precautions not to be, walking from the office to Raffles Square, then through a department store to its rear entrance, picking up my taxi one street over. Which left Sally. She hadn't got up from a pad in the sun to go in to pack, just to phone her colleagues. This meant that I was Lum Ping's guest.

It was one of the most unpleasant conclusions I have ever reached. I was still cold and I started shivering again. If my captors were that lot, they must have a good reason for taking me prisoner instead of just pumping me full of bullets. The reason could be interrogation sessions ahead.

We are all cowards if you can find the right spot. I have quite a few available. One is torture. I don't care to remember often my one major experience of this, but as I lay on that bed it came back, in some detail.

I suppose my sleep was natural, but the waking from it certainly wasn't. Someone standing at the top of the bed hauled me up into a sitting position by arms under my armpits, wheezing onto my head in the process. A second visitor stood looking down at me. Lamplight sketched an imitation face on nylon drawn over his real one. I had the feeling at once that, seen in the flesh, he wouldn't be very attractive either. A plain tropic business suit, white shirt, and tie were in striking contrast to the improvised mask topping them, giving the creature the look of a Martian trying to masquerade as a suburban commuter. When he opened his mouth to speak, the tautness of the mesh was broken and his false face disintegrated, really nasty to watch. He lifted one arm, pointing toward the table. Words came in gutturals, as though he was pitching his voice well below its norm.

"Why you do?"

My visitor's English was about second year of a local high-school level, but I guessed what he meant.

"I don't like drugs."

He took a step closer to the bed. The back of his hand cracked on my jaw. He was wearing a ring, a big one, and I felt this break skin.

"You think escape?"

"Do I look like an escaper?"

He hit me again, same place.

"You telephone?"

I didn't know what he was talking about and said so. The man holding me up had eaten a garlic dish recently and the aftereffects of this were half gassing me. The ring came in again to bring me back to attention.

"At Hok Lin house . . . you telephone?"

"No."

"Before leave, you go in house. You telephone?"

Sally must have been watching from an upstairs window.

"I went in the house to go to the toilet."

"Telephone in hall. You use?"

"Why should I?"

140

"Call police!"

"No!"

Another crack, same target area. My hands were free. I brought one of them up to my jaw, touching a stickiness. I didn't look at my fingers. Mask was a trained operator, his technique to establish one focal point of pain and build on it. Each time he hit me it was the ring that did the damage. I've kept all my teeth so far, thanks to expensive dentists, but if this went on, it could start abscesses.

"Speak! You telephone?"

"No."

He timed his blow to allow for the jerk away of my head, once again putting a piece of jade and its embossed gold support work right into an earlier excavation. The stickiness was moving down my neck to my chest.

"Where you tell taxi go?"

"To poli e headquarters."

That really surprised him. There was a wobbling in the mouth area as he sucked in a deep breath.

"You go see Kang?"

Since they could name the director of operations against them, there seemed no point in shielding the man.

"Yes."

"Kang no know you come?"

"How could he? I've told you I didn't phone."

"You tell Kang of girl Sheh Loh?"

"You know damn well I didn't. Otherwise Kang would have nabbed her in her grandfather's house."

"You go Kang. Why you no tell?"

"Because Hok Lin has been like a second father to me. I thought the truth about Sally would kill the old man. I still think that."

It occurred to me, a bit late, that by convincing these men I had told no one about the girl I could be signing my own death warrant. On the other hand, if I didn't convince them, I soon wouldn't have much of a jaw left.

It appeared my interrogator believed me. He signaled forward a colleague I hadn't had time to notice, also masked, who had been standing by the wall beyond the door. The third man moved into the light. He was of slight build, but had outsize hands for his size and race, if he was Chinese. He was holding a hypodermic syringe. The chemical in that cylinder could so easily have been developed for terminal sedation.

What happened then was a weak man's bid to perform like a Malay gone amok. I jerked my head back into Garlic Breath's stomach. His arms slackened. Half blinded by pain, I rolled off the bed, but managed to land on my feet. I must have completely astonished my captors, for I was able to recover balance, still free. The door to the hall was ajar. I'm not sure whether I actually ran, but I certainly struck out at Big Hands with the syringe. I think I got past him. I was tackled from behind. I went down using Cantonese, wasting breath. Two of them sat on me. The third put a needle in my thigh.

A taste of sickness was in my mouth again. It was still the same room with the greenish walls and too pale light from the canned gas lamp. There was a man standing clear of the bed with his back to me, bending over something on the floor. He wasn't masked. I had to move my head slightly to see what he was doing. Nausea increased. One side of my head seemed to have ballooned up and there was internal swelling pressing against my teeth, like dental padding. There was a weight against my cheek, too, a wet cloth.

I watched the man wring out another cloth in the basin brought from the cupboard. He straightened, squeezing out drops, then turned, the light full on his face. It was Lung, who should have been over in Sumatra investigating a shipwreck.

142

IO 🦎

The general manager of Hok Lin Shipping wasn't wearing a ring. He didn't seem to notice that my eyes were open. He came around the top of the bed and, with his body blocking the light, changed my compress. I moved my head slightly. He leaned down even lower.

"You must lie still," he said, as gentle as a male nurse in a recovery room.

I hadn't much desire to do anything else, though I did try opening my mouth, which felt full of enlarged tongue. With remarkable intuition Lung guessed that I wanted to be sick and he made a dash for the basin, bringing it to the bedside with water sloshing. He positioned the thing on the floor and then held me propped over to make use of it, which I did, half choking in the process. When that was over I lay back gasping, with liver spots floating across my view of the ceiling. I heard him walk away and the sounds of the basin being emptied into the chemical closet. Back beside me, he used that sedated voice again.

"Feel any better?"

It's always a bloody fool question when it's obvious the patient doesn't, and I had no comment. As a nurse Lung was a fusser. He replaced the towel, trying out at least three places for it on

143

my cheek. I was able to note that he was neatly dressed in a lightweight suit and wearing a tie. It seemed to be a uniform for them.

I tried a few words, though it wasn't easy to get them out.

"How . . . you get here?"

"You mustn't talk, Mr. Harris."

"How?"

"At gun point."

Swelling and a wet towel must have screened my skepticism. "Where from?"

"The main road beyond the street leading to your house." For another kidnap victim he looked remarkably unrumpled. "I couldn't get you on the phone. Someone did lift the receiver but didn't say anything. Then hung up. When I tried again, the bell just went on ringing."

That sounded authentic enough—Chong up to his usual tricks. Suddenly Lung went into a spiel, suggesting something memorized for a school speech day, getting it all out and over as quickly as possible.

"I went to your shop. The shopkeeper was there. He said you were away but he didn't know where. I don't think he liked it much when I insisted on going up to your flat, but he didn't try to stop me. I rang the bell for a long time. Nothing happened. I went downstairs again and asked where your servant was. The shopkeeper said he was out getting some messages. He said he'd no idea at all where you were, that you might have taken a plane for Hong Kong for all he knew. So I left. It was dark by then. I walked along your street and was waiting for a cruising taxi when two men came up behind me. One put a gun against my back. A car drew up and they made me get in."

Lung stopped as though he needed time out for breathing.

"When did you get back from Sumatra?"

"This afternoon about four. I went straight to my hotel and tried to contact you from it."

"Did you contact anyone else?"

144

"No."

"Could you have been followed?"

"I suppose so. I just never thought about it."

That didn't tally with Kang's assessment of the man's extreme sensitivity in these matters.

"What happened in the car?"

"They bandaged my eyes, then pushed me down on the floor. I was driven here."

"How long did that take?"

"About half an hour, I'd say. Maybe a little more. It's hard to tell when you're shoved down on the floor."

"You didn't think of looking at your watch?"

"No."

"When did you get here?"

"About an hour ago."

His story was tidy enough. The fact that I didn't believe it showed how deeply I had been infected by Kang's suspicions. A police theory has a kind of built-in potency which makes it strong enough to overlay all other theories. I didn't ask him about the results of his mission to Sumatra. At the moment, the matter just didn't interest me much. Lung volunteered no information, though he probably had a recitation ready on that, too.

"What day is this?"

"Friday."

Sven's funeral had been on a Saturday. I stared.

"Date?"

"The ninth."

My mind rejected the idea that I had been in this room for a week, but my body didn't. It was endorsing Lung on this. I put up a hand to my undamaged cheek. I had a good growth of beard coming on. Those compresses stayed fixed because they were shoved down onto spikes. The weakness I felt was from no food, not drugs. Knowing this was somehow good for morale. A starving man loses initiative. I hadn't shown too much of this.

I asked for some water and he took the glass, going over to the cupboard, then returning to prop me up. I rinsed my mouth before swallowing. There was a hint of chlorine in the taste, suggesting the Singapore water supply and more or less confirming Lung on the point of how far we were from the city.

Water in a very empty stomach had the effect of making me light-headed. I lay back again with a lot of questions at the front of my'brain but somehow no power to put them into words. All I could do was watch Lung. I did this from under lowered lids, half expecting him to react to my seeming helplessness by whipping out another syringe. He got up and started to move about, as though for the first time inspecting security arrangements. I heard a scraping that could have been a testing of those planks over the shutters. Then he brought the one chair close to the bed and sat on it to watch me, like a guard. I continued to disbelieve that he was sharing my captivity. A thin sourness, like bile from the stomach, was bitter in my mouth.

In defending this man to Kang I had really been defending my own judgment. Now, in a weakness that might almost have been the emotional vacuum leading to approaching death, I could look back with feeling set to one side, self-assessment stripped of all the usual necessary ego props. The diagnosis, as though delivered by an outside specialist on a fleeting visit, was that I hadn't been too bright in any of my recent living. Mercifully, perhaps, this sharp, clear definition soon blurred and I moved over into the weird hallucination that I was being laughed at from all sides, and from mouths wide open to let out sound that for some reason was pitched in too high a key for me to hear. Then, as well as Lung's eyes watching, there were other eyes, dozens of them, eyes in twin huge arcs of bodiless faces, some back in this room from beyond death, and all united in a demoniac gloating over a victim lying helpless from exhaustion on a bed.

I hadn't really lost consciousness again. I could lift eyelids and see Lung there as part of the nightmare. I tried to fix attention on him and so get rid of the other eyes, but they refused to go. I was also lucid enough to be able to tell myself that all this unpleasantness was drug-induced, which ought to have helped, but didn't. I was aware, too, that I was sweating, streaming as though I was slicing my way through jungle with a parang, and the remarkably rational thought arrived that I would soon need salt-replacement tablets.

A burst of gunfire didn't involve me at all. I heard it with the complete detachment of a man suddenly being obliged to endure someone else's Western on television. There was a lot of noise, but it was contained in a square box somewhere and could be switched off if I could find the right knob. The din ought to be switched off—the bangs were beginning to set up unpleasant vibrations.

"Mr. Harris! Mr. Harris!"

The other eyes and faces had gone. There was just Lung leaning over, trying to lift me. I didn't want to be lifted. I shoved his hands away. The towel slid down on my chest, cold against opened pores.

The scream was real. It came from just beyond a door and not from a loudspeaker, a howl of agony followed by the crackling noise of wood collapsing. The cry mounted to wild terror, then was cut off.

Lung pulled me off the bed. He started to haul me across the floor, my heels dragging. I tried to get purchase on the linoleum with bare feet, but couldn't. There were three more shots, then a man's voice shouting something. It became two words, repeated over and over in Cantonese, thinning to hysteria.

"Don't shoot, don't shoot!"

Lung let me drop. I tried to push myself up, but was caught by violent giddiness and just had to lie there. Then Lung used the two words:

"Don't shoot!"

His voice sounded like a child's. I lifted my head, not very far. The door to the hall was open. Just inside it were three men in

147

uniform, all carrying automatic rifles. One of them was Superintendent Kang. He seemed to have recognized me all right, in spite of my beard. He stared as though the spectacle of an almost naked man lying on dirty linoleum was one of the really big anticlimaxes of his professional career.

"My God!" he said finally.

To me that didn't sound like deep distress. He seemed to shake himself back into duty, pointing a gun barrel at Lung.

"Search that one!"

Kang came over. He bent low over me and then pulled back a bit, as though something had offended his nostrils.

"Paul!"

"I'm dizzy," I said, like a peevish geriatric. "You'll have to help me up."

But he didn't do it, detailing men for the job. There were plenty of men in the room now. I was carried to the bed and laid out for Kang's inspection. He still seemed to find it difficult to believe that I was me. I had the feeling he might reach out a finger to poke one of my ribs, which were certainly showing.

"Do you know how long you've been here?"

"Lung says a week. So do my whiskers."

"They feed you at all?"

"Not unless intravenously when I was unconscious."

"Was that most of the time?"

"You could say so. They used big ampules."

Kang turned. "Have you searched that man yet? Found anything?"

"Just his wallet and some money, sir."

"No weapon?"

"No, sir."

Apparently no hypodermic syringe either. I could see Lung now. He looked bewildered, nothing more. And if Kang still believed my general manager was Lum Ping, he didn't seem exultant about having nabbed him in circumstances that would need quite a bit of explaining away.

A sergeant came in and reported noisily that a man who had fallen through a railing was dead from a broken neck.

"How many of them are alive?" Kang asked.

"Only one besides this one here, sir."

"Take them to the van and lock them in. Leave two men on guard by it. They might have reserves and try a rescue."

"Very good, sir."

Lung didn't seem to realize that he was involved in all this. It was when two policemen took hold of his arms that he made his appeal to me.

"Mr. Harris! They're taking me . . . ? You can tell them . . ."

He didn't say what I could tell them and I didn't say a thing. Out in the hallway Lung protested again, with a wailing. Then that stopped, abruptly. Kang ordered two ambulances to be summoned by car radio, presumably one for the bodies, the other for me.

"You're not to worry about anything," he said.

"What made you raid this place?"

"You could call it a tip-off. I'll come and see you in hospital and tell you all about it. I haven't time now."

"I want to go home, Kang."

"Don't be a bloody fool. You're an admission case if I ever saw one."

He turned and walked out of the green room. Five minutes later noise had damped down. Only one policeman was left to keep an eye on me. He didn't seem to think a lot of my survival chances.

"Is there a naked tree in the courtyard of this house?" I asked. "One of those things with no bark?"

"Yes, sir."

I knew where I was.

The flowers might have been for a VIP, as though a grateful society was welcoming me back into its patterns. I stared at them. None of your cheap stuff, no cut-price cannas from civic

149

nurseries, or local orchids, but Australian roses, two dozen deep red flown up frozen, plus a jugful of carnations that could only have been grown in the Cameron Highlands. I opened my eyes from another spell on dope to a display that at once reminded me of Sven's funeral. Later I'd read the cards. Now I needed information.

"Nurse!"

Nothing happened. The door was shut. My room was paneled in jungle wood veneer and looked like a single cabin on B Deck of a cruise liner. It even had the attached bathroom, an open door showing pale lilac porcelain with tiles to match.

I had been given a pint or two of someone else's blood, the feed tube now detached but the apparatus left handy just in case I needed some more. There was a bell on the bedside table and I pressed it.

The girl who came in looked as though she had graduated from one of Lee Kuan Yew's strength-through-joy courses before she took up healing. Not many Chinese of her age and sex could be called strapping, but this one was and she moved with the confidence of someone who can turn over the heaviest patient without the slightest risk of rupturing anything.

"Well now, you're awake," she said in English, as though I had done the right thing bang on schedule. "Are you quite comfortable, Mr. Harris?"

"No. Turn off this damn air-conditioning and open a window, will you?"

"It's like *that*, is it?" she said, establishing a difficult-patient relationship at once. "It's against regulations."

"Nonsense. This is a private room and I want air. How high up are we?"

"Nine floors."

There was going to be some bill for penthouse-level accommodation and I don't carry hospitalization insurance.

"I want all the papers," I said.

"What?"

"The newspapers for a week back."

"You're going to have some food first. That's doctor's orders. You've been fed intravenously."

"So I see."

"Not just plasma," she told me. "And you'll be on liquids for a few days."

"Like hell. Nurse, those papers, *please.*"

"I can get you today's *Straits Times.*"

She went out, leaving me cold in air-conditioning. I heard the distant sound of traffic penetrating soundproofing and also the drone of a plane going somewhere. The flowers were giving out a strong smell as though just before leaving the shop they were sprayed with the scent they were supposed to carry naturally. I sat up against two pillows. The hospital nightie into which I had been fitted felt slightly scratchy. My bones ached.

Nurse came in carrying the day's news from the world and she turned off a switch without being asked to again, opening a tip-over window. At once heat came in from outside, for which I was grateful. It was a beautiful day, high clouds sharing the sky with hazed blue. I took the paper, opening it out, noting that my hands shook and I couldn't stop them from doing this. I was like someone halfway down the mountain from Shangri-La suddenly beginning to feel his second century.

"Now for some soup," Nurse said and left.

The world hadn't changed too much in my week out of it. The three lesser wars no nearer an end than they had been. There was Muslim trouble in the Philippines and Japan's annual economic growth rate had been cut from ten percent to nine point two. Tokyo was getting worried. For my part, I'm looking forward to the really bad year when they make only seven. I turned a page for the local stuff, but Singapore seemed positively somnolent—not a kidnapping in sight. I turned over again to an item that sent a marked jarring along still sensitive nerves.

CHINESE MINISTER ILL

Peking Politburo member Li Feng Tsu, on a goodwill mission to Southeast Asia, and now in Singapore, has been confined to bed in his hotel suite for the second day of his official program. It is believed that he is suffering from influenza contracted in Burma, though no bulletin has been issued and no request made for local specialist assistance. The Minister remains under the care of the personal physician in his suite. A verbal statement was given to our reporter that Minister Li's condition is causing no concern and that he is progressing satisfactorily. It has, however, been announced that all Minister Li's engagements for today and tomorrow, including tomorrow's full-scale military parade, have been canceled meantime, though it is hoped that His Excellency will have recovered by next week. Reliable sources suggest that the Minister's visit here will be extended to enable him to cover his full, if postponed, program.

Additions to Minister Li's official party arrived in Singapore by air from Peking late last night, these being Lieutenant General Chen Foo of the People's Army of the Socialist Republic of China, and two aides. When asked at the airport whether his surprise visit had anything to do with Minister Li's illness, General Chen replied that it did not, that he was merely taking this opportunity to study at close quarters the Singapore Defense Force's new techniques of military training within restricted geographical areas in which he was personally deeply interested. General Chen also stated that he would probably be remaining with the goodwill mission until its return to China.

I read the item again. I could smell the hush-up of something big just as strongly as I could smell newsprint. General Chen Foo had all of China in which to maneuver. Why the hell should he be interested in military training within restricted geographical areas? He was interested in Li Feng Tsu and I was suddenly quite certain this interest had nothing to do with the Minister's influenza.

Nurse came in with a mug of steaming soup.

"I thought you might like to drink this through a straw," she said.

"I gave that up when I stopped drinking Cokes. And that was some time ago."

"Have it your own way, Mr. Harris. The cup's hot."

"For the next course I'll have fillet steak. Rare."

"You won't, you know."

I was allowed to finish the soup before she started that terrible bed-tightening process which is the way they put in time when there is nothing else to do and must be the first thing taught them professionally, drummed in so hard they never forget it. In half a minute I could scarcely breathe, but I kept up the struggle.

"What's your name?"

"Miss Lin," she said formally.

"Do you know what put me in here?"

"I was told to ask no questions, and when I'm told that I don't."

She'd had security training as well.

"I'm not a chronic drug case," I said.

"How nice for you. I don't know when I've seen prettier flowers. They must have cost a fortune."

"What do the cards say?"

"There's only one. It says: 'Best wishes for a speedy recovery. Superintendent Kang.' "

A top policeman's secretary must have long suppressed a secret desire to run wild in the city's most expensive florist. It was years since I had felt so deeply loved.

"I've finished the soup, Miss Lin. Surely I get something next?"

"No," she said and went out.

A telephone within reach appeared to offer direct contact with the outside world. I lifted the hand-set, at once getting a voice from the hospital switchboard, a girl who sounded as though she had been brought up in Texas, which is an odd kind

of English to hear in Singapore. But everybody gets everywhere these days.

"How can I help you?"

"You can get me a city number."

"I'm sorry, sir, but the patient in nine three seven is not yet
fit to receive or send calls."

"You can let me judge that. I'm the patient."

"I'm sorry, sir, but those are my instructions. You're on the
red list."

"What does that mean?"

"Not to be disturbed under any circumstances."

"Even when I want to create the disturbance?"

"That's right, sir."

I didn't try to argue. I was under tight security up here on the
ninth floor and I knew who had ordered it: the same character
who had sent in frozen roses. Without doubt he meant to be my
first and possibly only visitor for the time being. The police,
when they want to, can make detention in a hospital private
room almost as tight as in a cell under their administration
building.

I had no clothes here. I had even lost the jockey shorts. A man
in a starched hospital nightshirt can't get very far with an escape bid even after a blood transfusion and a mug of soup. But
you don't get strength back lying waiting for it to come seeping
into wasted muscles. I struggled against those sheets like a moth
coming out of a chrysalis and finally got onto the composition
flooring, wobbling toward lilac plumbing. There was a shower,
but I decided on a soak, the hot water bringing body temperature up to the point where I was comfortable again. By the time
I was back in the nightshirt I felt human enough to tiptoe to the
corridor door and open this a crack. The long passage was
empty, with not even a policeman sitting on a chair tipped back
against the wall. I was at the far end of the passage from the lifts,
which was a pity.

Voices and laughter erupted: Miss Lin and two colleagues

154

coming out from a private lair, bringing with them wild mirth that was probably from one of those macabre medical jokes that sweep through all hospitals as though carried on internal telex. I shut the door and had to pay tribute to the soundproofing— merriment was immediately cut off. There was just time for me to corkscrew down between sheets.

"Been having a nap, Mr. Harris?"

"No, a bath."

"What? You got up?"

"Sure. And my legs are working. But otherwise I'm frail."

"I should think so, too. The doctor will be here in twenty minutes. We must get ready for that, mustn't we?"

I've never understood why nurses involve patients in these conspiracies to keep members of the medical profession secure in the feeling that they are at least second-rank deities, but it always happens. I even had my hair combed. I told Miss Lin I hadn't cleaned my teeth and she went out to get a brush, bringing me a glass and spit cup and paste, too. After that we were ready.

Even in a spotless white coverall the doctor was a bit of a letdown: small, Chinese, and worried about his own ulcer. Most of the medicos in my experience have been in considerably worse physical condition than their average patient, but bravely soldiering on nonetheless. This one stared at my chart and then, while checking my pulse, looked down on me as though I was just another fraud in the middle of his afternoon.

"Hm," he said. "Any pain in the stomach?"

I shook my head.

"Vertigo?"

"Not unless I dance about."

He frowned. "What has the patient had to eat, Nurse?"

"Soup, Doctor."

"Liquid diet for the rest of today."

He might have been prescribing for himself. He left soon for something more interesting and Miss Lin left with him, from which I gathered that she had a few other stables to look after and wouldn't all be on my bill. She didn't come back for twenty minutes, and then it was to draw curtains.

"The doctor says you should have as much sleep as possible. You can have one Somnorol."

"I don't want it. All I want is a little peace and quiet."

That surprised her. "What do you mean?"

"There has been pretty frantic noise from the next cell." I pointed to the wall over my head.

"That's impossible. Nine three six has been empty since yesterday morning."

"There was a distinct sound of manic laughter."

If she blushed, I couldn't see it in the dim light.

"You've been imagining things, Mr. Harris. If you need anything, just ring."

I was getting somewhere. If 936 was unoccupied, it seemed reasonable to assume that its phone wouldn't be on the red list unless this whole floor was reserved for police security cases, and we're not really a totalitarian state, whatever a hostile foreign press may say about that. Also, the afternoon before visiting hours is a sleepy time up on the top-price floor, with nurses as relaxed as they allow themselves to get on duty. There might even be a television soap opera about hospital life that none of them missed if they could help it. I waited perhaps half an hour, then tried out my legs again. Underpinning was better this time.

The corridor was empty. I got into 936 at remarkable speed. It was a tidy replica of 937 without the smell of flowers. The Texan answered the phone. For some reason I was sure she was a blonde. They have a great time in the Orient; scarcity value. Chinese men pretend not to care for them, but it's an act. I didn't ask to be given an outside line, just assumed I'd get it, and a moment later a bell was ringing in the free world. I was using Tong's number; there was no use trying my own. I got his wife and she did the switch-over to downstairs.

My shopkeeper accepted my story about why I was in the hospital without asking any embarrassing questions. He didn't even sound interested.

"I want home, Tong. I can't walk out in a nightshirt. Here's what I want you to do. Go out to the bazaar and buy a big fruit basket and the fruit to go with it. Before you fill the thing, put trousers, soft shoes, socks, and a shirt in the bottom. Chong will give you the stuff. See that it's properly hidden. Put a card on the thing saying: 'To Mr. Harris, room nine six seven, from Superintendent Kang.' Leave the basket with reception and if the girl asks any questions you're just the delivery boy. Have you got all that?"

"I'll write it down."

I could hear him wheezing as he did it.

"All right, Mr. Harris."

"And hurry with the thing."

"Yes."

He was grumpy again. It was becoming chronic, hearth troubles souring an otherwise beautiful nature.

"And tell Chong to lay in two pounds of steak. The best. He's not to try cooking it, I'll do that myself."

Tong didn't laugh. He was beginning to depress me. I ended the call.

By the time I was back in my own bed my heart was doing things that just might have interested an unhappy house physician, but I used deep breathing to calm it down and then lay wrapped in that peculiar self-absorption which the mere fact of being in a hospital seems to clamp down on the spirit, like their sheets on the body.

It's not good for morale to wake up from a nap to find yourself being stared at by a high-ranking policeman. Kang was doing this from a chair. He was slumped back in it, as though glad of the excuse to rest for a while, arms limp at his sides, one hand actually touching the floor. He has one of those faces which

157

fatigue returns to youth rather than making it a prophecy of old age, and from this he seems to demand a special, half-protective compassion. But I've never really been fooled.

He noticed that my eyes were open. He kept his voice low. "How are you feeling now?"

"All right," I said without making it sound very robust, intuition already warning me that I might need weakness to fall back on.

"The doctor tells me you had two shots of plasma."

"Maybe you have to learn to live with someone else's blood," I said.

There was a silence. I was pleased to note that in a dimmed-out room the one table lamp put a glow more on him than on me.

"What have you done to Lung?" I asked.

"Nothing."

Nothing almost certainly meant a long interrogation under hard white light with a team of questioners taking turns to fire words.

"Has he confessed to being Lum Ping?"

"No."

"Think he will in the end? Under your pressures?"

Kang said nothing. If I didn't watch out he'd stop respecting my invalidism. I switched from that tack.

"What made you raid that house where you found me?"

"A tip-off, of sorts."

"Who from?"

"A Mrs. Nivalahannanda."

"She ring you up complaining I'd broken a dinner date?"

"Not exactly. I thought you'd skipped from the island. And she'd been lunching with you just before you disappeared."

"So you went over our table chat with a fine-tooth comb and came up with a house I'd suggested she look at for a restaurant?"

158

"Actually, yes. Only I think you've guessed that it wasn't you I was looking for in that house."

"I guessed," I said. "I'm sensitive. And I don't think I've ever seen a more disappointed man than you. Who would you have traded me for? Li Feng Tsu?"

His head came up in surprise. "Drugs don't seem to have muzzed you."

"During the recovery phase the mind becomes sharply clear. What's happened to the Minister? Kidnapped, like me?"

"Yes."

"As a man with five hundred policemen on the security job, not to mention Li's own guards, you can't be feeling too good."

"I'm not."

"How the hell could it happen?"

"It happened in his hotel. We don't know whether he's alive or dead. There have been no messages from the kidnappers."

"But you're sure they're Lum's guerrillas?"

"I am."

"There was one man alive in that house where you found me after the shoot-up. What's he told you?"

"Nothing. He's a Singapore thug with a record a yard long. Not a guerrilla. Just specially hired for that job."

"So you haven't rounded up one Lum Ping man?"

"Not yet."

"Who is General Chen? Peking Security?"

Kang nodded.

"He just flew down here to take over when the bad news reached them?" I asked.

"He flew down here. He hasn't taken over."

"So you've been given twenty-four hours' grace? Before they start airlifting in People's Army troops to take over the search?"

"There have been no threats of any kind," Kang said.

I could see that he wouldn't like to bet there would be no threats later if Li wasn't found.

"Peking is playing along with your cover story?"

"So far."

At any time Peking could decide to break the news and let all hell loose in Singapore.

"Kang, have you any leads at all?"

"Several."

"I hope they're not like the one to Lung."

That should have made him angry, but it didn't, which gave me an unpleasant cold feeling. In spite of those lovely flowers, this wasn't just a visit to a sick friend. Kang was on duty.

"What went wrong with your security?" I asked, in a gentle voice.

"We overlooked the fact that we had a womanizer on our hands."

"What does that mean?"

"It means that at half past eleven at night Li came out of his bedroom on a heavily guarded hotel floor and walked to the lifts. He made it quite plain that he didn't need an escort because he wasn't leaving the hotel. The party security chief was asleep or Li wouldn't have got away with that—he'd have been followed. But he wasn't. He rode down two floors and walked along a corridor to the suite of a lady with whom he'd made a previous appointment."

Kang paused. I picked up my cue.

"The lady was Ranya," I said.

He didn't congratulate me for guessing right, just nodded.

"What happened to her?"

"She was gagged and tied to a chair. The perfect alibi for a whore."

Ranya had been right about the labels so quickly pinned on bachelor girls in our part of the world.

"You've jailed her?"

"No. She's in her suite."

Kang dealt with the problem of cell overcrowding by keeping his prisoners in bedrooms which they had to pay for themselves.

160

"How did the kidnappers get into the hotel?"

"They were already in it. As guests. Had been for some time, one of them for two weeks. Four Chinese businessmen with perfectly respectable bona-fides. We'd been checking new reservations for some time and had passed them."

Being honest about your own mistakes is one way to get on in the world, though it hasn't ever worked too well for me.

"You're sure Ranya was helping them?"

"I'm never sure of anything until I have the evidence."

There was one thing he was certain of, however: his purpose in coming to see me. He had made necessary checks on the state of my health, satisfied he couldn't be got at later for police brutality, and was now proceeding on a planned course. My questions had done nothing to deflect him from it. He answered them with a calm politeness that was beginning to make me feel cold again even though the air-conditioning had stayed switched off.

"Two of my policemen were killed by the kidnappers. Another two wounded. My men weren't looking for trouble coming at them from *inside* the hotel. Also, it was one in the morning. The kidnappers arrived within minutes of Li, but they didn't try to hustle him out. Actually, they drank the champagne your friend had ordered for her guest. It must have taken some nerve just to sit there keeping to a schedule, knowing that at any time someone might raise the alarm for Li. And the drug they used on the Minister may have taken some time to work. He was mobile, but his walk was spastic. They had to drag him through the kitchens. That's the way they took him out, past hotel staff still clearing up from a banquet. There was even a chef on duty. But everyone was apparently too stunned to warn my men. The two dead were shot in the back. Those were the first shots. Cold-blooded murder."

I had no doubts now about Li's kidnappers being guerrilla freedom fighters. These were the usual techniques, sickeningly familiar.

Kang lit a cigarette. The hand holding the lighter was steady. I wondered how much sleep he'd had in the last few days. That curiously expressionless voice started up again, the careful flat tone of a police witness in court.

"The escape car was a Mercedes. It arrived exactly on schedule, one half-minute before the kidnappers burst out of the hotel kitchens firing with three guns. Only one of my men was able to return fire, and that not for long. He says he saw the driver of the Mercedes. Swears it was a girl. We think he said he could identify her. But he's in this hospital now with a bullet in his stomach. We have to wait until he can talk again. He was also hit with a gun butt and has concussion. In a coma."

I looked at the ceiling. I couldn't look at Kang. He was my accuser even before a word was said, sitting in a chair smoking and talking and watching me.

"We found the Mercedes down by the bund. They'd changed cars there and probably again later. Their timing seems to have been perfect. The engine of the Mercedes was still hot when we got to it. It was a stolen car. Taken that night from a house outside the city. From a garage that showed no signs of having been forced. The car belongs to Hok Lin."

I don't think my face showed anything, but I still couldn't look at him. Maybe that told him what he wanted. What I felt like doing was crying out. I'd wondered if Sally loved her grandfather. Now I knew. They don't love anyone outside their hard faith. Not mothers or fathers or brothers or sisters. Conversion for them is as total as for that strange sect of Brethren in the north of Scotland where, when a man has joined the elect, he refuses to eat at table with a wife who has not. He doesn't leave her, he keeps up the front of family life, but behind it is hell. There had been a similar kind of hell in an old man's house and he hadn't known it. Or at least I hoped he hadn't known it. But her grandfather had been there to be used, even to that last indecency of taking his car, to leave that pointer straight toward a cripple who would die of shame. The Bible has it stated plain: brought down in sorrow to the grave.

"Paul, why did you go to Hok Lin's house on the afternoon you were kidnapped?"

"To see him. He was looking frail at Sven's funeral."

"You're close to the family?"

"You know that."

"Then perhaps you knew that the girl Sheh Loh Loyang had been a member of the Singapore People's Liberation Party?"

"No!"

"Kadok has been busy up in K.L. The girl was at a banquet given for Li Feng Tsu the night before he paid his visit to the casino on the mountain. She was there as the direct result of the Minister's request to meet some of the Chinese students in the capital. There was an informal session with Li after the meal when the girl was one of a group around him. Kadok has no record of what was said, but it would have been easy for her to suggest that the visitor might see more of local living than his fixed schedules permitted. Like a new casino up on a mountain. Li must have got the idea from somewhere, and apparently it wasn't put to him by any of the official party. He sprang it on them at the end of the next evening's dinner, quite suddenly. Lum Ping must have been gambling that he would do this. And he wasn't risking much if Li didn't. Just one trained rifle shot waiting up on a mountain. The girl."

I waited for what was coming. Kang allowed seconds of silence.

"You recognized the girl Sheh Loh Loyang as she came running down a path carrying a rifle."

"Yes."

The policeman stood. He stared down at me, a stranger.

"I warned you, Paul. You'll be kept in Singapore as the prosecution's chief witness at the girl's trial. After that Kadok can have you. As far as we're concerned, you'll be declared an undesirable alien."

After a minute I asked: "Have you been questioning Hok?"

"Only about that car. So far."

"Kang, believe me, he doesn't know about Sally. Can't you leave him out of this?"

"You're thinking of your business?"

"No! Damn you!"

"When we catch the girl, there can be no question of protecting her grandfather."

He walked past the foot of my bed without looking at me again. The door opened and then shut with a soft click.

II 🦁

When the door opened suddenly I thought it might be the Superintendent back to add a postscript, but it was only Miss Lin bearing a big basket of fruit. I'd been damn lucky that this hadn't arrived ten minutes earlier.

"Aren't you getting VIP treatment from the police?" she said, having read the attached card.

I could have found another definition for what I was getting from them.

"This is so huge, Mr. Harris, I'm afraid there just isn't room for it up with the flowers. I'll take it to the service bay and bring you a selection of fruit when you want it."

That made me sit up. "Just put the thing down by the window, please. I like to feast my eyes on all tributes."

She was visibly irritated. The imported pears would have gone nicely with her between-meals snacks, and in the tropics we all go mad about temperate-clime fruit, spurning the juiciest fresh pineapple for a tasteless defrosted apple.

Tong had done quite a good job. It looked professionally packed under its cellophane, bulk provided by still-green bargain-bazaar bananas and rambutans, over which was a layer of Australian exports—pears, grapes, and apples, thinly applied for

165

maximum effect. The basket sat on the floor looking like an allegory of friendship: Lift off the top layer and what have you got? Unripe bananas.

I bought a better relationship with Miss Lin with two of the pears and she went off happier, leaving the curtains still pulled because I was going to have another of those naps so vital to my recovery. As soon as the door had shut I got out of bed and dissected a present I'd have to pay for. The first piece of clothing brought out was a Hawaiian shirt. I own only one, wearing it sometimes on my roof terrace but never in public. Chong had shown his usual talent for doing the wrong thing. In that shirt I wasn't going to melt into the crowd down in the hospital foyer; even in our climate I would be as conspicuous as a nude at a tea party, for who visits the sick wearing the wild colors of rude health?

The shoes were all right, soft-soled, and so were the trousers, banknotes crackling in a pocket, but even bundled up that shirt shouted at me. The next problem was where to store my getaway gear. Fresh linen was kept on the top shelf of the built-in cupboard and Nurse might open that door at any time. Standardized hospital equipment offered no secure hiding place. Even under the mattress was no good, for during tuck-in rituals Miss Lin practically lifted the thing clear of its underframe. Finally, after repacking the fruit, I took everything to bed, lying with the shoes between my thighs and the rest of the stuff on my stomach under the nightshirt. Obvious patient mobility had eliminated the risk of all the lights suddenly being switched on and a couple of ladies surging in to give me a bed bath.

I lay with my thoughts and those clothes until seven. The thoughts did nothing for my convalescence. No supper arrived. At twenty past Miss Lin came in bearing a tray and offering an apology. She had left feeding me until later because of pressures to get her other patients ready for visitors and she knew I wouldn't be having any. The head chef hadn't worked too hard over my meal. It was a powdered-egg custard made sloppier by the addition of more milk. I didn't complain, just ate fast so she could take the tray out with her.

When I was alone I dressed fast, too. If Nurse came in for anything, my escape bid was over. Kang, learning of the attempt, would probably send a policeman to sit in the corridor. I waited, listening for visitors' going-away noise, as nervous as a man on the verge of X rays he is damn certain are going to reveal the suspected worst. I opened the door a crack.

You expect the rich to have plenty of visitors, but there couldn't have been any near-terminal cases on my floor, for the long corridor leading to the lifts offered only about half a dozen duty-done people going home. But a good many of the bedroom doors were open, which could mean more just on the point of leaving. I decided my moment was now.

Still it was lonely out there. The lifts seemed miles away. While I walked toward them, automatic doors hissed open and a waiting group was absorbed into the box beyond. I could be all of five minutes just standing in my bright shirt while that lift went down and came back up again. Almost certainly the other one wouldn't be working. I heard a voice from one of the rooms, loud and bitter.

"They keep making me walk! Something about adhesions. I keep telling them it's not a week since I left half my insides in an operating-theater slop bucket."

I looked back. I couldn't help myself. Miss Lin came out of a service room, surging down the corridor, then turned sharp left into what had been my accommodation. Like a fool, I hadn't even left the bathroom door shut, which might have held her up a minute or two.

I gave up the idea of riding down, making for what looked like a fire door. There was a sign on it saying: EMERGENCY. DEPRESS BAR AND PUSH TO OPEN. I followed instructions. There was a sound like felt being ripped off a billiard table as an air seal broke. I went through into something suggesting an up-ended concrete pipe, pushing the door shut again and leaning back on it, as wobbly at the knees as that post-operative case had sounded.

The fire-escape stairs went around and around an open well, a corkscrew with the stem removed. In any panic among the walking sick, a percentage of them might well have been shoved over into that hole, and as if belatedly realizing this, the hospital authorities had caused what looked like chicken wire to be stretched across the drop at each landing.

Just looking down nine floors made me dizzy, but I started the descent, keeping to the outer wall. I wasn't afraid of immediate pursuit from floor nine. Even if someone had seen me going through the emergency door, a man in a Hawaiian shirt wouldn't at once be connected with the former occupant of 937. I'd left the hospital nightshirt shoved well down between bed sheets and they wouldn't come upon that for a bit. What worried me was how long it took hospital authorities to get out an all-points call for an escaped patient, an unknown factor which kept me hurrying. The airtight doors on all landings were a potential threat and I nipped past each one like a kid playing musical chairs and determined to win. After five flights I felt an acute need for another blood transfusion, but kept going, prodded on by the thought that if I was caught in these circumstances I'd probably be put in the psychiatric ward for observation. I've always had a morbid fear of professional mind-benders. Even the semi-skilled among them can have you certified in almost no time. And Kang, now poised like a black angel over my life, would stop at nothing to have me neutralized. The only comfort I got out of the present situation was that he seemed to consider me still dangerous. I didn't see how I could be, but it nourished my ego slightly that he felt this.

On the second landing from the bottom I had to pause for breath, my lungs a bellows and feeling very giddy from continuous circling at speed. I was still propped against concrete when I heard the ripping noise of air-sealing being ruptured somewhere above, I couldn't tell how many floors up. There were voices. A man called out in Cantonese: "I don't think he's here."

A second voice held authority. "Go down and check to the bottom anyway."

I went all out down the well, breathing a wheeze. There was a shout:

"There *is* someone here!"

"I'll phone down from the ward! To get someone out in the court!"

I reached the main-level exit, which was steel, with bolts to loosen as well as another push-bar. While I worked on them, feet thudded above me. I fell out into warm night air.

Stars were bright. I was in an asphalted court used by ambulances. Two of these vehicles were parked, one with rear doors open and three men lifting down a stretcher. They didn't see me. It was a long run to the gate, a much shorter one to the ambulances. The stretcher party moved off toward the building. I went past the open back doors of one ambulance to the closed ones of the other, yanked down a handle, and crawled into darkness, finding the tip-up seat for a nurse, then groping about for the inside lock.

There was shouting. From the number of feet pounding about outside, it could have been a jailbreak. Kang would see it as that. The door beyond me was tested, twice. Then the pursuit seemed to move to the street and possibly around to the front of the hospital.

I was thinking about getting out of my hiding place when the door to the driving compartment of my ambulance opened, then slammed again. Someone got in the front passenger seat too. The handle of my door was jerked down. A man yelled: "This thing's locked!"

"Well, get in beside Nurse," the driver called. "And hurry up!"

The engine started. When we were out in the side road a siren began to whine right over my head. We traveled fast. I got an impression of bright lights through smoked-glass windows.

169

After five minutes I worked forward to a small communication hatch and slid this back.

"You can let me out here, please," I said.

Brakes screamed. I had the rear door open before we actually stopped. Someone jumped down from up front, yelling at me. People on pavements stared, but there was no actual pursuit.

The ship-chandler's was open for business at getting on for eight thirty, with hours to go yet before normal closing time. It was well lit toward the front, dimmer at the back. Tong emerged from shadow just as I passed under a bulb. He stopped.

"Tuan, you're all right?"

"Yes."

Actually I'd had to get out of a taxi and walk because I was feeling sick.

"I brought down whisky. You'd like some?"

He meant before I tackled the stairs. It seemed a good idea. I went into his cubbyhole, which backed onto the sail lockers. There was a kettle steaming and a bottle of my twelve-year-old malt on a low table with a gummy-looking glass beside it. I sat down on a chair and poured out a sound medicinal dose. He stood watching me.

"It might be a good idea if you put up the shutters now," I said.

He stared at the dressing taped onto my jaw.

"Tuan, what happened to you?"

"I had an accident."

He turned away. A moment later I heard shutters being fitted into their runners, then shoved along. I sipped the whisky. Beyond a steaming kettle was shelving for holding new canvas, this going up for twenty feet and in sections for different sizes, a movable library ladder giving access to the top levels. With the police very much on my mind, I had the thought that one of those bays would make quite a good emergency hiding place; in some of them there was considerable space between the

170

canvas and the wall. Quite a comfortable kennel, too, even for a long wait.

One of the bays was, of course, already in use as living quarters. This had always embarrassed me and I'd suggested to Tong more than once that we could partition off space somewhere to make a room for his assistant, but he had shrugged off the idea, saying the youth was perfectly happy with what he had, which was a lot better than he'd known at home. During most of my evening visits to Tong here the boy had been tucked back in his kennel asleep and I'd rather avoided looking at him, but the bay was empty now. It certainly seemed cozy enough, rather like a railway lower berth, with a quilt to lie on, a pillow, a folded blanket, and a shelf at the back for personal possessions.

There didn't seem to be many of these: some clothes squeezed in, a tin box on a pile of what looked like magazines, then a gleam of white plastic. I had to lean forward to see what this was. A crash helmet. I stared. Tong had a motor scooter, but it seemed unbelievable that he would allow a youth with a markedly low IQ to use it in Singapore traffic.

The last shutter banged into place. There was the sound of bolts being shoved home. Tong came back to the cubbyhole, taking a three-legged stool opposite my chair, settling to brew tea, pouring this almost at once, a pale yellow trickle into an arsenic-green handleless cup. He lifted the cup between fingers on one hand and stumps on the other.

"Chong laid in that meat?" I asked.

Tong sipped. "He's not here."

"At this time of night? Don't tell me he's got a girl friend at last?"

The shopkeeper shook his head. "He went away three days ago."

"*What?* But he's got nowhere to go!"

"That's what I said to him. But he wouldn't tell me anything. He was carrying a suitcase."

"What *did* he say?"

"That he was going away for a while. I think he was upset. Maybe because he hadn't heard from you."

"Chong's used to my going off without telling him."

"There's no use asking me questions, tuan. I haven't the answers. He just locked up his rooms and went."

"Not even a note for me?"

"I haven't seen one. It could be in your flat, I suppose. Or Chong's rooms. If you have a key to them."

"I did once. I think I've lost it."

I hadn't lost that spare key to my servant's quarters. There was a coldness in my stomach the whisky wasn't warming away and it wasn't from hunger.

"Did Chong give you his key to my flat?"

"He gave it to me."

It was the natural thing for my servant to have done, of course, but I was still surprised that he had. I would never have expected him to hand over those keys to anyone, even the shopkeeper. There hadn't been much contact between the two of them, no open animosity that I saw—they just ignored each other. Their flats shared a landing, but I doubted if either had been through the door opposite his own. Chong treated the shop as though it shouldn't be there at all, certainly not as the only access to my apartment from the street.

"I got the meat for you," Tong said. "It's in your kitchen."

"Then I'd better be getting upstairs to do some cooking."

He stood when I did, not looking at me as he asked a question:

"Is there some trouble with the police?"

"Why?"

"You wanted the shutters closed. It's early."

"There might be inquiries about why I left the hospital the way I did. But you won't be involved. You needn't be worried."

I had the feeling he was.

He came up the stairs with me. I took more time over the climb than I needed to, resting halfway.

"You should be in bed, tuan."

"It won't be long before I am."

The apartment was hot and this seemed to underline Chong's absence. I went into my bedroom to get out of the Hawaiian shirt and into a dressing gown. The mirror over the washbasin in the bathroom showed a face that was quite a long way from its somewhat battered best. They had shaved me in the hospital before putting the dressing on my jaw, but stubble was there again and this, plus a marked gauntness, gave me a real lost-weekend look. But it was my eyes I liked least, the eyes of a man who has suddenly had a glimpse of something he would have given a great deal not to have seen.

I climbed the spiral stairs to the sitting room, met by a smell of onions frying. The door to the kitchenette was open.

"Tong, what the hell are you doing?"

"Making your supper."

"I didn't know you could cook."

"I've learned many things. You sit down."

I wanted another whisky, but it had to be food first. I sat by the phone, lifted the receiver, and dialed. I didn't get straight through to the man I wanted—an interceptor asked my business.

"Can I speak to Superintendent Kang? The name is Harris."

"Just a minute."

In the kitchenette onions stopped sizzling. Kang was still in his gray downtown office. He was probably sleeping there these days.

"Well, Paul?"

"I wanted you to know that I'm at home."

"I guessed you would be."

"I plan to stay here. So there's no need to waste any of your men on the job of seeing that I do."

"I had no intention of doing anything so stupid."

"Ought I to call the hospital?"

"No. I told them not to bother about you. If you want to make a fool of yourself, that's your affair. I'd advise you not to try to leave the island. Otherwise you can do what you like."

"Are you still holding Lung?"

"How does that concern you?"

"I want to see him."

"You could always try ringing his hotel."

He hung up. I rang Lung's hotel to be told that a resident guest had not yet returned from a business trip abroad. I tried Ranya's hotel to find that she wasn't available either.

Tong came in with a tray. One look told me that you can lose four fingers and still manage to do a great deal over a hot cookstove. The centerpiece was a slab of meat the size of those Porterhouse steaks which used to be a good reason for traveling on American railways, one order enough to feed a whole family. The fillet was garnished with mushrooms and there was also a green salad. If he could cook like this, why didn't he just push his wife out of the way and get on with it?

I tried to get Tong to bring another plate and take half, but he wouldn't, claiming to have eaten already. He seemed restless in a domestic role, not knowing quite what to do with himself while I chewed, going out on the terrace at one point and just standing there. When he came back in again, I suggested it was nearly time for the television news and he switched on, standing to watch.

Most of our announcers rather ape the American style of newscasting, a breathless outpouring of words as though they had just arrived panting in the studio from a participant role in at least one of the events recounted. But this one wasn't like that. He might have been trained by the BBC, world horrors ironed flat by the massive weight of his indifference to them. The pronunciation of place names mattered, but nothing else seemed to. In due course we were told that Li Feng Tsu was still suffering from a high fever in that hotel suite where I knew he wasn't, but that his doctors were expecting a turn for the better any time now. The way the item came near the end, among the

174

brief snippets, suggested that it was now local policy to play down the importance of a goodwill mission. This could be a form of insurance against the very real possibility it would soon be necessary to announce that Li's body had been found. But if the Singapore government thought they could play this down if it happened, they were optimists. I couldn't see Peking being understanding about the finding of a Politburo corpse.

Tong watched the news as if events beyond the affairs of our shop bored him.

"What do you think of the kidnapping?" I asked.

He shrugged, saying nothing.

"I hear a Chinese general has arrived."

At first that didn't seem to interest him, either. Then quite suddenly he turned toward me.

"They've brought defense-force troops into the city. No one knows whether it's to help hunt kidnappers or to keep a watch on General Chen."

The change in Tong was startling, as though he just found it impossible to go on playing a role he had assigned himself. He wasn't smiling, but his eyes glinted with a sardonic glee much nearer to his personality norm than the pianissimo effects he'd been offering since my return.

"Where did you hear about the troops?"

"In the street. It's common talk. I'll go now, tuan. But I'll make your breakfast. Stay in bed."

It seemed I wasn't going to be allowed to miss Chong. I watched a self-appointed replacement disappear down the spiral stair. The set began to blast out the din of an overture to a Chinese opera.

Kang would never ask for defense-force assistance in his search for Li Feng Tsu. If there were troops in the city, they were here as a prophylactic against rioting that could so easily flare the moment the news broke that Li had been murdered. I didn't believe that General Chen had been dispatched from Peking with the idea that he should become a focal point in that

175

rioting; he was just their pretty big man on the spot. Mao's Marxists are nothing if not total opportunists. A situation just might arise in a strife-torn Singapore in which General Chen would feel he must play an activist role. This would see a recent olive branch chucked on the scrap heap and a pike picked up in its place. It didn't take too much imagination to see the General emerging as a man morally obliged to support a People's Liberation struggle against a fascist dictatorship, perhaps even willing to serve as the temporary leader of the freedom fighters.

The great strength of the Peking regime is that it doesn't really plan policy in advance, but just arranges its pieces on a monster board, ready at any time to take a pawn with a view to the later capture of a queen. Anyone who imagines that an interval for serving tea and biscuits, with smiles, means that intense attention to the game has slackened off is something of a sizable fool.

On my way to bed I put the chain on the front door. In my room I made straight for the bottom drawer in which I keep sweaters for Scotland plus a Walther P.K., a handy gun. Unfortunately I don't have a license for it, about which I have a slight guilt complex, so it lies there unloaded like an item from my more violent past that I had forgotten I still possessed.

The gun was where it should be. I turned to the matter of bullets for it, which were kept in a hiding place I considered highly ingenious even if it was my clothes cupboard. It must be more than ten years now since I have worn white tie and tails in the evening, an outfit that really isn't suited to our climate, but I keep this relic from other living, too. And it is well preserved inside its own cellophane slipcover with the further protection of moth-resistant paneling all around. I wonder how many men, even those who wear this get-up regularly, ever use those slit pockets at the bottom of the tails. I certainly never used to. It may be possible for the chap about town to reach around and haul up the slack behind him, producing a cigarette case and lighter from one of those pouches, but I've never seen it done. Also, it has always seemed to me the kind of pocket that a searcher would overlook, even someone taking his time. My suit has two of these, flanking the back slit. In each is a little flat pack of Walther P.K. ammo, padded in a handkerchief.

It was a decided shock to find both the packs gone. I came out from the cupboard appreciating the subtlety of the way I had been disarmed. I could be expected to be reassured when I found the gun where I'd left it, unlikely to bother about the bullets unless I really meant to use the weapon. Chong certainly hadn't taken them. His cleaning rarely penetrates into cupboards and never goes as far as airing clothes. I send my suits to the cleaners when I'm not tubbing the tropic ones at home. That ammo could only have been removed as the result of a careful and intensive search for it.

The spare key to Chong's rooms ought to be in my handkerchief drawer, a repository for assorted junk that I always mean to sort out for a big throwaway and never do. There were keys there, for trunks I've had junked and cars I once owned, but no sign at all of the one for a Chubb lock downstairs.

I went back to the sitting room, switched off the television, allowed myself a very small whisky, switched out the lights, and went to bed, leaving the chain on the front door. There was a second key to this apartment knocking about somewhere, the one that had been in my clothes when I was snatched by Lum's thugs.

I woke just after one A.M. with indigestion, using the only yoga I believe in, those seven deep breaths. They broke a windball—a relief, but my teeth felt furred. I went into the bathroom to clean them, not liking my face any more than I had earlier, but after that protein intake, even though it hadn't settled, I felt stronger. I shaved around the dressing, then had a shower, and with the sprays needling my body had a kind of vision, of Chong lugging his rattan suitcase en route for the outside world which

he hadn't really looked at seriously for years. Servants anywhere—the domestic variety, not those in the slick hotels—
tend to be opters out from living who have lost faith in themselves, or never had it, marking the time of their years in a
corner of someone else's pattern. Because of this they rate almost the special protection given to children. They can't be
allowed to drift off into situations they haven't the qualifications
or experience to meet head on, at least not at Chong's age. He
has a tendency to asthma, and when he gets excited his breathing is such a fight he can't push words through it. Once he had
stuck by me when everyone else had run away. Where the hell
could he have gone, and why? A moment later I knew the
answer. He hadn't gone anywhere by his own wish. If he wasn't
in those rooms downstairs, then he had been taken away because his quarters were needed for someone else.

I got out of the shower feeling sick again, this time from fear,
for an old man, for myself.

The phone rang. I put a dressing gown around my wet body.
"Hello?"

"Paul! Is that you?" It was Ranya.

"Yes."

"Oh! I've been trying to get you all week."

"I've been away."

"Where?"

"It doesn't matter. Are you all right?"

"No. I've been deported."

"You *what?*"

"I mean, I'm going to be. I've been ordered out of Singapore.
The police are escorting me to a Bangkok flight tomorrow at
ten."

Kang didn't just track people down, he functioned as his own
judge and jury as well. We tend not to notice how powerful old
friends have become.

"They've kept me in the hotel ever since . . ."

"I heard about it."

178

"Who from?"

"Superintendent Kang."

"That man! He . . . They wouldn't even let me in the sitting room of my suite. The policeman was in there. I just didn't know what was going to happen. And when I tried to phone I couldn't get you."

"I'm surprised you were allowed to phone."

"Well, I wasn't under arrest or anything. Just held for questioning, whatever that means. And there were plenty of questions. About three times a day."

"I'm sorry, Ranya, but there's nothing I can do. You can say I'm under a kind of cloud myself."

"What for?"

"It doesn't matter."

"Is it Kang with you, too?"

"In a way."

"I hate that man!"

"It won't do you any good."

"I know. I'll be on that plane. Oh, Paul, can I write to you?"

"Of course."

"The thing is, I haven't your address. You gave me your number, but it's not in the book and I couldn't find out from anyone where you actually lived. You see, I just don't know what's going to happen when I get to Bangkok. I've had the most horrible news. My husband has started some kind of lawsuit against me. I think that's Kang's excuse for just shipping me back. I could be arrested when I get there. Our law isn't for women. And if I'm locked up I won't be able to ring you. But I might be able to write. Maybe later you can help in some way. Oh, Paul, I'm so frightened!"

"The address is three four one Upper Gollongsang Road."

"Oh, thanks! I'll write that down. Just a minute."

"Are you phoning from your hotel?"

She didn't answer at once, and when she did the suffering had gone out of her voice.

"No. I've escaped. From my police guard. It was really quite easy. The man was stupid. I'm ringing from a booth in Raffles Square. But I'll get a taxi and be on my way to you in minutes."

"Ranya, no! Listen . . ."

"I've got to talk to you, Paul."

"Not here, you don't!"

"I'm, coming."

"You'll find a shopfront with the shutters up!"

"Then I'll batter on them until you have to open. I can make quite a scene when I want to. And you said you live in a Chinese quarter. That means plenty of people still about. I'll have a good audience. Better let me in, Paul. See you."

She hung up.

"The bitch," I said, sitting down on the bed.

12

It was quite possible that my talk to Ranya had been overheard by an outsider, and if my phone was tapped I didn't think Kang had ordered this check. I believed the policeman when he said he could get what he wanted out of me without resorting to electronic gadgets. He'd proved that often enough. Intuition, fortified by a good deal that was non-psychic, suggested an interceptor device in this building somewhere. It was unlikely the installation was located in Tong's flat. Mrs. Tong was always on the hunt for ammunition she could use in those regular barrages against her husband, and I was sure it was the shopkeeper's policy not to let his wife know more than he had to about his affairs. This would also apply to any guests of his enjoying free accommodation in my property. That restaurant a few doors from us would deal with the feeding problem and there was no reason why a housebound wife should ever guess there had been a takeover of my servant's rooms.

Anger has its tonic properties. It went a long way toward neutralizing fear and was certainly curing my semi-invalidism. Too many people recently had labeled me a fool. I'd known for long enough that in a sense Tong gave me this rating. The man never really bothered to conceal a half-derisive appraisal of my

181

patterns, but the very fact that he hadn't concealed this had given me the feeling that it was backed by an affection of sorts. You can be fond of a dog that a change in your circumstances makes it necessary to have put away.

Still in my dressing gown I went to the front door and opened it, very quietly, to a half-inch crack. We leave the staircase lights on all night, a disadvantage to me now. There was just no place on the lower landing where a man could hide—two doors and flat walls, though at my level the architect had provided a totally useless alcove two feet deep. This wasn't shadowed, but a man backed into it at the corner nearest the stairs couldn't be seen from below. I shut the door behind me and went to play sentry.

Sentries usually have a boring time of it, but I didn't. The action started almost at once. Acoustics on the stairs are good, something having to do with a rough cement finish and no well, just solid partition walls forming a sharp-angled tunnel in which sound is bounced from corner to corner. There were feet coming up from the shop, and fast, too. This noise stopped outside what could only be Tong's door, replaced by tapping, a signal routine, three times slow, a pause, then two quick. I didn't hear a door open, just whispering. This was urgent and once or twice became rather loud. One of the whisperers was the youth who kept a crash helmet as a fetish. The young man hadn't been about when Tong locked up the shop, his bunk empty. I wouldn't have thought he rated a key.

The whispering stopped. Feet went down the stairs again. I didn't hear any other movement and was tempted to have a quick look out. It was as well I didn't do that. More tapping started, this time on Chong's door, the same signal, three times slow, a pause, then two quick. After that came more whispering, only this time nearer to me. I picked up words here and there, something about a girl, then distinctly: "Police." It looked as though a phone call to me had resulted in a red alert. I heard shuffling on the landing, then another pair of feet went

182

down the stairs, also hurrying. Whispering started again, which meant that at least two men had been using Chong's rooms.

I felt exposed in my corner, practically naked and with no gun in my hand. I had a feeling the men below were armed and that one of them, Tong, might at any moment decide to come up the stairs to make a routine check on his patient. After the whispering had ended and a door shut, breathing went on quite audibly on the landing as though someone was just standing there to consider his next move. I held my own breath until a second door clicked.

Back in my bedroom I picked up the phone and dialed the number of my own ship-chandling business. The bell rang for all of a minute before Tong picked up the handpiece of his sitting-room extension. He sounded convincingly sleepy.

"I'm expecting a visitor," I said.

"Eh? What? But . . . it's nearly two!"

Late hours didn't usually upset him.

"The lady chose the time, not me."

"You should be sleeping, tuan."

"I know. But I'm afraid we have to let her in. She promised a scene if we didn't. Out in the street."

"If this is some tart, I'll deal with her. . . ."

"She's a business executive on the run."

He allowed himself to sound fully awake. "Who from?"

"The police. But I think you'll find she's covered her tracks so that they don't point here. She ought to be here any minute now. I'd rather you let her in. So she'll see I'm not alone in the building. Help within call if I shout."

I laughed. Tong didn't.

"I'll get some clothes on," he said.

It wouldn't take him long to do that.

"Don't bother to bring her all the way up, Tong."

I searched for a dark shirt and trousers, not finding either in a tropic wardrobe, having to make do with a brownish nylon sweater with long sleeves that was at once too hot. Up in the

183

sitting room I allowed myself one very small whisky, standing to sip it while single isolated thoughts came at me spaced out like bullets from a sniper's gun: that plastic crash helmet, ammo stolen, keys gone, Tong playing nursemaid but uneasy in the role, phone tapped and from this the reasonable certainty that my rooms were bugged, too. The bugging had probably been a hasty job, rushed through when it was known I was coming home.

I could make use of those hidden mikes, and I'd use Ranya, too. In a way she was a catalyst. Tong was now sweating at the thought of police behind her and what such a visit could mean to his guests. I had no doubt that he was more worried for them than for himself, as a good general ought to be.

I had no option but to involve Ranya unless I avoided the issue ahead for both of us by putting the chain on the door after she was through it and then going out on the roof terrace to scream down to the bargees. They would waken. In time they might do something. But meanwhile Tong and party would just leave. As I was beginning to see things, a hasty departure of the occupying forces from this building would greatly increase the chances of Li Feng Tsu being found a corpse. It is difficult to move fast with a doped prisoner.

I like to believe that I don't hate easily, but I was hating Tong now, hating him for all the things he was behind the man he had pretended to be. As his current victim, or on the edge of becoming that, I was at the top of a long column stretching away behind into a positive army of the maimed and butchered, thousands who had died in helpless terror plus those others who had also died feeling what I felt now, a black rage that had done nothing to save them. All I had to save me was my wits. I'd have preferred an automatic rifle.

If there was banging on shutters far below, I didn't hear it—just a girl's voice in my hall.

"Paul?"

"Up the stairs."

184

I don't know what I was expecting, probably a glitter evening dress with accompanying accessories and pigskin jewel case. What I saw was a very nearly unrecognizable Ranya wearing dark-blue trousers and shirt to match, no set stones, nothing in her ears, not even a ring on her fingers, and all she carried was a small loop-handled bag dangling from one wrist. She came around the last curve slowly, staring at me.

"You're angry?"

"Not as angry as you had reason to expect."

"Oh. What's happened to your face?"

"I had an accident."

"Paul, I had nowhere else to go."

"Let's skip that, shall we? How soon can we expect the police knocking on our shutters?"

"Not tonight."

"What guarantees can you offer?"

"The way I escaped."

"Tell me about it."

A bribe came into it again, a big bribe, too, this time a thousand dollars to a waiter. Ranya didn't throw money like that around carelessly. She had studied her waiter for days, the only visitor outside of the police she had been allowed to see. They exchanged words—not many with that door to the bedroom in which she was confined left open to a sitting room in which was a plainclothesman on duty day and night. Ranya, trained in the skills of character assessment, had decided that the waiter was venal. There was a door direct to the corridor which allowed the bedroom to be rented without the sitting room on occasion, and this of course was locked. But there are master keys and waiters are sometimes in a position to get hold of them. A thousand dollars tucked into a note were a sufficient inducement. After midnight, and when the door to the sitting room had been closed to protect her modesty, Ranya had simply walked out that other door and gone straight to her rent-a-car via an unwatched carpark entrance. With any luck her departure wouldn't be discovered until breakfast.

It was all very simple and neat, no flamboyance, a plan conceived and executed without panic haste. I gave her a bigger malt than I'd meant to and she thanked me, apparently still surprised by the relative warmth of her reception.

"Where did you go in the rent-a-car?"

"The airport. I checked the car in at the office there. Then I bought a ticket to Surabaya. There was a plane due out for there and it was going to be pretty full. Mostly pilgrims returning from Mecca. And making a lot of noise."

"You didn't go through passport control?"

"No. But it will be hard to prove I didn't. My name's on a flight list."

"Then?"

"I went to the washroom and stayed in it for half an hour. Then I took a taxi to Raffles Square, phoned you, and got another taxi. But not until I'd walked around a bit."

I could see her doing the walking around, dressed in blue, pavements still moderately crowded, looking like a waitress coming home late from special duty.

"I'm sure I wasn't followed, Paul."

"What happened to your jewel case?"

"It's in the hotel safe. Everything. If I am sent back to Bangkok, Nivalahannanda isn't going to get his hands on one piece. Not even a ring. I have the receipt in my bag. I'm going to give it to you."

"I'm a man desperate for ready cash."

"I have to trust you."

I wondered whether Tong, hearing all this from a little ear glued under a piece of furniture somewhere, would decide to cancel the red alert.

"Did you get hell from Kang?"

Ranya nodded. "Four times. Once for three hours. Yesterday

186

it was for one minute, to tell me I'd be leaving today. Paul, can you get me out of Singapore?"

"No."

"But you have boats and we're on the river here."

"At the moment I haven't even a canoe."

"All I need is to get over to one of those islands you can see. They're, Indonesia. I'm *not* going back to Bangkok. Nivalahan-nanda will see that I never get out again. He's that kind of a man. And the one thing he has is pull in the right places."

It seems to be difficult to really finalize a Thai divorce. Ranya was looking upset for the first time since she had joined me. She finished her malt, then got up from the settee, walking over to the terrace windows, sliding one back, looking out over the city that until a few days ago had been her hope. Then she turned.

"Paul, why haven't you asked me the question I expected to hear the moment I got in?"

"What's that?"

"Was I helping the kidnappers."

"It never occurred to me to ask it."

"Why not?"

"I just thought you wanted to sleep with Li."

She put out a hand to the steel frame of the glass panel.

"If you can believe that, why can't Kang?"

"He's a policeman. The obvious often escapes them. Something to do with their training."

When I took pajamas to the spare room, Ranya was in the attached bathroom with the shower running. I didn't knock. She was letting water pour down her body, not worried about getting her hair soaked. Unlike so many Oriental women, her legs weren't too short for her body. She stared at me, then turned off two taps. I threw her a towel. She made this into a sarong. I turned on the taps in the washbasin.

"Why are you wasting water?"

"The sound of it is supposed to throw microphones. Not that I think there's one in here."

"Somewhere else?"

"The living room."

She thought about that, and about what she had said up there.

"To the police?"

"No. Down to my shop. You don't happen to carry a little gun in your handbag?"

She shook her head. "I've never even had one in my hand."

She stepped out of the tub and sat on the loo cover, crossing her legs, pulling down another towel and using this on her hair.

"Would you recognize any of the men who took Li from your hotel room?"

"Of course. All of them. They weren't masked. They stayed for a long time before they took Li away."

"I think they brought Li straight to this building."

Ranya couldn't be stampeded into a reaction. She made a turban out of the second towel.

"Are they still here?"

"Yes. In two rooms one flight down."

After a moment she said: "I'd like a cigarette. I've smoked all of mine."

I had to go up to the sitting room for a box of what must now be slightly stale Benson and Hedges. I made a certain amount of domestic noise for the mikes, collecting glasses, running water in the kitchenette. From a cupboard under the sink I took a plastic bucket and dropped two big packets of soap powder into it, taking my load back to the bathroom. Ranya had dressed at speed and was again sitting on the loo cover. I gave her the cigarettes and matches, then turned on the hot tap in the tub, leaving this until it came almost boiling. I emptied the contents of the soap packets into the bucket, topped it up with hot water, stirring the brew with a long-handled back scrubber.

Ranya watched me, looking a bit like a member of the audience at a television cookery demonstration, forced to appear more interested than she was. It seemed probable that she was facing up to terror. She must be frightened. Even with rage as an antidote my guts were cold and churning. I seemed to remember that Kang had said something about the kidnappers using Lugers. It is the hand gun I fear most. The bullets make huge holes. Also, it's abominably accurate.

"What are you going to do with that?" Ranya's question was almost polite, as though she felt obliged to ask it.

"Pour it down a flight of stairs. It ought to make them difficult to negotiate."

"The stairs from your landing?"

"No. The next flight down."

"Beyond the kidnappers?"

"Dividing them, I hope."

"I don't understand."

"Before you came one of them went downstairs. I don't think he's come back. On some kind of guard duty in the shop. If I can also get my man Tong down those stairs, I believe that will only leave one man guarding Li."

"There were four at the hotel."

"I know. But their use of this building was an emergency thing. I'm pretty sure they streamlined their numbers for the change."

"What's happened to your servant?"

"My guess is that he's in the river with weights on his ankles."

She stared at me for a moment, then lifted the cigarette to suck on it. I set the bucket on the floor.

"You're going to try to get Li away from them?"

"Yes."

"You have a gun?"

"No bullets in it."

"They'll kill you."

I could have done without her flat realism. I tried to cover that bald statement with my plans and she listened to them, her face serious under the turban. Ranya looked a bit like a magistrate on a bench, not a cynic, just experienced at separating the plausible from the ridiculous. She assessed my chances, found them not good, and came up with an alternative suggestion.

"You think Kang will come here to collect me, don't you?"

"Yes."

"Why don't we just wait until he does?"

"By the time Kang gets here the kidnappers and my man Tong will have gone, taking Li with them."

"Why do you think that?"

"Because Tong was jumpy as hell at having me show up here. Then you arrived suddenly. There's a direct lead from you to the police."

"You made me tell my story upstairs to make this man feel safe again?"

"That was the idea. But I doubt if it worked. I think they're all waiting now for a boat to take them away. It's their natural escape route."

It was a moment before she asked: "Why must you save Li?"

"I don't give a damn about Li personally. I want to get Tong. He's used me and he's a killer."

"What about your telephone? Tapped?"

"You bet it is. If I even lifted the receiver at this hour they'd cut the line, if they haven't done it already."

She pushed the stub of her cigarette over the edge of the washbasin.

"What do you want me to do?"

"Stay in the hall of this flat while I make my sorties from it. Be ready to slam that door and put the chain on if I can get Li up here."

"And if you can't?"

"Guns banging will mean I've lost. Lock yourself in and get up to the terrace. Scream. To the barges. There's a good chance they won't come after you. They'd have to break down a door. That takes time. And there's not much point in killing you."

"I see."

190

Talk was unnerving me. I had to believe that there was only one man now with Li in Chong's rooms. Two, with guns, meant I hadn't a chance. I went to my room for flashlights, found two, tested them, then got a screwdriver from a hall cupboard. I pulled a plug from the baseboard in the guest bedroom and got to work on it, moving the red wire over into an unnatural marriage with the green, tightening them both down together. The entire building is on one circuit to a main fuse in the shop. I'd blown every light once with a faulty television connection and Chong had done it again with his vacuum cleaner. I put the plug back in its socket and went into the bathroom. Ranya was combing her hair at the mirror. I put one of the flashlights on a shelf.

"Don't use that unless you have to. They attract bullets. How long before you're ready?"

She put down the comb and picked up the flashlight. "I'm ready now."

"Then get out into the hall and wait there. You can have the door open a crack if you want to, but remember bullets will ricochet from all that concrete on the stairs. Use a house wall for cover."

She looked at me. It was the assessment again: this time my rating was Fool. I picked up the bucket and went into the bedroom, over to the plug. I heard her go past me to the hall. I put out a toe and flipped the switch on. There was a bang, a flash, and all the lights went out. I reached down and pulled the plug out of the socket.

Ranya hadn't switched on her flashlight. I put the bucket on the floor, set my flashlight beside it, struck a match, opened the hall door, and went out onto the landing. At the first step I struck a second match, going down four treads as it burned into my fingers. I swore.

A third match took me to the landing with two doors, then went out.

"Hell!"

I spent some time fumbling with the box. There was a click from Tong's door. Light blazed into my face. I shouted:

"Drop that damn thing!"

The beam lowered. I still couldn't see who was behind it, just colored dazzle circles.

"I'm sorry to wake you. But that fool Chong has been pulling out plugs by the cord again. I've told him not to twenty times. This time it's the guest room bedlamp. If you'll lend me that torch, I'll go down to the fuse box."

"No, tuan." His voice was quiet, like a man trying to keep sound from the rooms behind him.

I lowered mine. "Look, you go back to bed. Just let me have your light."

"I'll fix the fuse. I wasn't in bed."

I saw trousered legs and shoes.

"Then we'll both go down. I'll hold the torch for you."

"There is no need, tuan. Go back to your guest. She must be nervous?"

"Oh, all right."

I never saw his face. He lit me up the stairs. I went into the flat and shut the door, leaning back on it. Tong didn't quite believe me, but he needed light again in this building. I thought he would go down. Someone else in the shop might be able to fix a fuse, but I thought Tong would go to check up. I gave him half a minute, then opened the door again, a crack. I couldn't hear anything.

Ranya whispered: "He's gone?"

"I think so."

Hell would break if he hadn't, if he was just waiting there beyond the stair partition wall with a gun in his good hand. I was certain he had trained himself to fire with that hand. And he wouldn't need his light again. A glow from the city would silhouette me on the landing.

I lifted the bucket and flashlight from the floor. Ranya widened the gap. I went out, a black moving target. The stairs were a dark tunnel between two patches of neon-tinted glimmering, above and below. I went down a few steps into that shelter, pausing to listen, hearing nothing but my own heart. When I moved again, the thick solution in the bucket made a faint sloshing sound.

I got to the lower landing, the glow showing two closed doors. I hadn't much time to play with before lights came on again. Halfway down the second flight I tipped out the contents all along the step below my feet, then went back to the landing, pulling the torch from my trouser pocket. Chong's door was almost directly in line with my own. If Ranya was working with the kidnappers, this was her chance and I was a dead man. She had only to send down a beam of light and fire along it. There had been no chance to check her bag. Telling her exactly what I meant to do had been my biggest gamble. Maybe she hadn't shown fear because she had nothing to be afraid of, just a role to play.

I knocked gently, three times slow, a pause, then two quick. In the room beyond there was a faint thud, as though a man had run into something. I scraped my throat with a guttural rendering of Cantonese, a bid to imitate Tong's voice.

"A boat's coming. Here's light for you."

It got me in, but he must have seen suddenly that the shape was too tall. His breath hissed. I kicked the door shut. In pitch dark I guessed at the position of a gun hand coming up and brought the torch down. It smacked into metal, spinning away from my stung fingers. There was clattering on the floor. He came at me first with a groin kick, then a body follow-up. The kick missed, the follow-up took me back hard against the door panels. My breath whistled out. He tried to knee me. I twisted my body. He stood clear to give himself the weight and swung for a low punch. I moved into this, arms high, taking the blow on my pelvis before it was really powered. I chopped him, both shoulders. He grunted, sagged, but came up again, trying to use body weight to ram me back against the door. He hadn't an adequate leg brace and didn't do much more than rock me. I managed a neck lock with my right arm. His resistance to this was unskilled, a thrashing about, the man a gun killer, nothing more. I was lucky. I couldn't have stood up to unarmed combat with a trained opponent, and I didn't find it too easy to hold his head steady enough to skid my left thumb over sweating cheekbones to the depression under an eye. I pressed hard. He didn't yell, just bit me on a tensed biceps. That ended the bear hug. He flung himself back. I heard the thump of his body against Chong's massive deadwood central table. I expected him to use this as a launching pad for another assault, but he decided to hunt for his gun. Over the noise of my own breathing I heard his. He was working his way around the oval of the table. Then he was down on the floor behind it, flapping about with his hands.

The lift of that table was enough to bring on a heart seizure. Sweat jumped out of my pores. The man on the floor didn't seem to realize what I was doing, even when I had that huge lump balanced for the tip-over. I gave the table a final heave and it went down without much more than a scraping noise from two of its legs, a great weight onto the cushion of a body. There was no cry, just the whistling sound of air being pressured out of lungs, then a tiny whimper that might have come from a child or a puppy in a dream.

Lights came on, a roof fixture glaring. The window had a blanket blackout. Only an arm projected out from under that upturned table, fingers slack. He hadn't got anywhere near the Luger. I picked up the gun.

The door to the inner room was half open. There was bright light in there, too, and another blanket blackout. Chong used an Indian-type bed, a wooden frame with ropes across it for springing, no mattress, just a quilt. Lying on this, spreadeagled, was a man, wrists and ankles roped to the frame. I recognized crumpled Shantung silk tunic and trousers, not much else. He

194

was just another kidnap victim, no aura, his face disguised by strong black stubble. He had morning-after eyes.

My equipment didn't include a knife. I had to go back into the outer room to hunt around for one, very conscious as I did it of Tong, with a fuse fixed, mounting stairs again. I thought it unlikely he had heard any din from these rooms. I opened the door to the landing to be able to hear Tong coming up that last flight, then went back to Li. I put the Luger down on the bed and started sawing at a wrist rope. Li lifted his head, but couldn't keep it raised. I knew the feeling. No food, though drugs didn't seem to be a part of this scene. I got the second wrist free and helped him to sit up. He still hadn't said anything.

There was a step in the room beyond. I grabbed the Luger and swung around with it pointed. Ranya came through the door. She said, quietly:

"He's coming up."

I gave her the knife and went past her, out onto the landing. From below came the slap of slippers on treads, a man not hurrying. I had never seen Tong hurrying. I waited behind the shelter of the stair wall partition. The feet came closer. There was a yelp of surprise, then a thud. I looked out.

Light shone down on my skid solution. It had dripped step by step from that halfway point where I had poured it out all the way to the corner of the stairs and around it. Tong had fallen at the bend, but not as heavily as I'd hoped for. He was on his back, sprawled out against a wall, staring up at me. I fired to kill and missed. As the gun banged, he rolled. A ricochet seemed to follow him behind the partition wall of that lower flight, but it didn't find its target. I heard his tumbling descent, as though he thought I was coming after him, then his bellow for reinforcements.

Ranya was on the landing. Li's arm was about her shoulders. He was shuffling. The kidnappers could have been burning the soles of his feet, systematically, for days, a simple technique in persuasion which continues to get much better results than the more subtle psychological tortures.

Between us we hauled him up the flight to my landing and through the door into the hall. I put on the chain. On the stairs to the sitting room Li crawled on hands and knees, finding he could do this quite well. I stepped over him to get quickly to that phone by the sofa, finding this dead as I'd expected. I poured whisky and turned with the glass just as Li reached a chair, still crawling, and pulled himself up into it as might a child. His face was haggard with pain, but he still hadn't said a word. I gave him the glass.

"Could you eat something?"

He nodded.

I went into the kitchenette, opened a tin of beef soup, poured it into a pan and set it on the hot plate. I found a loaf Tong had brought in for me, cut three slices, and buttered them.

The attack would come soon. Even if they only had Lugers down below, it was a heavy enough gun to blast the lock. They could then kick the door back onto its chain and shatter the hinges. Tong would have had plenty of experience in these techniques. On our side we had an eight-shot gun from which one round had been fired, but we also had a concrete floor under us in which there was only a single round hole, for the stairs. I've been in worse defensive positions.

Li had finished his whisky. I took the glass from him and held out the cup of soup. He used both hands for it, trembling so much that he spilled some. I steadied the cup. He drew back his head and positively glared at me, as though this service angered him. Ranya stood staring down at the man, apparently expecting to be recognized at least. Li gave no indication that he had ever seen her before in his life, just kept lifting that wobbled cup to his lips, his eyes fixed on something in the kitchenette. There's no question about it, a total withdrawal from other human beings does give you a kind of dignity. The soup sipper was getting back into his aura.

196

I hadn't time to watch the process. I went out on the terrace to start yelling for help. There wasn't a light on any of the barges, but I was pretty sure I could wake the sleepers and was about to start doing it when a sound of battering on wood came over roofs from the street. There were voices, too, and then a shout. I made out the words.

"Open up! Police!"

The battering was on the shutters of my shop.

13 ❧

I lifted the Luger and fired a shot back over my roofs. Even there in the open the sound was impressive, and just to make sure they got the message down in the street I pulled the trigger a second time. The police stopped asking for admission. There was the sound of a heavy-duty engine being revved, followed by the noise a tank makes when it's attacking a frame house. But my shutters seemed to hold against the onslaught. The vehicle groaned in what could only be reverse gear.

"Paul! Why did you . . . ?"

"Police have arrived. But they haven't got a boat on the river!"

The barges below floated like huge emptied pea pods, most of them bow in toward the bank. On the one nearest my back door a light glowed under the stern hood, and then a bright, hard beam was directed up at my roof. I yelled at the man to cut out the dazzle, but his interest stayed focused on the foreigner's wild party. I looked down four floors to the projecting ramp and thought I could see figures on it. There was another crash from the front of the building and this time the engine went on roaring through a tearing of wood, suggesting a police Land-Rover being driven right into the heart of my business.

The man on the barge must have heard that row, too. He lowered his flashlight straight onto three men standing on the ramp. One looked up. It was Tong. For the second time within half an hour I fired to kill and missed. Tong jumped into the water. So did the others. Only one head came up immediately. I fired at the round blob. It didn't disappear. The fool on the barge seemed determined to keep his beam from doing anything useful, wavering it around and finally redirecting it up at me. I screamed at him to drop it. He did this suddenly, picking up two heads surfacing under the high, curving side of the barge. They were out of range for a Luger, but I didn't let that stop me, emptying the gun. Bullets pocked water a long way from targets. A body came up out of the river in what looked like a dolphin's jump, hands clawing for a hold on the narrow strip of the barge's deck. The hands held. In a pure gymnast's feat, illumined by a spot, the man pulled himself up and lay clear of the water, panting.

Suddenly the bargee ended neutrality, picking up a boathook and coming down the strip decking with it. But he didn't go for the man aboard. Instead he bashed down toward a head still bobbing in the water. The swimming man backed away and then turned and made for mid-river and the current.

There was a blast of light from the ramp. A machine gun clattered, an arrow of flecks pursuing the swimmer. He screamed, then choked on his own noise. The man on the barge was running when the light caught him, leaping from bow to bow. It was Tong. Other figures emerged from stern hoods, but no one made a move to stop the runner. The machine gun went silent. A moment later I heard the heavy engine in the street again, revving madly. A siren shrieked. I went back into the living room.

I opened my front door as Kang came up the last flight of stairs. He had the machine gun under his arm. He stopped two steps from the landing, staring at me.

"Li?" was all he said.

"Upstairs. Eating brown bread and butter."

The policeman came up the rest of the way. I couldn't see why he was angry at me. I was suffering from reaction. It took the form of acute fatigue.

"He's . . . all right?"

"Except for his feet. I think they fried them. Not that he's told us anything. He doesn't seem to react to English or Cantonese, or not much. When I offered him food he understood that. Ranya's probably trying him with French now."

For a normally inscrutable policeman the change in Kang's expression was remarkable. He had arrived looking like a man contemplating suicide to escape the shame of total bankruptcy. Now he might have learned that he had won a big lottery prize. He went past me toward the spiral staircase.

"Leave this door open," he said. "My men will be up."

I left it open and went into my bedroom, shutting that door. I looked at the bed with longing. I had the feeling I'd ruptured a major blood vessel to my heart lifting that table. I sat down on a chair and heard his men going up. There seemed to be great numbers of them, alien feet trampling through my apartment. A complete police takeover is a disturbing thing. It makes you feel disreputable. I didn't think Kang had any right to make me feel that.

The door opened and Ranya came in. She was looking more discomposed than I had ever seen her, as though she had not quite orientated herself as yet to the recent past, it being so far outside anything like her usual norm. She closed the door carefully and stood fumbling inside her handbag, finally producing from the bottom of it a cigarette that had once been in my box. It was bent, but she lit it anyway.

"The Superintendent told me I was to stay down here. I didn't want to be alone in the other room. Do you mind?"

"Delighted. Have the bed. I decided that if I stretched out, my muscles would seize up."

"Paul, are you all right?"

"No. Are you?"

"I feel . . ." She stopped.

It was somehow pleasant to see her at a loss for words, a weakness not noticeable in any of our other contacts.

"Thanks for coming down to help with Li," I said. "If you hadn't I don't think we would have made it up here before Tong's reinforcements arrived."

We might as well admire ourselves since no one else was going to. Ranya came across to sit on the bed. Then she pulled up a pillow, propped herself against it, and swung up her legs. In spite of the relaxed position, there was still a suggestion of tension about her. Her hand jerked out in search of an ash tray.

"What's happening in the sitting room?" I asked.

"Li Feng Tsu is doing most of the talking."

That was a surprise.

"In French?"

"I think it's Mandarin."

"And Kang seemed to understand?"

"Yes. Why not?"

"His father was a dock coolie from Canton. No money in the family to give the boy a classical education. Must have taught himself. But he would."

Ranya blew smoke at the ceiling. "It's like a court up there," she said.

"Whose?"

"Li's. He's sitting in that chair. They put his feet on a footstool. Even with that beard he looks like an emperor."

The old fascination was filtering in through shock. I hoped they'd take the emperor away soon, probably by boat. I didn't much like having my house as a detached palace.

"Paul, do you think I'm going to be put on that plane this morning?"

"No."

She stared. "What makes you so certain?"

"If he tries to, we'll blackmail him. With the story of tonight's events which you mean to tell journalists in all its details immediately after touchdown at Bangkok."

"I don't understand."

"Look, dear, Li Feng Tsu is going to be shipped out of here very soon, back to his hotel. It'll be given out that there's been another triumph of Chinese medicine and he's recovered from Burma flu. His shoes will be fitted with deeply padded insoles and he'll go through with his arranged schedule, a bit late, but still nothing left out. Including the military parade. The moment he's been shaved and put back on parade, he'll be radiating goodwill again. It's the kind of price you have to pay for greatness, keeping up the front even if you've just escaped being murdered. I'm sure he'll see it all through splendidly, supported by General Chen, who has arrived to strengthen the team. As you've pointed out, Li has something. Even if he won't talk English or Cantonese."

"You mean . . . nothing about the kidnapping will ever be known?"

"Certainly it won't. Unless we blow it."

"But who would believe us?"

"In these circumstances, and with the evidence I could produce, every foreign correspondent within five thousand miles. And it's not a story that will go stale quickly, either. Given a magazine treatment, it could even be used years from now. Believe me, Kang is going to want you here in Singapore where he can watch you. If you decide to become a local citizen, so much the better—your path will be smoothed before you. I can't see your husband ever getting his hands on those rocks either. Nor will you or I hear one word more about deportation. When we say smile, Kang will smile. And that's a lovely relationship to have with a leading policeman. I've been wanting something like it with Kang for a very long while."

"Blackmail," Ranya said, quoting me.

"There are times when one has to face up to the full implications of that word. This is one of them. Yes."

Ranya looked at a wall and through it toward her new future. I got up and opened a tip-over window.

"What's that for?" she asked.

"I thought it would be nice to hear the chug-chug of a police launch coming to my back door."

"How will they explain all the gunfire here tonight?"

"A gang raid on my safe."

It was a full twenty minutes before the boat came in, a very quiet boat. Ten minutes after that the processional started down from my sitting room. It sounded rather as though they were carrying a Minister Extraordinary, muted instructions reaching us through the door. I thought I made out Kang's voice once or twice. Then the stairs down echoed to feet before silence returned.

"I think we might reoccupy the sitting room now," I said.

Ranya and I were drinking whisky in the small hours of the morning when Kang came back up the spiral stairs. It's not easy to make an impressive entrance up curving steps. We saw his head first, eyes fixed on two people sitting on a sofa. We were both very much awake and could have been waiting to hear what our citation was going to be, nervously excited to know whether we rated third or second class of the Order of the Red Dragon of the People's Republic. Kang refused a drink and made it very plain very quickly that we didn't rate a thing except a good citizen's duty to be extremely discreet in a matter of national importance even though neither of us was yet a national. I made it quite clear to him early on that Ranya and I had done our homework for this lesson and suggested delicately that we all suddenly found ourselves in what could be called a new basic situation. He was unhappy about this, but still didn't reject out of hand my gentle claim. An understanding was reached which indicated drinks all around, but he still wouldn't have one. I got the impression once again that he was controlling raw anger with difficulty. Later, preferably by telephone, I would have one or two follow-up points to raise, the chief one concerned with how to protect the inevitably short future of an old man with arthritis. I had a feeling that it would be a long time before Kang and I again had a cozy little dinner at my expense. Something was lost between us that could never be rediscovered: he no longer had all the power on his side.

It was almost a sadistic release for the Superintendent to tell me in some detail, and with Ranya as the audience, how I had been duped. He moved about a good deal as he talked and might have been looking for mikes, except that he didn't actually peer under the furniture or climb up to check cornices. His men had been hard at work below, and the big find had been an operations room, nine feet by three, squeezed behind a false wall at the back of one of the shop bays. This had been fitted out as a highly sophisticated communications center. It didn't have a computer, but it had everything else: two-way shortwave radio, monitoring gadgets, and the most interesting device of all, an apparatus probably manufactured in Czechoslovakia which had been removed for inspection but was almost certainly an unscrambler designed to break top-secret police signals. To the operators of this kind of equipment the bugging of my rooms and tapping of my phone presented no problems at all. It was the police theory that the technician on permanent duty in my shop had been the simple youth I had usually seen wielding a broom. It was only a theory because his body had been one of two with bullet wounds taken from the river. The young man had been trying to follow his leader up the side of a barge when he had been shot. Tong had perhaps made his first mistake in dealing with me when he drafted a technician for emergency service as a tail. You can't shift people about like that in their roles even in an undercover urban-guerrilla organization. As for Lum Ping himself, alias Tong Tsun my shopkeeper, he had got clean away. An intensive search of the district and the city had been mounted, but I could see that Kang had small hope of any positive results. I asked about the man under a table.

"Concussed. Still unconscious, but he'll talk."

I got no credit for the one prisoner taken alive.

"I've lost a servant," I said.

"Describe him."

It was curious how difficult I found this, as though already the physical image of the old man was fading. I could remember his eccentricities better than his appearance. Kang made notes. Then he put the little book away and pulled out a wallet, removing a roll of bills, holding these out to Ranya.

"Yours, I think, Mrs. Nivalahannanda. The thousand dollars you paid to a waiter. He was my man."

She remained remarkably calm, the only sign of slight shock a straightening of her spine.

"So you wanted me to run for it? To see where I'd go?"

"We thought it might be interesting."

"You could also have arrested me for trying to evade deportation."

He said nothing, ready to leave the matter. Ranya wasn't.

"You had no idea Li was in this building. You just came to pick *me* up!"

Kang tossed the money onto the sofa.

"Tong had a wife," I said. "You've found her?"

"Yes. Locked in a cupboard in the flat below. She was in shock, but has recovered and gone away with her mother. The girl seems to have hated her husband. Probably not the only one of Lum Ping's wives to feel like that."

He turned away. We watched him sinking down a hole. The door to the flat slammed. I had the feeling that the rest of the building below that door was still in alien hands but would soon be left empty for me to re-people.

"Do you want to go to bed drunk?" I asked.

Ranya stood. "I'll go as I am, thanks."

She stood, then did an odd thing for a girl who had recently been planning to sleep with a leading member of the Peking Politburo. She bent down to kiss me on the mouth. The kiss could have become much more than sisterly, but my bones were aching.

I couldn't sit in the apartment, walking around it, pottering in the kitchenette, my restlessness like the feeling you get after a tropic storm, a sudden change in air pressure leaving you light-headed and jumpy.

Ranya had gone back to her hotel. My phone had been reconnected to the world, but I hadn't used it. I kept thinking of Chong lifting the receiver to shout: "No home!"

The living room was a mess. In the hunt for mikes they had pulled out half the baseboards and left me to call a carpenter to put them back again. They had found what they were looking for near the jacks for the phone plug-ins, even one out on the terrace, a careful wiring job that must have been done long ago as a check on me. It would have been easy enough to fool Chong with a story about men needing it for telephone maintenance. He would have protested but in the end allowed them to do the job.

In the kitchenette I made a ham sandwich from a loaf bought for me by a guerrilla general. The phone bell went. It was Bahadur in K.L.

"I've been trying to get you all morning!"

"The line's been out of order."

"There's a lot to tell you, Mr. Harris. Shall I catch the afternoon plane down?"

"No! You can talk now. We're on a safe wire."

"Sure?"

"Dead certain."

"All right. First, your manager, Mr. Lung, never went near the wreck of the *Chai Ming.*"

206

I took a deep breath, switching to another headache. "You're sure of that?"

"Yes. I paid a man to keep tabs on him all the time I was down at Mentawei myself. Lung never left his hotel in Padang except to go for walks and one night have a woman."

"This doesn't make a lot of sense."

"It makes sense to me, Mr. Harris. Lung didn't need to bother. He already knew what had made the *Chai Ming* turn turtle. This was a couple of crates of an outsize excavator which weighs about twenty-five tons when the thing's put together. Aft, also deck cargo, were two heavy-duty trucks. All this loaded at Benkoelen. After dark. I flew down there and was lucky enough to find a stevedore who had been paid double overtime. The registered cargo was already under covered hatches. We recovered the bills of lading from the captain's cabin. Water-damaged but readable. No mention of the excavator and two trucks."

"So you got a diver all right?"

"I sat in an open boat under blistering sun for two days while he went down below. Only the pair of us. I worked the boat gear. Also, the *Chai Ming* was not bound for Moekomoeko to load more copra, at least not until she had called at South Pagai to unload the deck stuff at a temporary pier. They're building an airstrip on the island. For the Army. Big opportunity for little side deals. When we got back to Padang, Lung had gone. Did he get to Singapore?"

"Yes."

"You've seen him?"

"Briefly."

"What did he report?"

"There wasn't really time for a report."

"I don't get that."

"Lung is under police detention at the moment."

"Good place for him. So the police are in on this?"

207

"Not exactly. Bahadur, no talk to anyone, not even Maria."

"You think I would?"

"I'm just underlining it, that's all."

"Sure you don't want me down there?"

"If I do, I'll ring."

"You sound tired, Mr. Harris. What's been happening?"

"Nothing much. I'm all right. See you soon. We'll talk then."

"All this is going to cost you plenty."

"That doesn't matter."

I took my sandwich out onto the terrace, chucking the bread and meat into the river. There were rumored to be fish down there still surviving the pollution. I lunched off whisky. I was drinking too much. I needed someone to talk to. There was no one around. Even the police were out of the building now. I'd hired an old man to act as watchman in the shop with shattered shutters, but it was closed for business. The rest of the day was going to be long, with a longer night after it.

I rang Ranya's hotel. She was in her suite of happy memories.

"Have dinner with me tonight?"

"Yes."

"Let's make it Raffles. I'd like to revive the good old days we're both too young to have known."

"All right."

"The bar we used before. About eight."

"Fine."

The apartment bell rang. I went down. Lung was on the landing. He had shaved but still looked scruffy, as though he had been sleeping in his clothes for some nights.

"I came straight here," he said.

"From a cell?"

"It was a room."

We went up the spiral staircase.

"Sit down. Gin?"

He shook his head, which surprised me.

"Then let's go out on the terrace."

He looked at the long chairs, but chose a straight-backed hard seat. I was the one who relaxed, for some reason able to do this now he was here. The sun on my face gave me the excuse to shut my eyes if I wanted to.

"Come to tell me about Sumatra?"

"No. To resign."

After a moment I said: "Because of what came out at Kang's interrogation of you? He hasn't told me about that. I don't think he means to."

"Then I will. I connived at fraud."

"Against the company?"

"More against you. I'm a coward. You may have noticed that."

"In a world of brave men," I said.

He looked up. "What do you mean?"

"None of us can be too sure how we'd stand up to the kind of blackmail Tsing Tai Tai was screwing down on you."

"You've found out?"

"What I didn't find out I guessed. I've sacked Tsing. He's out. Lucky for him I'm stopping at that. I have to. We can't afford a scandal among our directors right now."

"Mr. Harris, you did everything for me and I . . ."

"Let's not get sentimental. I brought you down from Hong Kong, where you had made quite a reasonable little world, and dumped you into one where you were never really accepted. I didn't even make a friend of you myself. I don't much with people in my businesses. It can cause discomfort. So you were alone here."

"That's my way!"

"It's no man's way, Lung. You were rejected by people with clans behind them because you hadn't one behind you. You were an outsider nudging in. And with my help, insofar as the business went. I was buying loyalty from a social orphan. I wanted you in my pocket, to use you that way."

"You had every right!"

"I don't think so now. Did you mean to tell me about what was happening with Tsing?"

"Yes."

"When?"

"In Kuala Lumpur. I came up to do that more than anything else. I didn't find out what was happening until I was in Java while you were in Britain. I went straight to Tsing Tai Tai when I got back."

"And he offered you a cut and said he'd crucify you if you didn't take it and keep your mouth shut?"

"I didn't take his cut!"

"You just postponed telling me?"

"Yes. Tsing said I'd never get another job in Singapore. And that he could implicate me right up to the neck, with proof that I had been his agent with those cargoes. It would have been easy enough to fake. Then when I heard from your cousin in England about the share buying for takeover, I put that to the front of my mind. I went to Lindquist about it, like I told you."

"But you didn't tell him about the extra cargoes?"

"No. That was for you, when I got the courage. But I never found it."

"Melodrama."

He stared at me. "What are you saying, Mr. Harris?"

"That you went along with a fraud, but not for very long and you didn't mean to go on doing it. Also, you made nothing out of it yourself. And if you think I'm going to the trouble of training someone else for your job, you're crazy. I'm not sacking you. It's not convenient for me. I've sacked Tsing. You I need."

"How could you trust me?"

I smiled. "I'll watch you."

I wasn't feeling too moral, for I was buying the man again. He got up and stood with his back to me, looking down at the river.

"All those whores aren't what you need at all, Lung. I'll hire a good go-between to find you a wife. With your prospects we may even be able to get one with a dowry."

I couldn't say for sure that the thing in the refrigerated drawer was Chong. It had been in salt water down at the river mouth for more than five days. One ankle was almost worn through by the rope to a weight, and crabs had gone for the face. It might be, it might not. That's what I told Kang. He led me out from the chill sterility into a long passage. At the end of this was a lift and we went up to his office. He produced a bottle of pinch-bottle Haig, special reserve for use after mortuary visits. I sat down in that room where the view was half screened as though the man who used the place didn't want to see too much of the city in which he was a power.

"I'm keeping Lung on," I said.

Kang moved in behind the desk. He might not have heard. "Had the old man any relatives?"

"Not that I know of."

He looked at me. "You feel responsible for what happened to your servant?"

"Oh, for God's sake! Of course I feel responsible! Chong's dead because I let that bastard into my building. And made a crony of him. Sat drinking tea with him at the back of the shop. Quaint character I'd picked up to fit into a corner of my business. Years from now I'll feel sick when I think about it."

"You couldn't see past that alibi of a murdered wife?"

I stared at him.

"Don't you try to throw that at me, Kang! You wouldn't have seen past that alibi either! I checked it just as carefully as you'd have done. And that guerrilla raid on a village happened. He had his own wife butchered just to make a cover story that would stand up to any checks."

"It mayn't have been only for that."

"What do you mean?"

Kang was judicial. "Lum has a real flair for smelling out thoughts of defection in the minds of his men. His reaction is automatic. He has them killed. That's how he's survived so long.

The wife he had in that village might have been growing tired. She'd been with him a long time and put up with a grim life. Could be that she felt they'd both reached retirement age. Lum wouldn't care for that idea. He also wouldn't like any suggestion that he was getting old. But he could see that she was, and with a tongue that might start wagging too much."

The Superintendent was probably basing his theory on historical precedents. Wife murder has quite often been a by-product of total power.

"Well, you know what you're looking for now," I said. "A man minus four fingers on his right hand. Though he may decide to have that arm amputated just to make things difficult for you."

Kang reached for a cigarette and lit it.

"What did he mean to do with Li?" I asked. "Start off by sending the Minister's thumb through the post to Peking? Or am I not to know?"

"I think it best that you do know. He meant to keep Li for two weeks right in the middle of Singapore with all the police and half the army looking for him. Just to show he had the power to do this. Li would then be freed."

"*What?*"

"Delivered up alive, he was much more useful to Lum's cause than his dead body would have been."

"As a demonstration of guerrilla power?"

"That, but much more. As a big joke."

Suddenly Kang didn't have to spell it out. Loss of face is still the worst thing that can happen to anyone in the Orient, even to Marxists, maybe especially to Marxists.

"You smothered the story of Li's kidnapping, Kang. Couldn't you do the same with the way he was found?"

"We could not. Li was to be left in a rubber forest just outside the city, tied to a tree, wearing nothing except a placard around his neck. We found the placard in the apartment beneath you. Clearly printed in big black letters on white. It said: 'This is Li Feng Tsu, member of the Peking government which has repu-

diated the true workers' revolution in Southeast Asia. Signed:
Lum Ping, Chairman, Malaysian Workers' Freedom Council.'
All Lum had to do before giving us and the press a tip-off was
photograph his naked victim wearing that label. He would then
make thousands of copies for wide circulation later. There is no
way in which we could have stopped those pictures going out
by the thousands all over Asia."

All over Asia there would have been laughter, echoing from
Hong Kong to Java, around to Rangoon, and over to Bangkok.
Laughter would have reached New Delhi. It would have been
the biggest loss of face to Peking since the Mao takeover. Not
many revolutionaries have had the wit or the understanding to
make use of the vast joke. Lum Ping did. His celebrity would
eclipse Che Guevara's, a real success story, a Far Eastern David
sending one stone from his slingshot straight into the forehead
of the Peking giant. There was a very good chance that Moscow,
wavering for so long over its policy for our corner of the world,
would suddenly decide to back the little David's bid for a
throne.

"Li told you all this?"

"Enough," Kang said. "Up in your sitting room he was a very
angry man. He's probably regretting now that he talked so
much. He was shown that placard as part of the pressures on
him. All he had to do in order to be returned to his hotel suite
was get in touch with Peking direct about a policy change
toward the guerrillas. The means for that direct contact were
ready and waiting down at the back of your shop."

"He wouldn't do it?"

"No. He's tough. They gave him nothing to eat, just water.
They burned his feet. He went on waiting to be rescued."

Kang leaned across his desk to stub out the cigarette. He
stared at me. "When you step outside my office door you've
forgotten all this."

I nodded.

The sunset was one of our more flamboyant ones, replacing earth color with the sky's. The water in the swimming pool, under assault from yellows in the heavens, turned to a weird magenta, ruptured by a line of pinkish froth made by a young Hok practicing the crawl. We kept seeing the boy's face at the turns, marked by an almost manic seriousness in training that somehow reminded me of Sally.

"You'll stay for dinner, Paul?"

I looked at the old man. "I can't, I'm afraid."

He lapsed into silence again. He hadn't been much interested in my talk about business. The area of matters that really concerned him was contracting almost visibly, giving me the feeling that each time I came it was to find the circle drawn tighter. It's unnerving to see the old just waiting, and the Chinese seem to move suddenly over into this phase, setting themselves to one side instead of having this done to them as happens so often in the West. Usually the families of patriarchs like Hok Lin do their best to delay an inevitable decision, but I was certain that the old man beside me had now made it. He watched the boy in the pool, one of his seed, loved because of that and probably for himself as well, but not loved as a girl had been who would never lie sunning herself on these slabs again, at least not in her grandfather's time.

"It's quiet today," Hok said. "The children come tomorrow."

"You'll enjoy that."

My own tone angered me, sedative for a terminal case. I hoped suddenly that I'll always have the strength to spit a resistance when it comes my turn to have the real world padded away because I'm not supposed to have the strength to face it.

Hok said, with sudden brightness: "Did I tell you we'd heard from Sally?"

"No."

"By telephone. She never writes, of course. From Tokyo."

"Oh?"

"I didn't know she was going. None of us did. But that's the

214

way Sally does things. She never asks family advice about anything, never has. Apparently she just caught a plane and flew
to Japan. Seemed surprised that we were surprised. She's going
to Hokkaido now, for the skiing. After that North Korea, she
says. I wonder why North Korea. Not a very attractive country,
is it? Been there?"

"No."

"I expect that's why she's going. No one else ever does." He
laughed.

In North Korea, Kim Il Sung is offering a personalized brand
of Marxism for rebels from the gospels of Mao or Moscow. These
days revolutionaries have a wide doctrinal choice. And as well
as sanctuary the country also offers schools for intensive training
in guerrilla tactics.

"I've always let her have too much money," Hok said. "For
some reason, one does with girls like Sally. But I don't see her
coming down on me for a dowry." He laughed, then added:
"She may settle later, but not in my time."

All realism hadn't gone, which was something.

"Ever think of marrying again yourself, Paul?"

"Not often."

"You should, you know. Who is going to light joss for you
when you die if you don't have a family?"

I looked at him. "Well, the joss burned for *you* one day is
going to add appreciably to our pollution problem."

He liked that and went off into a shout of laughter which
finished with coughing. Down at the far end of the pool the
young Hok pulled himself up steps and stood flipping water
from his body with the palms of his hands.

There were four tourists at a corner table in the Raffles small
bar, package-deal voices loud over the day's money's worth.
The two men pretended to fight over who was going to pay
for the next round. It wasn't much of a struggle—I knew the
thin one was going to. The fat one was clearly an expert at

the well-it-will-be-my-turn-tomorrow gimmick. He'd doubtless been traveling on it ever since their charter flight took off from Chicago.

Ranya came in wearing white to the floor and her emeralds. The tourist women didn't believe the stones were real.

I stood up. "I've been drinking all day on an empty stomach," I said, "and I'm cold sober."

"The last time I heard that, the man was under the table twenty minutes later. We'll eat soon."

She sat down. The barman believed in those stones. He took much longer over the order than he needed to.

"You're beautiful," I said.

"No. I make the best of what I have."

The tourist women were hissing at their men. I felt sorry for their men, even the fat one. After a meal the party would be going down to the night market to look at the boys dressed as girls. The tour guide tips you this as a special not on the prospectus.

We ate in the courtyard, our table next to a palm in a pot. A pink-shaded lamp made everything rosy, cloth, cutlery, Ranya's hands. Only the emeralds defeated the takeover. She made me eat soup, though I felt I'd been opening cans of nothing else for weeks, a bouillon to dilute alcohol. Our talk didn't recap. Ranya isn't greatly interested in yesterdays, even violent ones. For that matter, she isn't too concerned about this-mornings, either. Curiosity seems to move in front of her like a long shadow when the sun is low behind her back. She had been phoning property agents again.

"I think you should drop that," I said.

"I don't understand."

"The restaurant business is a waste of your talents. Tell me about your bus companies."

Transporting people hadn't been too interesting. You stayed solvent by keeping your costs down and your fares up, remembering to stash away capital reserves for replacements, though

216

I gathered that she ran her buses practically to the junkyard, the public in Thailand not being too demanding in matters of comfort. They expected travel to be miserable and Ranya gave them what they were expecting, at considerable profit to herself. I began to get the feeling that her valuable rock collection came directly from the buses, not her eating house. In her approach to food she was too much the artist to make real money. If you're going into catering as a proper business, it has to be chains of self-service places; the more of these you can open, the better your chances for cheap block purchases of supplies. I made this point. She didn't like it much.

"I *will* open my restaurant in Singapore, Paul!" Her jaw was protruding just slightly.

"If you must, you must. But how about a directorship on the side?"

"In what?"

"Something called Hok Lin Shipping."

"Your company?"

"Well, you could probably say it is now. We've had some sudden changes at boardroom level and I want new faces around that table. It would be a real pleasure to see yours there."

"You're drunk."

"The only effect alcohol has had on me today is to make me see a lot of things very clearly indeed. This is a firm offer. It will stand in the morning."

She didn't tell me I was crazy, just thought for a moment. "I know nothing about shipping."

"It's a bus company on water. You carry goods, not people. And you're always looking for potentially profitable new routes. I think your role would see you traveling a lot, but not on the ships. First-class air. I need someone I can trust, with a sharp eye. I've had some disheartening experiences with men in this connection recently."

"You would trust me?"

"Yes."

"Why?"

"For one thing, you'd be out to prove that anything men can do you can do better."

She nodded, then said: "I believe you're serious."

"Of course I'm serious. I need someone with experience and talent. You have both."

She sipped her wine. "You don't want me to live with you?"

"This is a straight commercial offer. And as a director in Hok Lin Shipping you'll have a ready-made position. No need to find a husband as a front for the world."

"Not even a lover?"

"Not unless you want one."

"You don't find me attractive?"

I took a deep breath. "Ranya, if I did, I can't help feeling that something would always come between us."

"What?"

"An image of Li Feng Tsu."

She laughed. "Maybe I didn't like him so much."

"Maybe you didn't," I said.

218

73 74 75 10 9 8 7 6 5 4 3 2 1

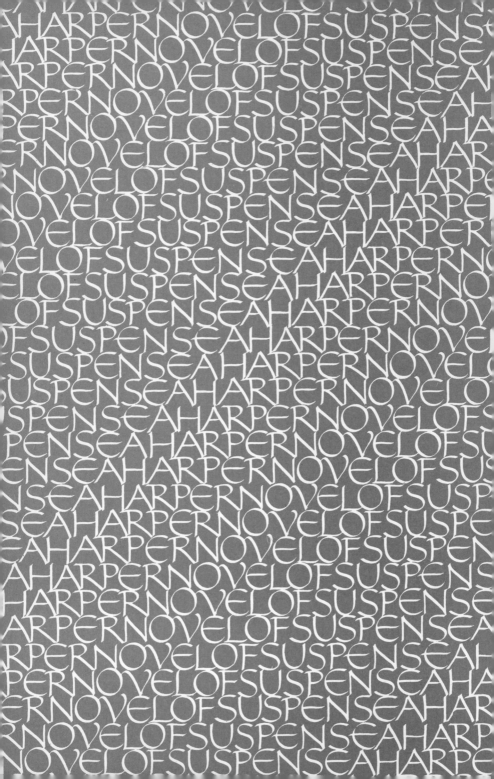